THE DELIVERER

ENDORSEMENTS

Rising star Jason William Karpf is back with his unique trademark blend of blockbuster action, fascinating yet terrifying futurism, and abiding faith. *The Deliverer* salutes dystopian classics *Mad Max* and *The Hunger Games* in creating a fallen world that seems far too possible. Protagonist Bren Van Allen reminds us of Marshal Will Kane from the western *High Noon*, a solitary hero who must overcome the moral weakness and overwhelming danger that surround him. The author's Hollywood roots are on full display, guaranteeing you a thrilling and thought-provoking read.
—**Lee Purcell**, Actor/Producer, Two-time Emmy nominee

Jason William Karpf's award-nominated fiction brings together contemporary culture and timeless spiritual truths. His latest book, *The Deliverer*, builds from our shared experiences in a divided America. Crafted with care, suspenseful, and thought-provoking, *The Deliverer* is highly readable and highly recommended.
—**James Strock**, author of *Serve to Lead*, *Ronald Reagan on Leadership*, *Theodore Roosevelt on Leadership*

In a futuristic America reeling from the devastation of Civil War II, Jason William Karpf delivers non-stop action

in his fast-paced novel, *The Deliverer*. More than excellent action scenes, he masterfully describes how Christians living in such a world could continue to minister and be great witnesses. Bren Van Allen, "The Deliverer," is given every opportunity to seek fame and fortune, but he holds fast to his convictions and helps bring the world closer to a much needed healing. If dystopian is your go-to genre, then *The Deliverer* will meet and exceed your expectations!
—**Travis W. Inman**, Author of *Earth Fire Series* and *Shadows: One Choice a Future Makes*

    The Deliverer is a fast-paced thrill ride that will leave you clinging to the edge of your seat until the very last page.
—**Andrea Chatman**, author of Selah Award finalist *Beneath the Deep*

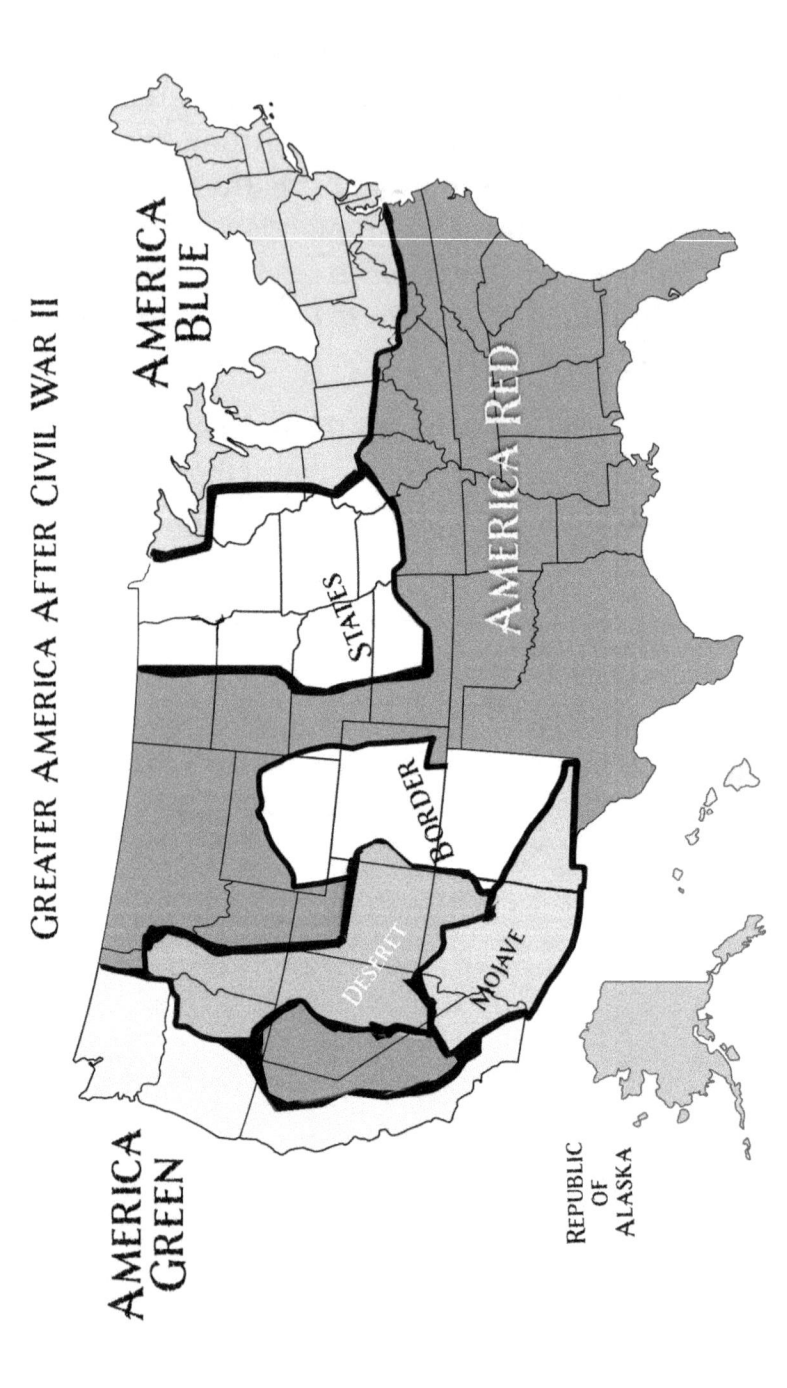

GREATER AMERICA AFTER CIVIL WAR II

AMERICA
BLUE

AMERICA RED

STATES

BORDER

DESERET

MOJAVE

AMERICA
GREEN

REPUBLIC
OF
ALASKA

THE DELIVERER

JASON WILLIAM KARPF

PUBLISHING THE POSITIVE
Plymouth, Massachusetts

A Christian Company
ElkLakePublishingInc.com

COPYRIGHT NOTICE

Cover and Interior Design: Derinda Babcock, Deb Haggerty

Editor(s): Judy Hagey, Cristel Phelps, Deb Haggerty

PUBLISHED BY: Elk Lake Publishing, Inc., 35 Dogwood Drive, Plymouth, MA 02360, 2022

Library Cataloging Data

Names: Karpf, Jason William (Jason William Karpf)
The Deliverer / Jason William Karpf

268 p. 23cm × 15cm (9in × 6 in.)

ISBN-13: 978-1-64949-675-1 (paperback) | 978-1-64949-676-8 (trade hardcover) | 978-1-64949-677-5 (trade paperback) |978-1-64949-678-2 (e-book)

Key Words: Christian Science Fiction Books; Dystopian States of America; Apocalypse Books for Adults; Christian Action Adventure; Hard science fiction novels; Science fiction adventure; Science fiction military

Library of Congress Control Number: 2022944145 Fiction

CHAPTER 1

AD 2033

"Daddy, don't go." Madison Van Allen pointed at her phone. "See? We're still on high-yellow alert."

Bren bent to his seven-year-old daughter's level and gently took the device. "Maddie, I said you could have a phone if you promised not to look at grownup stuff."

"The alert just popped up, honest," Madison said.

"I have to go. I have an important business meeting." Bren closed the notice and handed the phone back.

"I thought your last project was canceled." Bren's mother, Cindy, stepped out of the shadows. The family kept lights low to conserve power. The steel shutters resisted the sun as well as projectiles.

"New opportunity." Bren moved toward a hallway.

Cindy set her shotgun on a rack. She embraced Madison and made sure the girl was playing with her robot-builder app. The house's electricity consumption concentrated in the master bedroom where a ventilator and pain med drip blinked steadily. Bren knelt at his father's bedside.

"I said yes, Pop. Mammon finally won," Bren whispered.

Jack nodded feebly. Reaching toward the nightstand, he struggled to lift a holstered Ruger revolver with pouched full-moon clips. Bren took the weapon from his shaking hand. Jack caressed his son's face as the men shared a tear.

Bren pulled his Ford F-150 Lightning Platinum out of his parents' driveway. An Airstream Flying Cloud on the RV pad served as living quarters for him and Madison. Bren drove past shattered storefronts and barbed wire stretched like spider webs between concrete median barriers plundered from Caltrans. Loma Linda had been a thriving California community, home to a nationally renowned medical center. Now there was no more California—no more nation. Civil War II had brought home the American penchant for forever wars.

A news update played on the truck's touchscreen. Bren focused on the audio, trying not to take his eyes off the road to look at the accompanying images and maps. A chart of the former United States of America showed three major Americas—Green, Red, and Blue—and smaller breakaway regions. Territory marked Border States snaked between the blocs.

"Local update," the announcer said. The map zoomed to reconfigured California—America Green claiming the coast, the red-aligned states of Jefferson and South Jefferson dominating the interior, and the Republic of Mojave conjoining the southeastern deserts with the Phoenix megalopolis and Las Vegas. "America Green and Mojave have declared a ceasefire in the Inland Empire." The map zoomed in to show the area east of Los Angeles, its pretentious designation of "Empire" long predating the war. "High-yellow alert remains in effect. Residents are strongly urged to stay indoors."

Bren maintained freeway speeds through the desolation. His destination was a business park that had been spared the fighting. At the Van Allen Engineering suite, Bren popped the hood revealing the "frunk," the compartment that would've housed an internal combustion engine in pre-EV days. He removed a liquid-cooled cable of his own design and plugged in the electric truck for a full charge that would take five minutes.

Inside the dark, dusty office computer monitors awoke, bringing up diagrams and project management charts. "Canceled" marked some images in red block letters. Bren checked his email and deleted the message with an animated rat captioned, "Some people call them whistleblowers."

A video call rang through on his screen. Pastor Doug Wescott sat in a laboratory. A cross on a wall overlooked the banks of equipment.

"Brother, just calling to thank you for the design you sent," Pastor Doug said.

"What's the efficiency rating now on the hydro panels?"

"Fifty percent more than the previous benchmark."

"Water from thin air." Bren smiled. "Almost like manna from heaven."

"We could use more of your talents. We need you in the Revival Zone."

"Canada is locked up tighter than ever. We missed our chance."

"Got an inside scoop. Ottawa is signing a treaty with all the Americas. They'll allow the new e-Bahn to cross the border." Pastor Doug pulled up images showing the technologically advanced road under construction.

"The king's highway. I don't have enough money to keep the lights on, let alone buy a transit pass." A whistle sounded at the door, the motif from the Clint Eastwood classic *The Good, The Bad, and The Ugly*. "Moe's here. Gotta go." Bren ended the call.

The door swung wide. The visitor filled the entry, haloed orange by the smoky dusk. With a hypervigilant gaze and a Jericho PL in a drop-leg holster, he might've been a member of a Black urban militia. He wasn't. Standing out in a M-65 army field jacket in the heat, he might've become a target for a White supremacist militia, which would've been their grave mistake.

Moe Franklin saluted Bren, who saluted in return. The men fell into a bear hug. "Let's see what you brought to the party," Moe said.

Bren walked Moe back outside to the Lightning. Moe smiled. "Good vehicle for this kind of work," he said. "Fast, lots of cargo capacity."

Bren opened the driver's door. He pulled his personal carry Springfield Armory XD-E from the center console. Moe nodded at the compact .45 and opened the backseat door to view the gun rack mounted to the cab ceiling. The first rifle was another Springfield Armory weapon, an M1A Tanker, short barrel with a 20-round magazine. Moe leaned toward the second rifle for closer inspection.

"Barrett M82." Moe laughed as he admired the .50 caliber long-gun. "You're not gonna have time to set up a sniper's perch."

"Wanted something that could kill a car, not just a person."

Moe noted the oiled-leather rig on the backseat. He unsnapped the holster and pulled the Ruger partly into view. "Don't see many folks packing revolvers these days."

Bren refastened the holster strap. "My father wanted me to bring it."

"Daddy knows best. Put it on," Moe said.

Bren slid his arms through the rig. "Ready to roll."

The Lightning left the surface streets where Bren's office was located and headed west on I-10. Torched cars and craters marred the interstate, but Bren avoided the obstacles and maintained speed. Moe rode shotgun literally, holding a Mossberg 590M Shockwave. His pockets bulged with box magazines for the pistol-grip 12-gauge.

"My last run almost did me in. My truck needs an engine rebuild. Having trouble seeing." Moe pointed to his affected eye.

"You used to give better pep talks," Bren said.

"I'm trying to thank you for keeping me in business. When the world's going to hell, someone always manages to make a buck. Delivery drivers are managing."

"I wanted to manage the old-fashioned way, but my contracts dried up after the hearing."

"You did the right thing speaking out. An algorithm murdered those people, not our platoon."

"James 4:17. 'Remember, it is sin to know what you ought to do and then not do it.' Didn't have a choice."

Moe nodded. "Like you didn't have a choice going on this run?"

Bren shook his head. "I could've said no tonight." Moe patted his shoulder.

Ontario International Airport was a travel and logistics hub in the Inland Empire, with runways long enough to handle overflow from LAX. Bren eyed the military presence as the Lightning approached the complex.

Moe pointed. "Our cargo is at Gate 4E."

"I thought the airport was only being used for humanitarian flights."

Moe snorted. "Plenty of commerce mixing with the charity."

The Lightning eased into a line of Humvees and transport trucks. At the checkpoint, Moe gave the guard a coded hand signal and lowered his window. Tapping his phone, he transferred a crypto bribe to the guard's device. The Lightning moved forward. Skeletal aircraft scattered along the tarmac echoed the car wrecks on the freeway. Moe directed Bren to a parked Airbus A400M Atlas, its cargo ramp down.

The two walked between pallets offloaded from the turboprop, crates containing relief supplies, stenciled in French. An alert beeped on Moe's phone.

"This one ... and that one." Moe indicated the boxes with RFID tags—radio frequency identification—tripping his sensor. He viewed the Gallic labeling with a visual translation app. On the screen, the words became English: "Medicine. Keep chilled."

Bren and Moe muscled the crates into the Lightning's bed and lashed them. The guard waved the truck back through the gate. Once off the grounds, Moe motioned for Bren to pull over. He took small cameras out of his gear bag.

"What's this?" Bren looked down at the body cam Moe was clipping to his vest.

"Extra revenue," Moe said. "Guy named Kenny Turro has an online show about delivery drivers. He's following us live tonight. We get a cut of ad sales plus a bonus if we get enough Likes."

Moe affixed other cameras within the cab and launched the video feed with his phone. Kenny Turro appeared on the screen, wearing a hoodie, surrounded by the monitors and gear of a homebrew TV station.

"Ladies and gentlemen, live from Southern California or whatever they're calling it these days, it's the Sarge!" Kenny said. "The always exciting Moe Franklin is here with a special guest."

"Good to see you, Kenny. Meet Bren Van Allen, my teammate," Moe said. "We served together in the Army National Guard. He was lieutenant first class, platoon leader."

"But on the road, the Sarge is in charge, right?" Kenny said.

"We're breaking him in tonight, but make no mistake, the man has skills!" Moe said.

"Coming from you, that's quite an endorsement." Kenny turned his attention to Bren. "Say hello to the audience, new guy."

"Hello." Bren hesitated. He didn't savor internet celebrity on top of his notoriety as a whistleblowing former officer in the National Guard.

"Well, Moe," Kenny broke in, "it doesn't look like your friend's skills include public speaking. Hopefully, he can entertain us in other ways. Good luck tonight, Sarge."

The Lightning pulled onto the access road and returned to I-10. "Where are we going?" Bren said.

Moe entered the destination into the truck's navigation system. "Short run. Straight up Mt. Baldy."

Bren smirked. "You don't have skis in those crates? There's been no snow up there for years." He pressed the accelerator. Thunder rumbled overhead.

Moe laughed. "No, smart guy, no skis. And don't be talking about the weather. You'll jinx us." He checked the map. "Turn on Euclid. Take the off-ramp slow."

Smashed cars lined the Euclid off-ramp. A car with less damage blocked the lane. Moe motioned for Bren to move at a crawl.

"Porch Pirate blockade. They wanna nail us before we even get off the freeway." Moe racked the Mossberg. "When I say, punch it, hit the car in the rear. Less weight there, better chance to spin it."

The Lightning inched forward. A Porch Pirate popped from behind the car, leveling his rifle.

"Now!" Moe leaned out his open window. His shotgun roared. The Lightning's tires screamed.

The double-aught load threw the Porch Pirate backward. The Lightning clipped the rear of the blocking vehicle, the car spinning as Moe had predicted. A second car raced up the off-ramp. The next round from the Mossberg exploded the windshield. The car dived off the incline as the Lightning passed. Bren turned on Euclid toward the San Gabriel Mountains. A line of Porch Pirates peeled out of an IHOP parking lot.

The long straightaway prompted speeds exceeding one hundred miles per hour. The atmospheric river system known as the Pineapple Express pumped storm clouds from the Pacific. The pavement slicked. A pursuing car lost traction, crashing into a security wall insulating a large home from the street. Bullets reached the truck, shattering the Lightning's rear glass. Moe climbed into the backseat to deliver more rounds through the open window frame. He pulled down the Barrett.

"Wanna use your heavy artillery?" Moe said.

"You're already back there!" Bren said.

"I can't see well enough to aim a rifle!" Moe ducked as a bullet split the frame near his head.

Sweat dripping, Bren prodded the touchscreen icon for Autonomous Mode. The Lightning held course as Bren squeezed into the rear of the cab. He set the rifle's bipod on the seat back and extended the muzzle over the bed. The report in the enclosed space stunned Bren.

Fifty yards south, smoke rose from the engine bay of the closest Porch Pirate, raindrops and streetlights sparkling the plume. Moe whooped, and Bren aimed again. The next bullet shredded a tire, initiating a spinout that knocked two other cars onto the sidewalks. A signal from the dash interrupted Bren and Moe's cheers.

"Road conditions changing. Autonomous Mode disengaged," the computer voice said.

The Lightning slewed. Bren dived for the driver's seat. He brought the truck under control as Euclid Avenue bent toward Mt. Baldy. With too much momentum from the drag race to the foot of the mountain, a Porch Pirate missed the curve and churned through a parking lot.

THE DELIVERER

The mountainsides shone orange and brown, scoured in recurrent wildfires. Charred trees listed along the ridges. The rain came too hard for the naked heights. Dark rivulets poured across the roadway. Rocks agitated in the flows.

Bren craned his neck to check the tenuous slopes. Gaining on the Lightning, the remaining Porch Pirates adjusted their aim for the switchbacks. Maintaining return fire, Moe's hands ached, and the Mossberg's barrel steamed in the moisture. A car sprouted four muzzles and took point, forcing Moe to drop from the window opening when the guns fired. The Lightning's aluminum body panels rang in the new fusillade. Dashboard lights and the touchscreen blinked. Moe removed the Jericho from his leg and raised the pistol to the window, taking blind shots.

"Jesus ... Jesus ... help us!" Bren murmured as he urged the truck upward.

The mountainside burst, releasing rocks and earth. A boulder crushed the closest pursuer. Mud shelved on the road ahead. The runoff rose, necessitating Bren engage four-wheel drive. The tires still lost grip, and the Lightning pinwheeled. Moe flew headfirst into a rear passenger door. The heavy truck became mere debris as the mudflow sought the guardrail and the chasm beyond.

"Holy Savior, help us!" Bren yelled as the Lightning's slide quickened. The flow overran a culvert at a bend in the road. Rocks piled in the concrete corner, and the truck pushed backward against them. Bren jolted when he felt the back tires bite the solid surface. He pressed the accelerator and the Lightning responded, struggling away from the edge. The truck moved sideways, advancing each time the wheels found purchase. The treads finally touched pavement, and the Lightning reached a clear section of the road. There was no sign of Porch Pirates.

"Moe, Moe!" Bren called. When he didn't get a response, he looked over his shoulder to see Moe sprawled across the backseat, bleeding from his nose and an ear.

"Finish the run," Moe muttered.

Five miles later, the Lightning arrived at Bald Mountain Lodge, a vintage resort in a high canyon. Bren sneered at the parking lot filled with luxury vehicles, knowing a rich person's folly had nearly killed him and his friend. He opened a door to tend Moe, who was still bleeding and barely conscious.

"Too many crashes … too many fights. Doctor said I couldn't take much more," Moe said. "That's why I needed you—"

A security guard grabbed Bren's shoulder. "This is a private event."

Bren spun and drew the Ruger. Other security came running with guns ready. "I have a delivery," Bren said through gritted teeth. He nodded toward Moe. "He needs medical attention."

"Several doctors here tonight," the first guard said. "Talk to Mr. Conroy, the host."

Bren ran down the hill to the main building, a rambling log construction. Sounds of a party leaked into the night. He transited the entrance into another time. A jazz band played "Minnie the Moocher," complete with an animated, scatting singer channeling Cab Calloway. Guests cosplayed in pinstripes, short flapper skirts, spats, and kohl-rimmed eyes. Shimmying to the slow swing, dancers packed a glass floor over a mountain creek. The rocky channel had gone from trickle to torrent during the storm.

Bren moved through the jostling crowd to a middle-aged man holding court. Mr. Conroy sported a monocle, slicked-back hair, and a pencil mustache grown for the occasion.

"Mr. Conroy?" Bren said.

"Are you my delivery person? You look familiar. We were watching the coverage. Thrilling!" Conroy pointed to the anachronistic big screen near the dance floor.

"I have to find a doctor," Bren said.

"Very well, we'll pick one out. In the meantime, join the fun. We're celebrating the hundredth anniversary of the repeal of Prohibition!"

Bren waved off drinks and curious women. Security guards entered with the crates. They pried the lids, revealing cryogenic containers. The large metal capsules hissed opened in a cloud of frost. Conroy extracted a chilled Dom Perignon and held the bottle over his head

"Who needs a refill?"

Bren tensed with rage. "We almost died. Don't you have enough booze up here already?"

"'Booze,' my dear man? You've brought genuine champagne. Not much left since the vineyards died. Drink this, and you can bottle your pee for top dollar."

The crowd of guest around Conroy laughed then shrieked when Bren seized the man's double-breasted lapels, sending the six-figure magnum of champagne crashing. Security pulled him back.

"Let him go." Conroy aimed his phone at Bren. His mobile device beeped. "There, a tip for your trouble." He turned to a security guard. "Find Dr. Winston." He walked to the bandstand, waving his arms. "Play that hi-dee-ho song again—from the top!"

Bren stood alone, exhausted, forgotten, as the party resumed. He saw the guards carry Moe on a stretcher from the main entrance to a side room. Bren hurried to his friend. The pair were alone, their pain orchestrated with the musical lament of fast-living Minnie and Smokey, her addict boyfriend.

Bren took Moe's hand. "Lord Jesus, watch over your warrior, Moe. Save all the souls lost on this mountain tonight."

Dancers watched the cataracts rise beneath their feet. A dislodged cabin surfaced like a submarine. Guests screamed and scattered as the ridge beam cleaved the glass floor. The canyon rumbled. A wave of mud, rock, and long-dead trees snapped the stilts that suspended the lodge over the creek. The building tilted.

Bren looked up from the unresponsive Moe. The side room's wall split along a seam between logs. Bren slid down the floor. He negotiated the twisted doorway and headed toward the cries of the ballroom. The building became a chute feeding guests to the flood. Bren reached for clutching hands. The wood planks beneath him gave way.

"I love you, Maddie!" Bren breathed as he lost his grip.

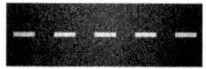

Bren woke to the gentle, rhythmic sounds of water. He opened his eyes and gasped. The unseen flow wouldn't close over his head. Bren lay in a white bed in a white room. Medical equipment stood in place of a nightstand, but the chamber smelled of salt air, not the antiseptic cloud of a hospital. A bearded figure entered the room.

"This can't be heaven," Bren said.

"My presence proves it. I'm—"

"Jerold Cox. Billionaire."

"Trillionaire. Market's up this morning." Cox stepped aside as medical personnel entered and checked Bren's vitals and injuries. Bandages wrapped his head. His chest and left leg throbbed.

As the doctor guided him, Bren swung his feet out of the bed and put weight on them. The holstered Ruger sat on the nightstand. He touched the handle of his father's gun.

"In addition to saving you, we salvaged your weapons and truck," Cox said.

"What about the people?" Bren said.

"Only a few survived," Cox said.

"Moe Franklin?" Bren said. Cox shook his head.

"I want to talk to my family." Bren managed a couple of steps.

Cox activated a media wall. "Of course. They already know you're alive."

The video call connected. Madison and Cindy, eyes red-rimmed, lit up when they saw Bren. Cox left the room with the medical team. The Van Allens were content to gaze at each other, tears streaming.

The elevator opened at the observation deck where Cox waited. Bren stepped out, leaning on a nurse.

"Let me officially welcome you to my yacht, the *Disco Volante*," Cox said. The pleasure craft was longer than a navy cruiser, the cambered surfaces of the streamlined boat evoking a flying saucer, inspiring the craft's name in Italian.

"Why am I here?" Bren grasped a railing and stood without assistance. The nurse departed.

"Your livestream came to our attention," Cox said. "The audience loved you, and rightly so." He held up his phone and played a carousel of clips from Bren's delivery night. "I wanted to reach out. A rescue mission became the best way."

"I didn't like being on TV. Guess I should be grateful."

"You'll warm up to it. But Turro is right about one thing. You need media training," Cox said.

"I'm not going back on the tube. I'm not doing another delivery run."

"You not doing another run the way you did ... on your own, seat of the pants. High-end delivery needs to be legitimized. My company, eQuality, plans to take control of the market. We need talent to do so. We need you."

Bren turned away from the ocean view, locking eyes with Cox. "If you really watched my video, you know I'm a Christian. Not an assassin. Not an errand boy for decadence. I have no place in your plans."

"Yes, you do. Sentiment spiked when you prayed—when you called out to Jesus. That audience segment is underserved. You can serve them."

"Christians shouldn't be watching that garbage." Bren walked along the railing, testing his leg.

"But they are. Be their example in a broken world." Cox brought up a new display on his phone. "My marketing department has created branding for you."

He brought up a poster with Bren's face photoshopped onto an action pose. The headline read: "Bren Van Allen. The Deliverer."

Bren shook his head and managed a laugh. Turning away from Cox, he studied the water. "Jesus is the deliverer."

"Moses too. You'll be a distant third," Cox said.

Bren exhaled. "I made the money I needed. I'm out."

Cox began his close. "You covered your immediate needs. You can bring your business loans current. You can pay the lien on your parents' house. You can put food on the table and buy electricity for your father's medical equipment for another six months. Then what?"

Bren bristled. Cox knew his personal life, but there were no secrets in the digital era after all, especially for a trillionaire. The *Disco Volante* was halfway to Catalina Island, affording a magnificent view of the mainland coast. The storm had done its customary job of rinsing the filthy air. The once-Golden State would look the part again for the next few hours, but the cycle of droughts, fires, mudslides, and blackouts would persist while the continuous war flared within its shifting borders. Bren gazed over the railing but knew he couldn't afford to be seduced by the vista, lulled by a California myth long since exploded. His old life was over.

"I want to get my family out of California." Bren glared at Cox. "But you already know that, like you know everything else about me."

"And now you have a means," Cox said.

"Expecting gratitude?"

"Never." Cox brought up a contract on his handheld. He passed the device to Bren. "I've added a signing bonus. You'll need it. Moving your family will be expensive, very expensive depending on how far you want to go," Cox said.

"The Lord directs our steps."

CHAPTER 2

AD 2038

The Lightning took the two-lane at eighty. Upgrades over the years, like the sway bars that belied its bulk in the turns, had kept the pickup ahead of most threats. Some original features received scant attention, such as the Antimatter Blue paint scheme gone dull. The neglected cosmetics threw the corporate decals into sharper relief. An eQuality, Inc. logo was an honor for a delivery driver and a target for Porch Pirates.

Bren alternated his gaze from the road before him to the intervening heads-up display projected onto his windshield to his rearview cameras. A video call came up on the main touchscreen.

"Hey, Bren, got time to go live?" Kenny Turro sat at a news anchor desk receiving touch-ups to his hair. He'd traded his hoodie for a Bernini suit. His show had moved from his mother's basement to a world-class broadcast facility.

Bren shrugged. "They haven't started shooting yet."

"We'll catch that too," Kenny said. The stage manager counted him in. A rock instrumental played as titles filled the screen: *Delivery: Dead or Alive!* Kenny flashed his winning smile. "And we're live with the Deliverer, Bren Van Allen. How do you feel about today's run?"

"I'm proud to be carrying medical devices." Bren remained calm as he watched for interceptors.

"A need, not a want. Just the load for our voice of morality in the daily delivery battles." Kenny gave a conspiratorial grin. "Think you might have some kills today? That's the biggest complaint the fans have about you. Not enough offense."

"I show up on time, with deliveries intact. I stay alive for the next run. That's all the job requires."

"Will there be a day you won't turn the other cheek?"

"Kenny, if you think I'm such a pushover, why don't you fire up your ride and meet me on the road. See what happens." Bren smiled at his challenge.

"Snappy response. Once upon a time, I couldn't get two words out of you."

A female voice came over the truck's speakers. "Porch Pirates are six hundred yards behind. Closing fast."

"Looks like the Deliverer is about to engage." Kenny brought up multiple feeds from cameras on Bren's body and truck. "Keep watching live on *Delivery: Dead or Alive!*"

A squad of Porch Pirate vehicles approached the truck. On the touchscreen, a grizzled face peered over a steering wheel. "You have quite the rep, Deliverer."

"Can't say I know you." Bren accelerated.

"Name's Lonny. Got my whole crew coming for you. Hacked your manifest. You got a cool load of precious metals."

"Components of medical implants for children."

"Do I look like I give a—"

Bren switched off Lonny's feed. Gunshots rang.

"Autonomous mode," Bren said into his smartwatch.

The truck held course with his voice command. Bren pushed a red button on the side of his driver's seat. The rear of the cab swung open, and Bren's chair slid on rails into the cargo bed. A translucent ballistic shield unfolded behind the tailgate. Bren's chair swiveled and locked into place. The Barrett sat atop a carbon-fiber armature. Bren poked the muzzle through a gun port in the shield.

Bullets from the pursuers thudded against the shield and reinforced tailgate as Bren peered down a digital scope. Lonny drove a black Dodge Charger, a carbon-fiber replica of the hitman car seen seven decades earlier in the movie *Bullitt*. Bren locked on the closest vehicle—a decommissioned Ford Explorer police interceptor. A round from the Barrett split the left front wheel, and the Explorer rolled over.

A pickup truck paced the Lightning. A Porch Pirate attempted to leap from his bed into Bren's. Bren seized an Enforcer, a manual battering ram used by British police. The steel striking plate swung into the Porch Pirate's chest, reversing his arc. Bren resumed position at his rifle, thinning the immediate ranks with carefully placed shots.

"Talk to me, Raveena," Bren said into his smartwatch.

"You can't outrun them or outgun them," the female voice replied.

"So, what's your better idea?" Bren squeezed off another round, cracking an engine block one hundred feet away.

"Your favorite Plan B. A shortcut. You'll want to get behind the wheel for this."

Bren pressed the button on his seat and slid back into the cockpit. He saw the shortcut on his touchscreen—straight up a rocky slope beside the road. "Can we handle the incline?"

"Yes, if you pick a good line. Most of their vehicles won't make it."

"Most?"

Bren veered off the road and slowed, allowing the Lightning to slip into four-wheel drive high. Porch Pirate rounds crazed the bulletproof rear window as the truck climbed the slope. A boulder scraped under the Charger, lifting the rear wheels off the ground. Cursing, Lonny jumped out and continued firing at the Lightning. The truck switched to four-wheel drive low as the rockfall steepened. A Suburban lacking the Lightning's upgrades and Bren's driving techniques slid sideways before tumbling to the bottom, taking out a Porch Pirate Jeep.

"Sparky, it's up to you!" Lonny said.

"I got him," Sparky said.

A Baja Bug bounded up the rocks, a V-6 howling in its elongated tail. The Bug passed the Lightning and pitched to a stop. Sparky emerged with a grenade launcher. Excited to score the kill, the young Porch Pirate fired. Bren dodged explosions but surrendered his line. The Lightning's wheels spun.

"He's slipping! Stay on him!" Lonny said to his crew.

Bren tapped icons on a secondary screen. The front winch activated, shooting a harpoon attached to the steel cable. The harpoon pierced the Bug's hood and embedded in the skid plate. The winch turned, yanking the car off its wheels and sending Sparky flying. The enemy vehicle wedged into a rocky cleft, anchoring the cable. The Lightning's wheels turned diagonally in "crab mode" and regained momentum. The harpoon disconnected, the winch line rewinding.

The Lightning disappeared over the top. Moments later, boulders rumbled toward the remaining Porch Pirates. Lonny called a retreat, his squad decimated. Sparky stumbled down the hill.

"He wrecked my Bug! You know how long it took to build!"

"We've all lost a ride we loved." Lonny put a hand on Sparky's shoulder. "Welcome to Porch Pirate life."

Bren slowed on the backside. A group along the ridge had sent the boulders to stave off the Porch Pirates. They cheered Bren's arrival while peering over the rise to confirm the attackers were gone. He waved as he drove on toward their settlement.

A second group flagged down Bren at the town clinic. They welcomed the Deliverer with more cheers and prayers. Several watched replay footage from his battle minutes before—cameras in the truck's bed capturing vehicles taking .50 caliber hits, a tiny camera mounted on the harpoon showing release and impact. A live feed from his body cam dominated the telecast, broadcasting the settlement's joy.

"I want to thank Trillium Scientific for donating this greatly needed cargo and for sponsoring my run today," Bren said to the broadcast audience. The manufacturer received the dual boost of a humanitarian gesture with great marketing exposure. "And I want to thank Jesus Christ for bringing me to my customers once more." Bren turned to the clinic director, Dr. Luna. "Twelve ocular implant systems as specified."

Staff members retrieved the metal suitcases containing the medical devices. As Dr. Luna reviewed the manifest on a tablet, Bren surveyed the landscape. The valley was a patchwork of gashed rock and grassland.

"Looks like mining reclamation," Bren said.

Dr. Luna signed the screen with her finger and nodded. "The mine has been on our tribal land for over a century. It was the center of our economy. Now, coal is banned. We're taking the land back a piece at a time."

One of Dr. Luna's assistants ushered Bren into the clinic. Lamps burned low in the admitting area where a dozen children waited, trembling.

"Twelve implant systems. Twelve angels trapped in the dark." Dr. Luna carefully shone an exam light at their faces.

Each child had milky white eyes, sunken, dead. "A birth defect linked to mining toxins."

The doctor opened a case. Six pairs of implants rested in a recessed tray, each a tiny tube capped with an artificial iris and retina. "The latest design. It emits an invisible laser stream to capture shapes and motion."

The doctor brought one girl forward. "This is Sara. We've implanted a prototype. All she needs now is the neural activator, which you also brought." The girl's eyes were agate-colored, reflecting the micro-machinery within.

"I'm scared," Sara said.

"This is the easy part." With gloved hands, Dr. Luna removed the minute neural activator from its compartment. She exposed a port surgically implanted in the back of Sara's head.

"You're very strong," Bren said. "You remind me of my daughter Maddie. Can I hold your hand?" Sara nodded and took the Deliverer's grasp.

Dr. Luna inserted the neural activator and sealed the port with a flap of synthetic skin. She moved to a wheeled computer station to bring the implant online. Sara's eyes were closed tight. She opened them slowly. The computer showed what she saw—the world, similar in resolution to a 4K video game, a miraculous vision.

Sara looked up at Bren. "You're beautiful," she whispered. Bren sank to his knees and hugged the girl.

Kenny watched the body cam footage along with his Greater America audience. "As usual, the Deliverer is full of surprises. Another successful run. Let's get reports from our capital bureaus."

A digital map behind Kenny showed the American map. America Green ran from Seattle to San Diego. The image zoomed to Portland, the capital.

A female correspondent consulted a dashboard of social media metrics. "America Green continues to enjoy the Deliverer's ingenuity and use of technology. They remain distrustful of his evangelical Christianity, blaming the faith for precipitating Civil War II. Some of our leaders want to indict the Deliverer as a war criminal."

Kenny smirked. "Nice." He brought up another talking head. "Jefferson City, talk to us."

The view switched to Jefferson City, once the state capital of Missouri, now the national capital of America Red, geographically the largest spinoff nation, stretching from Spokane city limits to Key West. A male correspondent referenced another social media dashboard. "As much as the left coast hates the Deliverer's faith, America Red loves it." The correspondent brought up specific bar graphs. "The theory that he's a spy for the DC establishment is still getting play. But he also gets respect for his past military service and expertise in firearms."

"If he wasn't so stingy with his bullets," Kenny interjected.

"We're not all bloodthirsty down here. Big sentiment spike when he comforted that little girl."

"Thank you, Jefferson City," Kenny said. "And now to the old capital, Washington, DC."

The remnant of the original USA bent from the Great Lakes through New England to the mid-Atlantic states. The final commentator came with the quaint trappings of a public affairs program—dark suit, shot of the National Mall in his background. "America Blue reports fifty-three percent approval rating for the Deliverer. Low marks for religiosity.

High marks for his sense of fair play. Highest sentiment scores for his public calls to reunify the country."

"We can all dream, right?" Kenny said.

CHAPTER 3

Huge silver bracelets glinted in the dark room. They jangled when Olivia Durand shifted her bronzed arms. The light from the media wall played on her swept hair, which was deliberately silver to match her jewelry. "Can you keep a secret?"

A vaguely mechanical, lightly accented voice responded from the shadows. "One of the few things I can still do."

"I'm a finalist for the Prix de Gloire, digital category." Olivia brought up the website for the competition. "The winner receives five million and a teaching residency in Geneva." Photos and videos showed the conservatory and its world-class dancers.

Olivia clicked images of a luxury domicile and its amenities. "Furnished apartment at the conservatory. Top-rated security. The elementary school is one of the best in the world. Josh would learn so much."

"I thought you were a dancer. You sound like a real estate agent now."

"I am the pupil of Vadim Ilyanovich Orlov. If I cannot dance, I shall die." Olivia put a hand on her companion's shoulder. The old man, contorted in a wheelchair, appreciated the touch but didn't react physically.

"So said Anna Pavlova just before her death." Vadim's speech synthesizer sounded from under his chin. "I've used those words too. It's taking a long time to carry out the threat."

An elderly woman entered the room with a tray of sandwiches, white hair in a spiky cut, wispy frame clad in leather. "I heard that. We don't need a drama queen around here."

"You're the only queen in this house," Vadim said. The woman nodded as she switched away from the Prix de Gloire content. Vadim's synthesizer conveyed his agitation. "Roxy, what are you doing? Olivia was showing me her escape plan to Switzerland."

"I'm sorry, sweetie. Special broadcast. Don't want to miss it." Roxy patted Olivia's hand. *Delivery: Dead or Alive!* filled the wall.

Olivia looked at Roxy, perplexed. "I didn't know you watched this stuff." Roxy motioned for quiet.

Kenny smiled into the camera. "It's time to announce our theme song for this season. You, the fans, have spoken. A big hit from the early days of MTV—'Kiss and Crash' by Roxy Steele!"

The raucous tune started behind highlight images and show credits. Roxy squealed and hugged Vadim. "Baby, they're playing our song!"

Roxy clicked a link which brought up the 1982 music video. Her twenty-five-year-old self wildly strummed a fluorescent Telecaster while singing about passion and peril on the road. The chorus ended with the line, "When I fall for you, how much will it hurt?"

Dancers encircled Roxy. A tall, muscular, shirtless man led the troupe. The man was also an actor in cutaway shots, kissing Roxy in a 1963 Corvette Stingray speeding down a neon-lit highway. Villains, inspired by the contemporaneous blockbuster, *The Road Warrior,* pursued the lovers in a flurry of studded jackets, designer chain mail, and post-apocalyptic vehicles. Roxy froze the video. The digital ID confirmed the smoldering lead dancer was young Vadim. He looked into the camera with a calm confidence, a prophecy of Roxy's lyric "When I fall for you."

"The only person who could ever upstage me. I figured I'd better marry him," Roxy said.

Olivia laughed and clapped. The regular broadcast played in a window alongside the paused music video, muted. Olivia looked at Bren's publicity shot and enlarged the image, intrigued. The Deliverer was the TV attraction of 2038. He may have lacked Vadim's eighties uniform of big hair and crimson leathers, but he shared the same knowing expression, a silent statement of "I got this." Their ages separated by more than fifty years, both men still promised the world with a smile. Roxy arched a brow at Olivia's juxtaposition of the portraits. The women shared a laugh.

"Dad, there's something wrong with the media wall. I can't watch my favorite show." Seven-year-old Josh Durand repeated the hand motion required to change the programming.

Gabriel Durand climbed the stairs to the loft. His silver hair matched his younger wife's though the cause was natural, not chemical. He stared at the media wall, irritated. "Isn't this the show about delivery drivers?"

"It's the wrong one. This is *Awesome Road Buddies* for preschoolers. You know I watch *Hyper Mighty Delivery Heroes* for kids my age." Josh pointed in protest at the cloying computer-animated renditions of famous drivers who sang about safety and sharing. "The wall says I'm blocked."

Gabriel entered the parental control code. He grimaced, finding home electronics daunting even for a tech executive. The wall showed a menu of the drivers' shows sponsored by eQuality:

Awesome Road Buddies, which Josh had outgrown.

Hyper Mighty Delivery Heroes, drivers with secret superpowers battling evil scientists and extraterrestrials in mythic anime.

Good Rides, Good Choices, a live-action animated series about a fictional teen auxiliary to the main drivers, fighting bullying and jamming to the latest pop hits.

Delivery This Week, an edited review of actual deliveries, omitting foul language and gore.

Delivery: Dead or Alive!, the uncensored primary program hosted by Kenny Turro.

Gabriel reset the parental controls and clicked on a show.

"Dad, that's *Delivery: Dead or Alive!* That's the grownup version. Mom doesn't let me watch it." Josh spoke in a near whisper as he stole looks at the action.

"Then pick out the show you're supposed to watch. Use your headphones." Gabriel went downstairs.

Josh started to switch programs when a highlight reel for the Deliverer came up. The powerful Lightning enthralled him. He marveled at a body cam shot of Bren riding his seat to the tail gunner position, the camera view switching to a feed from the Barrett's digital scope showing pursuing cars targeted and hit.

"I thank God for the opportunity to be an eQuality driver," Bren said in voiceover. "I bring joy to people. I can provide for my family and build a future for them. And I can share the gospel in ways I'd never imagine."

"What about that family?" Kenny said. "Do you miss them when you're on the road?"

"Terribly. But we're not the only family split up during wartime. A lot of families can never get back together," Bren said. "When you see me fighting, I'm fighting to get home."

The reel ended with Bren standing next to his truck at dusk, another run complete. Josh smiled at the image.

The Lightning approached a small lake. A mansion stood on an island in the center. A drawbridge lowered, allowing the truck to drive to the house. The homeowner emerged, toting a Galil Ace rifle with illuminated night sights. The sun was still shining.

"Where are all the Porch Pirates?" the homeowner said.

"They took a lot of damage during my last delivery," Bren said. "I'd say they're regrouping."

The homeowner frowned. "That's too bad. I was hoping you'd lead a bunch here. Wanted to get you over the bridge, and we'd pick 'em off together."

Bren shrugged. The entire family came out to receive their packages and take selfies with the Deliverer.

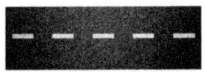

The next morning, Josh walked out his front door wearing his backpack. Today was an in-person class day at the Entrada elementary school. Other well-scrubbed and well-appointed children appeared along the cul-de-sac. The school bus arrived, a cheery tram with open bench seats like the vehicles that brought excited guests from sprawling parking lots to theme park gates.

Morning cup in hand, Gabriel closed the front door. He walked the five-thousand-square-foot house, every inch designated to ensure his privacy and continuity of thought. In the ground-floor study, he checked reports from the factory he'd contracted with in Ukraine. Chip matrix output was meeting his early goals.

Gabriel descended to the basement. As he refilled his mug in his living quarters' kitchenette, he checked messages on the small media wall. "Missing you" appeared with a woman's image. The woman was not Olivia. Gabriel moved to his lab, which dominated the basement. He opened the security door with a biometric sensor. The corporate logo for Warder, Inc. floated on the multiple monitors. A video call rang, and Gabriel answered on the main monitor. Olivia was calling while driving.

"I expected you to check in twenty minutes ago," Gabriel said.

"Sorry if I'm not keeping your schedule." Olivia narrowed her eyes, a look daring him to comment.

"Stay on the route I reserved for you," Gabriel said.

Olivia viewed the road ahead—populated with Border State patrols. A car burned at a blockaded intersection, a reminder of the violence awaiting both authorized travelers and bandits. A digital road sign indicated directions to the e-Bahn. Olivia had the family transit pass. She could make a run. Olivia hated herself for the impulsive thought. Not without Josh, whom Gabriel had forbade joining the visit to Vadim and Roxy. Olivia would not deviate from her route. She wanted to get home quickly, just as Gabriel wanted her to do.

"Go, Deliverer!" Josh watched *Delivery: Dead or Alive!* on the media wall. He replayed highlights from the run just completed, including a recap of every round Bren had fired from the Barrett.

Olivia came through the door and called to her son and husband. Neither responded. She climbed the stairs and dropped her bags outside the loft.

Olivia gently removed Josh's headphones. "What are you watching?"

Josh hesitated. *"Delivery: Dead or Alive!"*

"The adult feed? I said you could only watch the kid's version."

"But Dad ..."

Olivia reached for the remote. Josh grabbed first.

"Mom, look at what the Deliverer did." Josh clicked on the highlight reel. "He owned those Porch Pirates. I bet he's almost as smart as Dad."

Olivia glanced at the footage of the Deliverer in action, his photo alongside the video thumbnails. She paused at the video of Dr. Luna and the townspeople sending off Bren with fresh farm products and more prayers. Olivia took the remote from Josh and reinstated parental controls. The program faded out.

Gabriel ascended the stairs, lips pursed. "I have an important call in a few minutes. I need quiet."

Olivia picked up her bags and headed to the master bedroom. "I know. Every call is 'very important.' Sorry I was being too loud."

Gabriel followed her into the bedroom. "If you want the house run a certain way, you shouldn't leave."

"This has been my first time outside the gates in over a year." Olivia threw her bags on the bed and began unpacking.

Gabriel disappeared into the sprawling closet. "You could've visited your old teacher online."

31

Olivia suppressed the urge to yell. "He's dying. A Zoom call won't do it." She saw Gabriel reemerge from the closet with two ties dangling from his fist. "Didn't you take enough ties when you moved to the basement?"

Gabriel held up neckwear choices in a mirror. "I thought you appreciated not being disturbed when I come to bed late."

"You haven't disturbed me in a long time."

Gabriel looped the final selection around his collar. Turning from the mirror, he held out a hand. "The transit pass."

Olivia looked at him—if she could, her eyes would burn holes through him.

"Or do you have other terminally ill teachers I don't know about?"

"I have nowhere else to go." Olivia withdrew the puck-shaped device from her suitcase. Ignoring Gabriel's waiting palm, she dropped the transit pass on the duvet.

CHAPTER 4

The eQuality, Inc. logistics hub resembled a half-century of outposts modeling Ali Al Salem Air Base in Kuwait, the middle of nowhere transformed into improbable crossroads. Bren joined a line of delivery drivers wending through HESCO barriers, stacked shipping containers, and checkpoints. As the vehicles inched forward, his mind drifted ...

Eight-year-old Bren stomped across a carpet of shed eucalyptus bark. A dusty lot stood behind the trees, shielded from the fields holding Heritage Days, which his family attended every season. No lit-up rides, no garish concession stands occupied the secluded corner—merely a jam of rusty horse trailers and tilting campers. The band Southern Culture on the Skids played over tinny speakers.

Bren prowled the narrow paths between the parked vehicles. His boyish sense of the forbidden told him he didn't belong, making the reconnaissance more exciting than strolling the midway.

"Where'd you come from?" Aluminum steps shimmied under the old man exiting his RV.

"Heritage Days." Bren pointed over his shoulder with his thumb. "I saw all this stuff when we were driving in. Is this part of the festival?"

"You might say," the old man said. "We're working the event. Cowboys for the rodeo. Carneys running games and rides. The folks who cook and sell the food. This is where we stay."

"I'd like to work here. I could ride the Cyclone every day and eat all the funnel cakes I want."

The old man smiled. "It's a hard life. Towns all over the country have something like your Heritage Days. We hit as many as we can to earn a living. You wanna live on the road?"

"Sounds cool!"

Bren's parents called out as they jogged toward him. They took his hands in iron grips.

"Sorry," Cindy said to the old man.

"This is not for us." Jack pivoted the family toward the proper attractions ...

Thirty years forward, Bren was the nomad, admitted to a packed commune, expected to put on the show. The line of vehicles moved, and Bren could see his Airstream Flying Cloud parked with the other drivers' rigs. The sleek aluminum trailer wore its abuse like the Lightning, like the rolling stock at Heritage Day 2008. Bren saw himself deteriorating like the prophetic carney if he lived long enough.

Bren parked next to his trailer and surveyed the recent damage. Kevlar under the aluminum panels had maintained integrity. Bren took photos of the bullet holes. The service bay would be ready to dig out the slugs and patch the holes with aluminum putty mixed to his specifications. A diagnostic app showed internal systems intact. Turnaround would be brief.

An orange Mustang Shelby GT500 lurched to a halt, headlight and chin spoiler drooping from a crumpled quarter-panel. D.D. Guthrie exited the battered car with her own damage—left arm hanging awkwardly, a gash in her form-fitting jumpsuit. D.D. cursed under her breath as she tossed her crash helmet in the backseat, releasing her long hair dyed in rainbow streaks.

Bren inspected D.D.'s left shoulder. "Dislocated again?"

"Partial," D.D. leaned back against her car. Bren took her wrist and moved the arm in a circular motion that gradually increased. She yowled when the ball popped back.

"I'd hug you, but it hurts too much." D.D. shifted weight to her feet. Technicians prepared to tow her car to the service bay. "You give me a real fender. No carbon fiber. Detroit iron!" The techs nodded at her order.

"You need a little servicing yourself," Bren said.

"I don't want people seeing me in a hospital bed." D.D. smirked as she put a familiar hand on Bren's face. "Imagine fans finding out you're human."

Smiling, Bren took D.D.'s hand from his cheek and gave a gentle pat. "Can't let that happen."

The drivers assembled in a hangar. Towering displays married stock market exchange boards with Ginza Strip signage—the latest driver rankings driven by AI assessment, customer reviews, and fan sentiment. Bren's data row hovered at the top. D.D.'s sank steadily, several cells lit in cautionary yellow.

"You're downgrading me?" D.D. exhorted the display. "That'll lower my take." She confronted the data manager walking the floor. "I was top five before tonight. What are you doing?"

"We're not doing anything. The algorithm decides." Reginald, the data manager, checked his tablet. "AI determined you made a poor choice with the evasive maneuver that smashed your fender. You lost time and passed up a clear shot at this Porch Pirate vehicle." Reginald showed an image of a flatbed truck that had pursued D.D.

D.D. jabbed the screen. "I got four yahoos in the back aiming 12 gauges. Yeah, I'm gonna bug out and find another way to pop the driver. Sorry if some computer didn't see it the same way." She strode to the middle of the floor. "I take home too much money, and eQuality doesn't like that!"

The ranking session concluded, Bren took a stainless steel and Lucite box to another hangar. One of the parting gifts from the townspeople, the box cradled three dozen eggs suspended in metal hoops, suitable packaging for such precious cargo. Bren set the box on the counter of the logistics station inside the building.

"Requesting cryo-drone shipment," Bren said.

"Someone's getting a fancy treat." Mia, the logistics manager, nudged a tablet toward Bren to collect shipping information.

"Breakfast for Maddie and Grandma," Bren said.

"Won't get there until noon. Air traffic is a mess in the city corridor."

"Lunch then."

A refrigeration transport the size of a coffee table hovered toward the station. Mia opened the frosted belly and secured the box inside. The drone rose into the swirl of small craft inside the hangar and flew out the open doors.

Bren took a long walk in the hot night back to the drivers' area. The logistics hub never slept as trucks, drones, tiltrotors, and an occasional jet kept common cargo moving. The elite packages would have to wait. Their human factor did sleep.

Bren made breakfast in the trailer kitchen as he spoke into his phone. "Whatcha doing this weekend?" The automated mount swiveled to keep him in the shot while he opened the fridge.

"The youth group is going to the refugee camp. We're helping at a feeding station. I made inventory and distribution lists like you use, Dad." Madison added her project documents to the video call view. At twelve, she already displayed impressive management skills.

"Those camps can be rough. Stick close to the pastors," Bren said.

"This girl is very responsible, unlike a certain little boy who always wandered off." Cindy peered over her granddaughter's shoulder to get a better look at Bren's food prep. "Are those fresh eggs?"

Nodding, Bren cracked three of them into a skillet. "A gratuity I got on the last run. I kept some and sent the rest to you by cryo-drone." He checked his smartwatch. "You should get delivery around noon. Keep an eye on the balcony."

Madison instinctively looked toward the sliding glass doors. She and Cindy were high in a former office building, erected when people had worked at desks downtown. Their apartment was carved from an executive suite and included the perk of a fresh-air landing.

"Any info about the new hub?" Cindy asked

"Still a rumor until it isn't," Bren said. "Lots of money to be made in the Border States. Lots of risk with sides shifting all the time. But if it's real, and I get picked for the starting lineup, I'll go."

"I miss you, Dad," Madison said.

"I miss you too, Maddie. I'll get back to the city soon as I can. And remember, we'll be together all the time when we move to the Revival Zone."

"When are we moving?" Madison said.

"You know. When we can afford a transit pass to take the e-Bahn." Bren stirred the eggs in the skillet, regretting the line of conversation.

"Let's say goodbye. Your dad needs to rest before his next run," Cindy said.

"You always say the same thing. There must be another way to get there. We didn't need the e-Bahn when we moved here," Madison said.

"That was different. We'll be crossing the most heavily defended border in the world," Bren said. "We have to double back across Greater America to the immigration center at Surrey, British Columbia. NATO rules for entry."

"You're the best driver. You could get us there." Madison fought tears as her grandmother comforted her.

"There's no other way." Bren was solemn.

Olivia and Gabriel intersected in the kitchen. She wore a steel-gray leotard and leggings, complementing her hair and bracelets. She selected fruits and vegetables, grown blocks away in the community aeroponic farm, and dropped them in the juicer. Gabriel settled for local produce as well, brewing a packet of roasted grain and genetically modified guarana as a coffee substitute.

"Don't plan any more trips," Gabriel said.

"I told you I wasn't." Olivia pulsed the juicer.

"I'm heading to Ukraine to review the production facility. I have meetings with potential backers after that. Obviously, I'll need the transit pass." Gabriel locked eyes with his wife. "A Zoom call won't do it."

"There's no sense asking when you'll be back," Olivia said. "What do you want me to tell Josh?"

"Tell him to spend every possible second with *his* children. I'm making him a man of leisure, so it'll be easy." Gabriel glanced about. "Where is he, by the way?"

"Sleeping over at the Lightfoots. He won't disturb you." Olivia pressed a button under a counter ledge. The kitchen island retracted, compelling Gabriel to retrieve his steaming cup from its surface.

"Panic attack, darling?" Gabriel's jest came whenever she opened the passage.

"Far from it." Olivia finished pouring her juice and descended the spiral staircase now visible through the kitchen floor.

The panic room contradicted the spirit of the Entrada community. The fortified enclave was one of the safest places in the Border States, as the marketing had promised. Still, every basement featured a reenforced retreat, an expected luxury amenity long before Civil War II. In this forgotten cellar, Gabriel allowed Olivia to store her art—her art being herself.

After warming up, Olivia removed reflective appliqués from a small case. She put the red stickers on her cheeks, torso, and limbs. The media wall activated. A line of life-sized characters filled the screen, heads bowed, eyes closed, standing in shadow. With a gesture, she summoned a figure forward on the screen. Stepping into the light, the avatar revealed itself as Olivia's likeness but in costume and makeup.

The corporeal Olivia entered a motion capture field, a lattice of lasers tracing her face and body, ruby beams bouncing off the appliqués. She turned into a fourth arabesque, and the avatar duplicated her movement in real time. Olivia looked over her shoulder into the digital re-creation of her eyes. The avatar was a watercolor left in the rain, pastel shades of pigment and fabric draining from the body.

Olivia sent the image back to first position and conjured the avatar in the center—the Metallic Woman, arms sheathed in fearsome exaggerations of her beloved bracelets, hair literally electric-blue and separately animated, body painted and paneled.

A music track started—percussive, atonal. Olivia built into a grand jeté, the metallic woman drawing her life force, synthesizing her leap. The dancing intensified as the music crescendoed. A small red bulb ignited at the far side of the room, similar to a "quiet, please" light outside a soundstage. Gabriel's latest conference call was underway on the floor above. Olivia doubted her music or any audio signature ever escaped the bomb-resistant chamber. Still, she stopped the track and sent the Metallic Woman into waiting. She sat against the media wall and wept, the avatars standing sentinel behind her.

The door to Gabriel's study was shut, its media wall active. Like his wife, Gabriel took pleasure before his display, pacing the room, summoning documents and images with gestures. A woman, mid-thirties, appeared on the conference call app at the wall's center, her digital name tag reading Naomi Pham, eQuality, Inc.

"Mr. Durand, I assure you, eQuality is very interested in your technology," Naomi said. "But remember, we're one of the biggest companies on Earth. You're a startup."

"Is that supposed to intimidate me?" Gabriel said.

"No. I'm saying we move at different speeds," Naomi said.

"I want to talk to Cox himself. If he's moving at my speed, he can reach me at the plant in Ukraine. If he's moving at his speed, he can leave a message while I'm negotiating with his rivals."

Olivia looked toward the corner of the room. The barely perceptible outline of a door etched the textured surface. She glanced up at Gabriel's silence light, which still burned. She moved to the panic room's server, a powerful, standalone unit to control life support and communications. The computer was programmed to anticipate problems.

The panic room's voice agent spoke, "Olivia, the door is locked from the outside. As I've said before, this is dangerous in case of fire. Do you want me to open it?"

"Yes, please." Olivia removed the tablet interface from the dock.

The door clicked open. Olivia entered Gabriel's lab. Computer monitors displayed the logo for Warder, Inc., Gabriel's startup. A bank of 3D printers lined a wall— industrial models, not the consumer variety found on the upper floors.

"Unrecognized computer system operating in proximity," the voice agent said. "Do you want me to launch countermeasures?"

"Yes, please."

The panic room computer had a potent anti-hacking program to protect against cyberattack while residents were sheltering. "Countermeasures" mode allowed concealed control of hostile systems. Both the computer and Olivia considered Gabriel's network hostile.

"Privacy-compromising file on tablet screen," the voice agent said.

Olivia already knew the file from the first time she'd hacked Warder: "Subject: Olivia Durand." She saw the update: "DNA Uptake Scheduled." The cryptic, invasive datum didn't rattle Olivia. She would be ready.

CHAPTER 5

A group of drivers sat in camping chairs outside the Airstream. Each had Scripture on a phone or in print. Bren stood in the center of the circle. An online audience watched a live feed.

"Romans 8:28. 'And we know that God causes everything to work together for the good of those who love God and are called according to his purpose for them.'" Bren looked up from his Bible. "Everything—good and bad. What are some examples from Scripture of bad things turned to God's purpose?"

The study group perused their texts. D.D. walked past the trailer. Bren pointed to an empty seat. She frowned before walking away.

"Job, he's the king of bad times," a driver said. "God used him to teach humanity and Satan a lesson. 38:33. 'Do you know the laws of the universe? Can you use them to regulate the earth?' He wrote the laws. He reminded Job, then restored him."

"Genesis 50:20," a second driver said. "'You intended to harm me, but God intended it all for good. He brought me to this position so I could save the lives of many people.' If Joseph's brothers hadn't tried to destroy him, he wouldn't have become the guy running Egypt. He ended up saving them."

A driver with a gray ponytail sat in thought—Roadie, who drove a battle-scarred van that used to haul rock bands to their gigs. "What about the bad in us, the bad things we do?" he asked. "Does God need another Cain, another Judas? Am I just a cautionary tale?"

"How bad are you?" Bren was thoughtful.

"People call us modern gladiators. The Romans had gladiators. They were evil."

"Maybe we're the Christians getting thrown to the lions."

"Maybe we're Caesar's killers." Roadie looked at Bren with imploring eyes, hoping to be talked out of his despair. The other drivers shifted in their seats.

"Saul of Tarsus was a killer. He found redemption on the road." Bren paused. His words resonated for the entire group, including himself.

A man waved from the edge of the trailer encampment. "Hey, it's the Deliverer!" Bren dismissed the study group as the man approached. "Can I get a selfie? My kid's a huge fan. Me too."

"Not used to seeing fans inside the wire." Bren smiled and brought his face into frame.

"I'm working here. Harrington Transport. Leasing space at the hub." The photo app clicked, and the man introduced himself. "I'm Jeff." He shook Bren's hand. "God bless you."

An older man strode into view, wearing the same company uniform as Jeff. As he folded chairs, Bren watched Jeff jog toward the man, who grabbed Jeff's shirt in one fist and nearly struck him with the other. The pair hustled away.

"Aren't you supposed to be on the bidding floor?" Mia was at her workstation, orchestrating the morning flight of drones.

"Exchange is down. Gives me time to stretch my legs." Bren came to the desk. "Just ran into someone who said he was with Harrington Transport. Didn't think eQuality was in the habit of leasing hub space."

Mia nodded. "Harrington's been landing the past couple of days. Running C-17s."

"Military normally flies those."

"Some C-17s are privately owned. Couple of the states had fire sales."

"What have they offloaded?"

"Nothing much, far as I can tell."

Bren craned his neck to look out the hangar doors. A C-17 sat across the tarmac, cargo ramp closed. A lone Humvee was parked under the nose.

In his study, Gabriel finalized his travel plan to Europe. Flights from the former USA were infrequent and bound in red tape due to makeshift treaties between the various Americas and European nations, creating prolonged delays for bomb and virus screenings. A bigger negative was the threat of being shot down before reaching the Atlantic coast. All three American air forces were on constant alert, and numerous independent militias had anti-aircraft weapons and distrusted anything leaving a contrail.

Gabriel's British citizenship would ease entry into Canada, which had stable relations and regular air travel with Europe. Crossing the 49th parallel by ground was not a simple matter. NATO had established a defensive line along the border to prevent Civil War II rolling north. In 2029, the Battle of Puget Sound to seize ballistic missile submarines had exemplified one such spillover.

Gabriel opened the app for the e-Bahn, the safest means of long-distance transit across the three Americas and the Border States. While the countries remained in conflict, they allowed construction of the interconnecting road system, with new routes and extensions opening thanks to overseas investment. The wealthy had demanded some ability to travel.

"Planning transit to Winnipeg," Gabriel said.

"Acknowledged," the voice assistant said.

Gabriel would avoid the old roads, which were minimally policed and repaired, making them ideal backdrops for *Delivery: Dead or Alive!* His privileged route, the e-Bahn, had supplanted Eisenhower's interstates. Green hydrogen fired the furnaces and kilns that had produced the new highway's steel and concrete. Private security was posted along the guardrails. An inductive charging system built into the road surface replenished EVs while they drove. As the premier infrastructure in Greater America, the highway received constant enhancement.

"Do you want to review the upgrades along your route?"

"No." Gabriel didn't need reassurance about the road's speed, safety, or security.

"Please present transit pass for reservation," the voice assistant said.

Gabriel held up the prized puck. The internationally recognized token had granted Olivia passage on the better patrolled conventional roads to see her teacher. For the first leg of his journey, the e-Bahn extending into Canada would lay open for his vehicle. After that, he would sail through the airports in Winnipeg, Kyiv, and any other major city. While priced comparably, the transit pass transcended yachts and mansions as a status symbol. Big boats and houses were much easier to come by.

"Please wait for confirmation," the voice assistant said.

Despite its extreme value, stealing a transit pass was pointless as biometrics restricted usage to the issued party. The same biometrics would detect stress levels if an owner were taken hostage, alerting authorities. And without the pass, driving the e-Bahn was impossible. The bored guards didn't have to lift a trigger finger to dispatch trespassers.

Gabriel skimmed a gallery of e-Bahn attempts made without a transit pass. In each recording, a spike of artificial lightning roasted the vehicle. The built-in charging system executed violators. Gabriel never made time for the popular entertainment of *Delivery: Dead or Alive!* but the e-Bahn's public service videos afforded him a brief guilty pleasure.

"Pass verified. Reservation confirmed," the voice assistant said.

Gabriel put the transit pass on his desk. The object lit up as Olivia passed the study door. She glanced reflexively. Smiling, Gabriel shut the door.

Olivia stood in the panic room studio, watching the light that signaled for silence. The bulb finally glowed red. Tablet in hand, she unlocked the lab and entered. A moment later, the panic room computer hacked the Warder network. Olivia opened a cabinet marked Prototypes. Two plastic divider boxes held a series of small cases. Olivia took the second-to-last case in the box to the left. She put the case for her laser appliqués in its place. The switch wouldn't stand close inspection, but an inventory gap would be obvious.

Looking through the open door, Olivia saw the "Quiet" light still burned. She brought the tablet to one of the 3D printers. The printer app appeared on her screen. A lab monitor displayed "Warder Consumer App—Beta."

A video of an attractive woman played. "Welcome to Warder. Quantum technology that brings you peace of mind. Time to print your Warder chip. Open your chip case and center the interior of the right half under your printer extruder."

Olivia tuned out the presentation as she had already researched the process through previous hacks. She prepared the case at the printer.

"Your printer should already be adjusted and loaded with chip compound, per the previous instruction module," the woman in the video continued.

She breathed deeply and slowly tapped *print*. "The chip you're now waiting for is a compound of silicon, gallium, graphene, and proprietary materials." The woman narrated over an animated image of molecular strata. "A breakthrough formula that combines quantum computing with home printing."

The plant in Ukraine manufactured Warder's compound formula, which Gabriel had shipped to the home lab via low-priority transport. Olivia remembered his insistence on this tactic. A flashy and costly courier like the Deliverer would have been too conspicuous.

"Every atom has its place in the Warder chip, an amazing quantum architecture." The animation transitioned to microscopic nozzles emitting compound, forming the chip's micro processing components. "Be sure to collect your DNA sample no more than five days after the chip is printed. The uptake receptors lose their sensitivity after that, making the chip unusable."

Olivia was confident about collecting her sample within the window of opportunity. She knew Gabriel would be leaving soon for Europe.

The printing app indicated eighty percent completion. Eighty-five. Eighty-nine. Olivia focused on the print job graphic, the circle inexorably closing to signal conclusion. She didn't notice the quiet light go off. She had no idea how long Gabriel had been off his call when she glanced back into the panic room. Ninety-three. Ninety-four.

Olivia heard a noise. She turned off the monitor playing the video. The basement stairs creaked. She stared at the printer app. Ninety-eight. Ninety-nine. The graphic circle closed. Olivia withdrew and sealed the case. As she rushed to the open door, she backed out of the Warder network, leaving no trace. The click of the combination resetting on the panic room door overlapped with Gabriel unlocking the main door.

Gabriel activated lab equipment. He looked quizzically at the monitor that didn't turn on and pushed power. He turned his head to the panic room door. He unlocked the door. Olivia sat in front of the media wall, stretching.

"I've confirmed the day I'm leaving," Gabriel said. "Something wrong with the computer?" He nodded at the undocked tablet on the ground next to Olivia.

Olivia looked at the tablet then raised her gaze to Gabriel. "No. Just adjusting the humidity level."

"Yes, you must get quite warm doing your routine." Gabriel started to return to the lab. He stopped and faced Olivia. "This is my most important trip yet. You won't go anywhere, do anything unnecessary while I'm gone."

"Is that a question or an order?"

"Neither. Simply a fact."

Gabriel reentered the lab and locked the door. He went to the cabinet and withdrew a case. He paused.

Olivia snapped the tablet into the dock. She picked up the gym towel she'd tossed in a corner, the chip case barely concealed in its folds. She stuffed towel and case into a workout bag, eyes on the door. She heard Gabriel start a printer. Bag in hand, she hurried up the spiral staircase.

"Now!" Sparky said.

He gunned the El Camino in front of the Lightning as a Porch Pirate jumped from the bed. His face plastered the windshield, wild eyes staring into Bren's. The Porch Pirate clambered onto the roof, seeking handholds in the rack. The Lightning veered from the El Camino. Losing his grip, the Porch Pirate rolled along the roof and landed in the bed.

Bren swerved violently, trying to dislodge the intruder. The Porch Pirate flattened and braced against a sidewall. He looked up. The Barrett rested in its mount against the tailgate. The Porch Pirate crawled to the weapon. He stood high enough to pull the rifle free and aim at the cab. The rear bulkhead burst open, and Bren's chair sped down the rails. He fired a double-tap.

The Porch Pirate dropped the Barrett and toppled backward over the tailgate. Bren remounted the rifle, eyes on the spot where the body stopped bouncing. Lonny's Charger barely missed the corpse. Sparky swerved to avoid the Charger and went in the ditch. Bren rode his chair back to the steering wheel. He returned his .45 to the center console and resumed manual control of his truck. The muscle cars on his tail fell back as he turned onto a rutted dirt road.

Kenny's broadcast played on the touchscreen. "You saw it live. The Deliverer with a takedown." He looked toward Bren. "Anything to say?"

"Hail, Caesar." Bren was stony, searching the road ahead for the next threat.

Madison watched her father's latest battle on her phone. She took a knee. "Lord Jesus, Dad didn't have a choice. Please forgive him and watch over him. Please forgive the man who just died. I'm sure he had people who love him too. Make everyone stop hating and killing each other. Amen."

Madison rejoined her pastors and youth group. They moved down the sideline of what had been a football field in a domed arena. The roof was a nine-acre sieve, surrendering the cavern below to bleach and rot. Still, the space was a haven to thousands who'd been displaced by massacre, famine, drought, disease. In their despair, the refugees reconstituted the former United States, the shattered stadium the new melting pot.

The church group wheeled wagons of donated food and water to a feeding station. Madison offloaded the goods with the others. A boy came alongside, waving his phone.

"Maddie, your dad just pulled the sickest move!" The boy was well-meaning, a fan. Madison nodded absently and hefted a case of bottled water.

CHAPTER 6

"We're both so busy in the basement." Gabriel watched Olivia top the spiral staircase after another studio session. "Perhaps we have more in common than we realize."

Olivia closed the kitchen island over the stairway. "You've always made it clear how different we are."

"Opposites attract. Forgive the cliché."

"You're forgiven."

Gabriel had become almost tender in the past forty-eight hours. Olivia knew his departure was imminent. She showered and put on makeup and a negligee at a dressing table deep in a closet labyrinth. She walked back to the shadowy master suite. Gabriel stood in the doorway.

"I see Josh is on another sleepover."

"I made a point of it." Olivia's smile came slowly.

A year had passed since Gabriel and Olivia had slept together. He took Olivia's hand to lead her to the bed. Both their free hands, gently curled, held a Warder chip patch. Moments later, both felt for a stretch of bare back to adhere the device. Olivia wouldn't have noticed her DNA sample being taken if she hadn't joined the subterfuge. Two scorpions in a mating dance stung each other, victory to the female who harbored the whole truth. At the end, Gabriel pulled Olivia into a lengthy embrace, the moment to remove the patch.

The Durands retreated to separate corners of the rambling suite. At her dressing table, Olivia removed the chip case from its hiding place. She played a Warder instruction video downloaded to her phone. Sound muted, the spokeswoman demonstrated how to load the chip patch into the recess inside the case. Olivia steadied her breathing as she positioned the patch, keeping watch on the walk-in closet door. The chip patch molded to the recess. Electronic pathways spread from the emplaced material, resembling a nervous system. Olivia's hand trembled, and she thought the device was stirring. She reburied the case in its hiding place.

Olivia emerged from the dressing area, closing her robe, as Gabriel left the master suite. "Thank you," Olivia said. Gabriel smiled over his shoulder, certain of his undiminished appeal.

The next morning, Gabriel stepped into his Buick RoadFortress, the two rows of back seats replaced by a mobile office featuring monitors, a small desk, and an ergonomic work chair with a seat belt. As the gullwing door closed, Gabriel was already absorbed in the displays. Josh came to the window, tears close to the surface. He tapped on the glass to get his father's attention.

Gabriel lowered the window. "Years from now, you'll remember this as the day your life changed." The glass resealed, and the autonomous Buick left the driveway. Josh cried as his mother pulled him close.

After an hour on expensive toll roads, the Buick reached the on-ramp to the e-Bahn. Digital signs read "e-Bahn—Your Tax Dollars at Work," "Serious Injury or Death Will Occur for Unauthorized Drivers." A third sign displayed dense legalese absolving the government of blame.

The pavement shimmered platinum and violet, the inductor layer to transmit power. Gabriel's transit pass blinked green, and the notice e-Bahn Travel Approved appeared on the touchscreen monitoring vehicle performance. Burned-out cars dotted the shoulders with corpses strapped in their seats. The skeletons of man and machine served the same purpose as crucified lawbreakers lining the road between Rome and Capua—a warning to obey.

Ignoring the grisly scenery, Gabriel examined the case containing the chip infused with Olivia's DNA, the microprocessor visible through the translucent top. An app opened on one of Gabriel's screens, Warder Tracking Dashboard. Subject: Olivia Durand. A map of Entrada appeared. A dot synced to Olivia's heartbeat within the diagram of the family home.

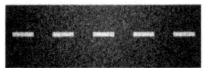

In her studio, Olivia held the case with Gabriel's chip. Subject: Gabriel Durand appeared on her phone app. Gabriel usually had no digital footprint. He routinely evaded tracking by conventional means. His invention was unconventional. Olivia watched his heart rate increase as his marker sped north.

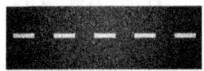

At dusk, Bren pulled into the checkpoint line for return to the hub. Social media continued parsing his Caesar reference from the day before. He glanced at sentiment charts. When he got closer to the checkpoint, he noted the beefed-up security. Closer still, and he recognized a face among the new guards.

Bren stopped the Lightning for visual inspection. "Jeff, I didn't know you worked security." He was friendly to the man who'd requested the selfie.

Still in his generic corporate uniform, Jeff held an M4 rifle. He gave Bren a small head shake. Getting the message, Bren disengaged and drove on after receiving the all-clear.

One more C-17 taxied to a growing fleet, and the landing lights of another pierced the fog. Humvees crisscrossed the field. Bren kept his eyes on the air and ground vehicles while he parked the Lightning. He took out his phone to call Madison.

At the same time in the city, Madison and the church group wheeled empty wagons through downtown when her father's ringtone sounded.

"Where are you?" Bren asked.

"We went to the refugee camp again. I'm almost home," Madison said.

"Find Grandma. If you hear air raid sirens, it won't be a drill. Get to the basement."

"What's happening?" Madison's fear grew as the phone connection sputtered.

"Military action. From what I can see …" Bren looked at the phone. The call had dropped.

The church group had gathered around Madison by the end of her conversation. The pastors ran with the rest of the children. Madison bolted to her building's security gate. She urged the biometric sensors and locks to hurry. She ran into the elevator and punched the button for her floor. The lights flickered and the car lurched. Madison slammed the metal wall to curse her mistake—Dad always said never take the elevator in an emergency. The doors began to part. They froze and the car went dark. Bluish backup lights switched on. Madison pried the doors open with her back and one foot.

"Grandma!" Madison ran into her flat. Cindy appeared from a back room with a flashlight. "There's going to be an attack."

"Are you sure it's not just another black—" An air raid siren cut off Cindy's question.

Madison and Cindy grabbed their go-bags and returned to the hallway. Neighbors poked their heads out. They followed the Deliverer's precocious daughter to the stairwell.

Bren drew Roadie close. "Military action's coming."

"What do we do?" Roadie said.

"Tell people to spread out the vehicles so we make less of a target." Bren climbed into the Lightning. "Everyone should stay calm. If we get jumpy, troops may suppress us. I'm gonna take a closer look."

The Lightning rolled slowly out of the camp, headlamps doused. In contrast, the drone hangar's lighting flashed brilliantly. Bren heard shouts in the distance. The beams from the open doors dimmed. The lights weren't failing. Something was eclipsing the illumination.

As he drew near, Bren envisioned the nightly bat flight emerging from Carlsbad Caverns. Drones billowed from the hangar, a chaotic, twisting mass. The huge doors rolled shut, ending the machines' exodus. A drone buzzed the Lightning.

More drones crashed into parked C-17s and Humvees. Screams, explosions, and automatic weapons fire reverberated across the field. A stream of the craft climbed into the main flight path. The latest C-17 was on final approach. The oncoming drones funneled into the plane's four jet intakes. The engines disintegrated, snapping the wings. The fuselage hit the ground, sliding on its belly before bisecting a parked plane and exploding.

The Lightning penetrated glass panes set along the hangar door's bottom edge. Mia and another worker hid under office furniture. The remaining drones wheeled overhead. The truck slid to a stop on the concrete floor. Mia and her colleague piled in.

"Someone hacked the drones." Mia was bleeding, terrified.

Bren gunned the truck toward the hangar doors. A large drone came head on. The Lightning swerved, and the drone's wingtip glanced off the cab. The truck spun, taking out more glass with its exit.

Troops and ground vehicles spilled from the surviving C-17s. As the drone barrage subsided, the force organized to leave the hub. Fifty-thousand feet overhead, a pair of ancient B-52s dropped their payload. What appeared to be iron bombs split open in descent, disgorging paratroopers in wing suits. Once free of the high-altitude cocoons, the wings inflated, and gun barrels and mini rockets projected from their membranes. The paratroopers streaked toward the hub.

The Lightning barreled across the field while the battle unfolded. Two explosions shook the truck. The roof cam locked on the incoming threat. Bren appraised the night-vision view on the touchscreen. A paratrooper dove for the Lightning.

Seconds later, Bren manned the Barrett, inserting a magazine marked Tracers. He chambered the first round as the paratrooper switched from rockets to guns. Bren's passengers screamed when bullets ricocheted off the cab roof. He aimed skyward. The first round missed, but Bren noted the distance between its orange trail and the flash of the airborne automatic weapons. The second round hit the paratrooper center mass. The wing suit ignited. The paratrooper's corpse continued gliding and burning, a moth embracing the flame.

Bren brought his chair back to the steering wheel. He pulled up at a bunker and urged his passengers inside. Returning to the airfield, he reached back to unlatch the Springfield Armory M1A from the ceiling gun rack. Paratroopers, their wings shed, formed small units to pin down troops and destroy equipment. The soldiers from the C-17s fought back with their ground vehicles and heavier weapons.

The Lightning turned toward the encampment. Several paratroopers were in a firefight with drivers. At the fender of her Mustang, D.D. crouched with a Typhoon F12 shotgun, holding off two soldiers. The Lightning's electric hum was inaudible in the din. Coming to a halt, Bren slammed one soldier from behind with his driver's door. He leaped onto the second, flattening him with a foot to the jaw. Rifle in hand, Bren jogged to D.D.

"Who's fighting who?" D.D. said.

"With all the C-17s, I'd say America Blue is conducting a military operation. They're under counterattack, and we're in the middle," Bren said. "Bunkers at the west end of the hub."

D.D. reloaded. "I'm not sitting in a hole while they wreck my stuff."

"At least drive down there. Get out of the line of fire." Bren rose to survey the camp.

D.D. peeled out for the far end of the hub. Other drivers followed. Roadie tended a comrade with a leg wound. Bren helped him put the injured driver in his van. As Roadie pulled away, Bren heard a groan. Jeff sprawled between trailers, bleeding heavily.

Bren slung his rifle and withdrew bandages from the first aid kit hanging on his belt. Jeff clutched his arm.

"Help me—" Jeff's voice was fading.

"I am." Bren applied a dressing.

Jeff shook his head. "Help me call my son." He held up his phone. Bren tapped the screen and positioned the phone in Jeff's trembling hand. A boy appeared in the poor connection.

"Dad?" The boy recoiled at the sight of his father's bloody face.

"I just wanted to see you," Jeff said.

The boy cried as Jeff's voice trailed off. Bren adjusted the phone to include himself. "I'll stay with your dad. I'm praying for him. You pray too. He loves you."

The call dropped. Bren couldn't find Jeff's pulse. He prayed as gunfire ebbed. The drivers' camp was largely deserted. A column of soldiers rumbled out of the hub, fighting off the airborne attack. Hearing a close burst of machine gun fire, Bren pulled the M1A off his shoulder and searched for remaining threats. He lowered the muzzle when he came upon his Airstream. He ran fingers over bullet holes. He withdrew his phone and summoned a grainy image of Madison huddled with Cindy in the building's bomb shelter.

"I just wanted to see you." Bren shared a tear with his daughter.

Gabriel's Buick arrived at the 49th parallel. The e-Bahn fed into a broad, non-electrified highway, its multiple lanes swallowed by an imposing concrete and steel structure, the Manitoba Provincial Border Station. Defenses bracketed the crossing—triple concertina wire fencing, tank traps, and minefields at the immediate threshold, with a flight line of CF-105B Arrows less than a mile north. The fortification had arisen from the Canadian Build the Wall campaign.

The Buick stopped inside the building. Flags for NATO and Canada hung from the ceiling. A Danish soldier approached the car, checking Gabriel's information on a mobile device. Soldiers from other European nations stood nearby, Colt Canada C8 carbines in tactical carry.

"You just made it," the soldier said. "We're closing the border until the fighting stops. Communications are patchy. There's a satellite boost station straight ahead. Anyone you need to call?"

"No." Gabriel rolled up the window and the Buick continued.

CHAPTER 7

The meeting hall held shadows and echoes, but no humans. Jerold Cox came forward. He stood six feet tall, two inches more than his actual height. Clara Ruskin, broker general for America Blue, joined him, sporting a new hair color and a preview of the stem cell face lift awaiting in Chennai, India, once she was able to take her long-planned medical vacation. Randall Bates, chair of the Border States governors' council, was the last to arrive. The injuries he'd sustained in the recent military action were hidden beneath his digital enhancement. Holographic ID appeared below each face. Chairs materialized for the avatars. The virtual reality meeting came to order.

"I have a TV interview soon," Cox said. "The audience is expecting good news."

"Two-thousand people dead." Gov. Bates summoned a battle-ravaged street as the VR background. The avatars stood as an island in a flow of casualties. "Will that make your audience happy?"

Broker General Ruskin dispelled the image with a hand motion. "My government has reached agreement for a new enterprise district with the Border States."

"Nothing like bombing your way to the negotiating table," Gov. Bates said.

"You were closing on a trade deal with the Chinese," Raskin said. "Very un-American."

"I thought that term was obsolete." Gov. Bates winced in pain. His avatar flickered, converting to his actual likeness in a hospital bed. He frowned in concentration, and his uninjured rendering returned.

"The fighting has passed. Let the commerce begin." Cox placed the trio at the ruin of a huge shopping mall. "eQuality has selected a site for its first fire hub, close to contested borders but an excellent logistics location." Cox gestured. "She was a beauty in her day." The mall images regressed thirty years. Fresh concrete repoured into walls and floors, and shoppers filled the promenades. Virtual humanity swept past the trio once more. "Thank you for the update. Meeting adjourned."

Cox removed his VR Ray-Bans. He sat before a media wall. The intro for *Delivery: Dead or Alive!* filled the display.

Kenny Turro addressed the audience. "We're live with Jerold Cox, CEO of eQuality, Inc., with a major announcement."

"eQuality is back in the Border States with its premium service." A series of images appeared beside Cox's closeup—eQuality drivers fighting off Porch Pirates, delighted clientele taking deliveries. "Our new customers will know the timeless thrill of packages on the front step, delivered with speed and style. The weather may change, the map may rearrange, but joy from eQuality is always in range." Cox smiled upon reciting the slogan.

"This has been a long time in coming, Mr. Cox," Kenny said. "When will you announce the starting lineup of drivers?"

"Soon. We're selecting the best of the best from across Greater America. AI analysis is nearly complete." Cox illustrated his point with a nod to a dense field of numbers being crunched. "We factor in social media sentiment too, so let eQuality know your favorites."

"Stay tuned to *Delivery: Dead or Alive!* to learn who's on the eQuality dream team!" Kenny said.

The interview concluded, Cox exited French doors. His Nova Scotia estate featured an infinity pool at the end of a winding path flanked by tropical landscaping and discreet security personnel. A physically flawless woman sunbathed on a chaise lounge. Cox caressed her before disrobing and diving. Hot, restless North Atlantic waves broke just beyond the pool's edge. Under the surface, Cox looked through a plexiglass seawall into the natural body of water. Reddened shrimp bobbed against the barrier, cooked within their shells during the current heatwave. Bloated, blanched fish drifted among them. Cox donned a snorkel mask mated to an air hose. He pressed his palm onto the glass, activating turbines to blow away the displeasing display of dead sea life.

Drivers milled around in the assembly hangar where big screens and IT systems covered bullet-pocked walls. They looked up to the displays as the *Delivery: Dead or Alive!* theme blared.

"Here is eQuality's lineup for the new Border State hub!" Kenny said. "From Mackinaw City, Michigan, Paul "Mongo" Mayfield!" A publicity image of the huge driver filled the screen, his nickname in an "earthquake" font accompanied by an explosion sound effect. Rapid-cut clips of Mongo's exploits rolled—careening in his Ford Bronco, tossing hapless Porch Pirates in hand-to-hand combat.

The image switched to Mongo in a cramped kitchen. His six children and pregnant wife stood with him. The kids cheered as they saw themselves on a monitor. "We're live with Mongo at his home," Kenny said. "How does it feel to make the cut, big guy?"

"Very cool," Mongo said. "Looking forward to good times and great deliveries."

Kenny read the next name. "From Talladega, Alabama, Derek Reno!" With his cowboy hat and lush mustache, Reno mimicked the old-time movie star Burt Reynolds, a car culture icon from the 1970s revered by the lethal counterpart of the 2030s. In the publicity shot, two drivers stood behind him in jumpsuits with Team Reno printed across their chests. Clips showed Reno piloting an MRAP—a Mine-Resistant Ambush-Protected vehicle built for action in Iraq, more recently retired from a police department. In hardened Maverick pickups, the other Team Reno drivers forced Porch Pirate cars into the MRAP's path for spectacular destructions. In another clip, Reno laid in wait as a delivered package rested on a front step. A Porch Pirate took bullets in the back when trying to steal the parcel. Customers came out of the house, ecstatic with the kill on their property.

Reno stood in a NASCAR-style garage for his live shot, helmeted teammates at his sides. Welder's sparks flew in the background as his MRAP received modifications. "Team Reno is coming! No other driver and no low-life Porch Pirates can share the road with us!"

A heavenly choir sounded behind a photo of "god rays" piercing clouds. Kenny announced, "From Loma Linda in the former state of California, Bren Van Allen, The Deliverer!"

Clips of the Deliverer celebrated his driving, marksmanship, and tenderness with the girl who received the ocular implant. A camera operator approached Bren on the hangar floor.

THE DELIVERER

"I thank my Lord and Savior, Jesus Christ, for this opportunity," Bren said. "I'm ready to earn my customers' trust."

Cameras remained on announced drivers, taking fans behind-the-scenes. In the kitchen, Mary looked up at her husband, Mongo. "How long you gonna be gone this time?"

"Can't say, honey. But that's why I gave you all these children, so you wouldn't be lonesome when I'm on the road," Mongo said with mock earnestness. Mary swatted her husband. The kids joined in. Mongo laughed as he wrestled with his family. His social media Likes rose accordingly.

In the Talladega garage, Reno walked toward his MRAP on the lift. The blockers removed their helmets, revealing themselves as a young man and woman. Ronni, the woman, got in Reno's face.

"You forgot two of your talking points. That camera time is precious. We gotta get our message out," Ronni said.

"See how mean your sister is?" Reno said to the male blocker, Robert, who shrugged. Reno leaned toward Ronni. "I'll review the script." The pair kissed.

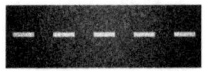

Olivia studied Gabriel's Warder chip marker. The dot moved east from Winnipeg at speeds that only a Boom Overture supersonic jet could reach.

"Mom!" Josh called from upstairs.

"What's the matter?" Olivia hurried to the loft where her son watched *Delivery This Week*, their content compromise following his exposure to the main program.

"The Deliverer is coming to the Border States! He can bring us stuff now!" Josh ran to his room. His wallpaper printer whirred, the machine designed to extrude dinosaurs, rocket ships, or other decorative whimsies.

Excited, Josh affixed the new sheet over his bed. Imbedded filaments drew a micro-current from the wall surface, activating electrophoretic ink. The image moved and smiled at observers. Bren's poster, complete with his tagline, Pray for The Deliverer, now stood guard in Josh's room. Olivia locked eyes with the paper phantom's shifting gaze while Josh begged her to book an order.

The starting lineup broadcast continued. Several of Bren's immediate counterparts, including Roadie, made the cut. Hurt and fury rose in D.D. as she paced, waiting to hear her name called.

"I didn't make the cut," she muttered.

"Hang in there. They'll need more drivers for the Border States. Rebuild your scores." Bren reached out to comfort D.D. She knocked his hand away.

"I don't have time to kiss eQuality's virtual butt. I've got student loans and an ex sucking me dry with support payments. I need to stay in the top tier! I need—" D.D. choked off her rant and stormed out of the hangar.

On Sunday morning, Bren sat at the dinette inside his Airstream, a cup of coffee on the table. When he donned his Virtual Reality Ray-Bans, he now stood in a black expanse, virtual coffee in hand synced with the tangible cup. He waved at Madison. The two avatars hugged. In the real world, the frames of their glasses transmitted neural signals to convey the sensation of contact.

"I still hate VR hugs." Madison's avatar shuddered after the embrace, triggering a laugh from her father.

A church sanctuary replaced the void, filling in like a time-lapsed puzzle. A banner unfurled on a wall, Project Archegos. The congregation materialized around Bren and Madison, greeting each other and chatting. The leader took the pulpit, the holographic ID appearing above his avatar reading Pastor Doug Wescott.

"I'd like to open in prayer for Bren Van Allen." Pastor Doug motioned, and Bren came to the stage with Madison. "Lord Jesus, watch over Bren in his new assignment. Amid the mayhem, he proclaims your name."

One member stood. "I move we take an offering to purchase a transit pass for Bren and his family. He needs to get off the road and come to the Revival Zone."

Bren shook his head. "This virtual sanctuary is filled with people trying to make it to the Revival Zone. My family will earn its way, like everyone else."

Pastor Doug quieted the murmuring avatars. "We'll respect Bren's wishes. All available funds are going to new programs, which we'll now review." Images from Project Archegos's labors filled the sanctuary screens—a research vessel off a rocky coast, a field planted with sustainable crops, a scientific lab.

"Yes, let's have a full account of the devil's workshop." An avatar's amplified voice boomed from the back of the room.

"This session is for members of Project Archegos." Pastor Doug already knew the interloper's identity—his sibling and rival.

"'For you shut the door of the kingdom of heaven in people's faces. You won't go in yourselves, and you don't let others enter either.'" The avatar levitated above the congregation although such stunts were considered poor taste per virtual reality decorum, particularly during a church service. Its holographic ID read Pastor Larry Wescott, Parabellum Church.

Pastor Larry landed on the stage. "You run off to Canada. You put faith in science and technology instead of the Lord!"

Bren stepped forward. "You hacked our meeting. Seems you're pretty comfortable with technology."

"If Jesus can descend to hell to save souls, I can make my way here." Pastor Larry turned toward the congregation. "How can you call yourselves Christians when you interfere with God's master plan? Trying to change the weather, change the harvest. Concocting vaccines and potions. The Bible forbids sorcery."

"Proverbs 25:2. 'It is God's privilege to conceal things and the king's privilege to discover them,'" Bren said. "Seeking knowledge is not sorcery."

Pastor Larry's eyes narrowed. "So eager to bite the apple."

Bren nodded at the point. "We've never appreciated the Garden. Got kicked out of the first one, and now we're destroying the next best thing. We're running out of time to get it right."

Pastor Larry sneered. "I see, brother, you're happy to turn your pulpit over to your celebrity spokesman."

"Bren is a minister. Everyone here is a minister," Pastor Doug said.

Pastor Larry looked down at Madison. "As a 'minister,' how do you tolerate your father being a murderer and blasphemer?"

Madison iced. "How do your kids like a dad who's a fat Pharisee?" The congregation roared.

"You'd know your place in my church," Pastor Larry hissed in Madison's face. The neural transmitters clasping his real-life head imparted the impact of Bren's forearm and shoulder. Pastor Larry's avatar flickered and staggered. His feet left the stage and he hovered, a ball of rage.

"Think you're so superior, so safe in your hidden forest," Pastor Larry bellowed. "You'll all learn your place!"

The doors burst open and members of the Parabellum Church streamed into the sanctuary by the hundreds, the shouting avatars clad in blood-red T-shirts with the church's logo. Bren put his arms around Madison. Pastor Doug made a sweeping motion.

Bren lurched in the dinette chair. He yanked off the Ray-Bans and caught his breath. His phone buzzed, and he read the text.

MADISON: Am I in trouble for saying "fat Pharisee" in church?

BREN: That wasn't half as bad as the names I was thinking.

CHAPTER 8

"I'm totally psyched. D.D. Guthrie is delivering to me!" D.D.'s new customer gushed liked a teenage devotee, but the exuberance was unsettling coming from a man in his seventies.

"So, you're a big fan?" D.D. forced a smile toward her touchscreen.

"I've downloaded all your videos, even the naughty ones." The old man nodded. D.D. cringed. The revenge porn from her ex-husband refused to die. "Maybe we can make some new videos."

"Look, mister, this is just a standard delivery."

"I paid triple your market rate. I've already gotten clearance from neighborhood security for you to stay the night."

"What do you think I am?"

"I think you're Pinky Tuscadero, the daredevil driver on *Happy Days*. She was Fonzie's girlfriend. I wanted her to be my girlfriend when I was a kid."

"I've got a few other deliveries on this run. By the time I get to your house, I expect you to be cool, like Fonzie."

"I'll pay extra—"

D.D. ended the call and shut down communication and sensor systems. She eased the Mustang onto the shoulder, stepped out of the car, glanced left, right, left again. Certain she was alone, D.D. lifted a bundle from her trunk, which unfolded into a long, translucent strip. She laid the strip across the road, the asphalt showing through to camouflage the object. D.D. shielded her eyes to confirm an approaching vehicle and winced upon recognizing the Lightning.

Bren stopped the truck and got out. "Expecting someone?"

"Not you." D.D. moved for the car door.

Bren reached out to take D.D.'s hand as she reached for the door handle. "Everything okay? I saw your system links went down. I'm glad I found you."

"I'm fine." D.D. pulled from Bren's grasp. "You don't want to be late for your next delivery. Might lower your scores."

"You're an easy target sitting out here. What's going on?"

"All of a sudden you care about me?"

"I've always cared about you, D.D."

D.D. scoffed. "I believed that for one night."

Bren looked down and exhaled. "We were about to go too far—"

D.D. paced. "You put your brand ahead of me. The Deliverer, the big Christian role model. Gotta protect that rep. But not me. I'm the bad girl. I have nothing to lose. Especially now!"

Bren reached for D.D. "Let's get back on the road. I'll shadow you."

D.D. pulled away. "You need to turn around and leave." Her eyes narrowed. "Your specialty."

Bren reached for D.D. again. She drew her Desert Eagle and aimed at him. Bren stood silently before getting back in his truck. The Lightning made a U-turn and disappeared down a side road. D.D. backed her Mustang off the shoulder. Resuming road speed, she ran over the chemical spike stripe, releasing the acetone mixture and soaking the tires. D.D. recoiled as the stench penetrated the cockpit. The rubber designed to resist bullets bubbled off. D.D. rode on steel belts and rims. New vehicles approached. Lonny and his Porch Pirates surrounded the slowing Mustang.

The vehicles stopped, and the drivers got out. D.D. towered over Lonny in her boots and crash helmet. She removed the helmet with a sigh, her resignation contrasting with Lonny's smiling expectation.

"We gotta make this look good," D.D. said. Lonny nodded to a large Porch Pirate who swung his elbow into the back of D.D.'s head. Blackness engulfed her.

At a rusting filling station a few miles away, a Porch Pirate swerved into the driveway. As the vehicle slowed to a roll, D.D. tumbled out semiconscious. The driver sped away as the proprietor came running. D. D. rose, rubbing her throbbing skull, and waved off assistance.

The golf course was one giant sand trap, the intermittent strips of grass resembling a comb-over. Still, the nine-hole was a luxury, irrigated with illegally diverted water. Lonny and a squad of Porch Pirates hiked across the dunes and patchy turf. D.D.'s elderly customer waited at the last tee. Lonny produced a long, slender package. The customer unwrapped his order—a Nike Vapor Speed driver, out of production since before the war. Tiger Woods' signature glinted on the head.

"Normally, I don't do business with crooks. I really wanted this club." The customer eyed the length of his prize. "But there's something I wanted even more—D.D."

The customer moved to his cart. "She said I was like Fonzie. Know what happens when you mess with the Fonz?"

He stuffed the driver into a golf bag, his hand reemerging with a 20 gauge Winchester nested among the shafts. The first round dropped the Porch Pirate standing next to Lonny. He and the others scrambled as the customer revved his cart and continued shooting on the move. The bandits returned fire. The customer slumped over the wheel, and the cart nosed into a water hazard. Lonny and the Porch Pirates ran for their cars parked beside the fairway.

Two security officers flanked Reginald as he approached Bren. "We need your recent dashcam files."

"My last run wasn't scheduled to be televised. Per the drivers' collective bargaining agreement, that means it's proprietary data." Bren maintained a wide stance and crossed his arms.

"The contract also states eQuality can seize any files in a fraud investigation," Reginald said.

"Am I under investigation?" Bren said.

"Not yet. But if you keep stalling, you will be. You'll automatically lose your place in the Border State starting lineup. You wouldn't want to disappoint your fans." Reginald enjoyed taking drivers down a notch. His bluff called, Bren looked him in the eye, slowly raised his mobile device, and released the footage with a tap.

D.D. sat in a conference room across from Reginald. Security personnel filled the remaining seats.

"My communications and sensors were malfunctioning," D.D. said. "I couldn't detect the spike strip before I was on top of it."

Reginald opened a data display on the media wall. "The files we retrieved verify your system failures. No chemical readings, no camera record." He looked at D.D. "There are other absences. No rape or murder when the Porch Pirates captured you."

"Guess they were more interested in the cargo. They got a good haul, including my Mustang and weapons." D.D. stayed cool, checking her usual impulse to tell off an authority figure.

"Better to be lucky than good, as they say. But we have footage that says you're neither." Reginald brought up Bren's dashcam video. D.D. averted her eyes. "An argument with your old friend, Mr. Van Allen." The video showed D.D. pulling her pistol on Bren. "If we go to the beginning—"

With the rewind, the view from the Lightning showed D.D. in the distance walking back to her parked car. Reginald stopped the video and zoomed in on D.D. "You seem rather calm. Your car is parked and intact. Add a hyperspectral filter." The video changed colors. A small cloud wafted over the stretch of road. "And we see an acetone plume from a spike strip a few yards behind you."

D.D. remained seated as security ringed her. "We could press charges for staging the theft of your cargo, but Mr. Cox doesn't like undermining customer confidence with negative publicity," Reginald said. "You're permanently banned from the eQuality network. We'll provide an air taxi to your destination of choice."

D.D. stood. She glanced at the media wall as the guards escorted her out of the room. The video paused on Bren looking back at his truck after disembarking. D.D. glared at the image.

The air taxi hovered over a desolate stretch of road. The electric rotors ebbed, and the pilotless pod settled in a dusty billow. D.D. climbed out with a backpack and a pair of duffle bags. The air taxi lifted off. When the dust settled, Lonny and his Porch Pirates came into view. D.D. walked toward the band and spotted her Mustang among their parked vehicles, wearing a fresh set of front tires. A grinning Porch Pirate sat on the hood, cradling D.D.'s Typhoon semiauto shotgun. Lonny had her nickel-plated Desert Eagle in his waistband.

"I sent your cut," Lonny said.

"That's not why I'm here," D.D. said.

"Want your car and guns? We'll be happy to sell 'em back."

"I'll collect my property in a bit. I've got a new proposition for you."

"You got nothin' to offer. We heard eQuality kicked you out."

"Their loss, your gain. I know their tactics and systems. We're going to the Border States and hit their expansion."

"We?"

"You'll need a new leader. Unless you wanna stay a two-bit outfit chasing scraps." The Porch Pirates turned their eyes to Lonny.

Lonny drew the Desert Eagle. "That is quite a proposition. 'Course, something would have to happen to me first."

"Careful. My big gun kicks. Might knock over a little guy like you."

Lonny boiled as the bandits laughed. He laid down the pistol and squared off. With her superior reach, D.D. landed two quick jabs. Blood trickling from his nose, Lonny dived for her legs. As D.D. toppled, Lonny grabbed rainbows of her hair. She stood with him clinging to her back. D.D. slammed her bantam opponent against the fender of her car. She spun, drove a knee into Lonny's chest, and threw an overhand right that sent him into the dirt. He crawled for the Desert Eagle. D.D. pulled a boot knife and jumped on him.

Lonny grimaced at the blade poking him under the jaw. "What do we do first?"

D.D. brought her lips near Lonny's ear and whispered, "Destroy the Deliverer."

Olivia, very excited, tried to appear calm as she conducted a video call with Madame Verneuil, an official for the Prix de Gloire. "We've received the link to the final version of your entry. Thank you," Madame Verneuil said. "Should you win, how many will be in your party for your trip to Geneva?"

"Two ... myself and my son, Josh," Olivia said. "You said you could transport us out of Greater America."

Madame Verneuil nodded. "We've negotiated NATO clearance to fly directly from your location to Canada. Then, it's a Boom Overture to Europe."

"Next to having Josh, I've never wanted anything more," Olivia said.

"We appreciate your spirit, Madame Durand. Good luck."

Olivia ended the call and opened the Warder app. Gabriel's chip marker limned a trip from Kyiv to Istanbul. Olivia refilled her wine glass and opened the website for the Toyzz Shop at Istanbul Airport. The emporium had a wide selection of airplanes. Olivia selected a squadron spanning a P-51 from World War II to a B-21 with lights and sound-effect buttons that obliterated any stealth pretense. She entered her revocable trust fund information for payment. Gabriel had established the fund years before when she'd first threatened to leave him. He would receive an alert if she tried to buy a getaway car or transit pass. He paid no attention to her ordinary "shopping," even with exorbitant shipping fees.

Olivia typed in the recipient: Josh Durand. She typed in the sender: Gabriel Durand. She instructed the store to print and include the attached note. A cursive emulator app typeset the document in Gabriel's hand:

Dear Josh.

Been doing a lot of flying lately. Now you can fly too!

Love. Dad

Olivia requested standard shipping, an unglamorous series of container ships, armored ground transport, and final-mile drones between Turkey and the Border States. The transaction complete, she brought up the Deliverer's official website. A banner on the homepage read Coming to the Border States. A digital countdown showed five weeks, three days, and six hours.

The site sold branded merchandise and took deposits for future deliveries. Customers could add videos to their payments. Olivia summoned the camera icon.

"Mr. Van Allen, I'm Olivia Durand. My son, Josh, is a huge fan. His dad let him watch *Delivery: Dead or Alive.* Now, his dad has left. But you're here. Josh put your poster over his bed. He talks about you all the time. Maybe you and I can replace his vanished father—for a moment at least." Olivia took a long drink. "For starters, Josh is getting a gift by ordinary transport. But I want his next gift to be really special. Maybe I'm not the only sad woman leaving you messages in the middle of the night. But can you look past me and see a little boy? Can you see him smiling? I can." A tear rolling, she stopped recording and placed a deposit equal to the cost of a three-bedroom house.

THE DELIVERER

Sleepless in the Airstream, Bren reviewed his social media feeds. He answered a few posts to maintain a personal touch with his fans. He stopped when Olivia's video message appeared. He opened the file and watched, not knowing why he plucked this content from the flow.

CHAPTER 9

"Incoming." Raveena's calm voice came from the touchscreen.

"Fire or social media?" Bren peered past the heads-up display on the inside of his windshield.

"Both."

"Friendly or hostile?" Bren tightened his grip as the steering wheel relayed disruptions in the pavement. The new enterprise district came with mangled infrastructure. The Lightning covered the corrugated asphalt at an aggressive pace.

"Both." Raveena chuckled.

"Not helpful." Bren kept the truck steady as a mortar round—the hostile fire—landed on the right shoulder. A Hellfire Romeo missile—the friendly fire—bisected the road twenty yards ahead and destroyed the mortar position. "I thought the army had it locked down. I don't appreciate towing my house through a hot zone." Looking at the rearview camera feed, he checked his Airstream bobbing on the hitch. The truck's electric motors hummed at full output, keeping the load at speed, assisted by the additional electric powerplants of the trailer's eStream system.

"Still mopping up." A colored map of recent combat operations filled the main touchscreen to verify.

"Cox wants us open for business in a hurry."

"Have to keep the corporate overlord happy."

"How about the real bosses? Let's have the sentiment report." Bren flicked the screen from combat maps to social media pie charts.

"Positive sentiment holding steady at 71 percent," Raveena said. "Approximately four-thousand posts congratulating you on deployment to the new fire hub. Your fee is up two points at market open."

"Christian keywords?" Bren said.

"Present in 38 percent of positive posts, 90 percent of negative." Raveena shared fresh graphs illustrating these metrics. "The anti-Christian remarks are either direct denunciations of the faith or simply general insults to boost another driver. You're still being criticized for your low kill rate."

"Same old." Bren noted the alert in his heads-up display—five miles to destination.

"I can reduce the number of devotions in your feed, bring up more action shots."

"Negative. Content mix remains the same."

"If I'm going to be your moderator, let me moderate." Raveena's image came on the screen, long black hair pulled back, topped with a headset. Concern replaced the bantering spirit from moments before. "I don't want you to lose your top ranking."

"You and me both. The higher my ratings, the higher my fee, the sooner I can get off the road."

"But you're gonna do it the hard way ... your way."

"God's way."

In the previous century, the concrete lotus had been a lure, designed neither to be missed nor resisted. Yet the mall had turned mausoleum well before the first shots of Civil War II. While the complex would now shift from retail to distribution—pushed farther back in the marketing channel, removed from the customer—Jerold Cox and eQuality had restored its purpose.

Bren came off a cloverleaf. Several boarded windows had surrendered their plywood to make a spray-painted sign: Welcome to Fire Hub Sears—a nod to the mall's former anchor store that had slid first into the socioeconomic abyss. Bren transited security checkpoints and was directed to a far lot.

The asphalt plain was refashioned as an RV park with water and electric lines installed throughout. Bren backed his truck and trailer onto the pad marked Reserved for The Deliverer. He began unhitching the Airstream when a huge hand fell on his shoulder.

"Well, if it ain't the Deliverer. Hope you don't mind ol' Mongo drafting you." The big man smiled.

"You're one of the few people I'd trust behind me." Bren shook Mongo's hand. "Been a while."

"How 'bout a brewski?" Mongo bent down to assist Bren with positioning the jack and unhooking the brake cable and safety chains.

"Bit early, don't you think?" Bren said.

"I don't know what time it is anymore. Haven't slept in two days."

"I have something to ease your mind. Better than alcohol."

"I know. Jesus Christ. Still don't think he'd waste his time on a guy like me."

"You kidding? He loves a challenge." Bren lowered the electric jack and released the hitch ball. Mongo laughed.

At a distance, Derek Reno cupped his mouth. "Hey, Mongo! Team Reno could use another blocker."

"He means 'human shield,'" Bren said.

Reno walked to the men. "Ditch the choirboy, and let's talk. The beer in my trailer is actually cold."

Mongo's gaze switched between the Christian and the hustler. "Looks like I'll be drinking alone." He and Reno went separate ways.

With a grin, Bren moved to a storage compartment on the side of the Airstream. He reached for the shore power cable to bring electricity to the trailer. On the open compartment door, The Van Allen Family, 2026, was written in black permanent marker. Below were two signatures, Bren and Hailey. A baby handprint in finger paint was the third mark ...

On the happy day twelve years prior, Bren had driven up in uniform, just having finished maneuvers with the National Guard. Hailey was in uniform too, her nurse's scrubs. Tiny Madison rested in her arms, strawberry blond tufts inherited from Mama. Bren honked the horn of the Lightning, the gleaming new Airstream in tow. He jumped out and kissed his wife and daughter.

"How did we afford this?" Hailey ran a hand along the aluminum skin.

"I sold the rights to the Gleaner drone design," Bren said. Hailey looked concerned. "Don't worry, I can always invent something else cool."

"I've got a ton of PTO. How about Big Sur next week?" Hailey said.

"And beyond." Bren jangled the plastic keys in Madison's chubby fists. "The governor just approved sending the Guard to Texas to help stop the secession. The country's falling apart. We may need to bug out."

"At least we'll be doing it in style." Hailey squeezed tight against her husband ...

Bren traced Hailey's signature. Returning to the present, he removed the cable and connected power to the Airstream's flank. He wanted to rest before the first run, but relaxation would have to wait. After hooking water lines to the trailer, Bren conducted a quick diagnostic of the Lightning. All systems were in working order, no damage from the mortar explosion. He brought his firearms into the Airstream for checks and cleaning. Sitting at the dinette, he alternated gunsmithing with social media, a practiced workflow during his downtime. He uploaded stills from his truck's cameras of his arrival at the fire hub.

A fan shared a shot taken by another driver of Bren with Mongo and Reno. "Don't you just hate Derek?" the fan posted.

"1 John 2:9," Bren typed in response.

Bren joined the new social media group Fire Hub Sears Delivery Drivers. He posted an invite for Bible study. Roadie was first to give a thumbs up. A notice showed a text message from Madison.

MADISON: Didn't want to bother you. I know you get busy after you pull in.

BREN: You never bother me. Just catching up on posts.

MADISON: You ought to let me manage your social media.

BREN: I have a moderator for that. You just focus on school and church.

MADISON: I could make you sound more cool online.

BREN: Then people would know it wasn't me!

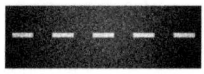

"Lovely VR." Cox sat at a patio table behind an English cottage, surrounded by a thick, verdant garden.

"I'm actually sitting in it," Gabriel said. "My father's home. He recently passed, and I'm getting his affairs in order."

"I won't keep you long," Cox said. "I am interested in your technology. I need proof of concept."

"I've prepared samples of the chip matrix and the printing technology. I've installed safeguards to protect certain proprietary elements."

"Naturally."

"But you'll be able to determine viability."

"Ship the samples to eQuality's R&D facility in Auckland." Cox stood. "Condolences for your father."

Cox removed his glasses, ending the VR session. Gabriel doffed his pair, and the real garden with brown and shriveled plantings replaced the fake one. He remained at the table, a Machiavellian smile forming on his face.

The siren jolted Bren awake. Loudspeakers announced: "Cargo docking in thirty minutes." He quickly showered and donned his tactical gear. " As he did before every run, Bren kneeled in the kitchen and prayed. "The Wayfarer's Prayer," derived from the Jewish Talmud—the ancient wisdom was always relevant on the road.

"'May it be your will, O Lord my God, to conduct me in peace, to direct my steps in peace, to uphold me in peace and to deliver me from every enemy and ambush by the way.'"

Bren joined fellow drivers in a fast walk from the RV lot to the center of the mall, security waving them along the path. The drivers avoided the construction work restoring the shattered campus while a crew on a boom lift hung building signage for eQuality.

The center of the concrete lotus had been a flower core of sorts, a courtyard where shoppers could recover from their exertions and let their children experience greenery. Except for wild ivy tracing perimeter pillars, the plant life had died with brick-and-mortar commerce. But the old mall's hollow heart had undergone a makeover like its fanning, echoing halls. A prefab pad covered the denuded soil. A shielded mission control projected from the top floor overlooking the void, a skybox for the day's sport.

Between the loading bays and the mall's center, the drivers assembled in a gallery where camera images ranged from interviews for major broadcasts to selfies for social media feeds.

"We're here for the exciting opening of Fire Hub Sears, eQuality's new distribution center for the Border States." Kenny was onsite for a live shot. "And here's the Deliverer himself, Bren Van Allen." He thrust the mic at Bren. "Any change in tactics for this new territory?"

"Not really," Bren said. "Just going to do what it takes to satisfy my customers."

"So dependable!" Reno drew the camera away from Bren. "This guy would've rocked at Federal Express. Or the Pony Express. Maybe that's why he carries a six-shooter." He poked at Bren's chest holster.

"Actually, it's an eight-shooter." Bren removed his primary handgun from the holster. "Ruger Super GP-100, .357 magnum." He opened the cylinder and presented the weapon to the camera. "Higher capacity than a traditional revolver but just as dependable—to use Derek's word. My dad gave it to me before my first run."

Reno scoffed. "Very touching." He stepped back and held out his arms. "You can tell a real pro by his equipment."

The black bandoliers wrapping his body blended with his leathers. With a wrist flick, the bandoliers turned translucent and glowed dull purple. Hundreds of 9mm rounds filled the tubular wraps. With another flick of his wrist, gauntlets shoved compact machine pistols into his palms. With nanofiber constrictions, the bandoliers loaded the guns, evoking belt-fed automatic weapons of the last century-and-a-half. Drivers and videographers gasped. Reno's social media scores spiked.

"No Porch Pirate has ever stopped Team Reno. If you want your orders delivered with a vengeance, call on us!" Reno bowed to cheers.

Loudspeakers announced: "Prepare for landing." Steel blast doors sealed the gallery. A bleary Mongo sidled to Bren.

"I got a bad feeling," Mongo said.

Bren gave a reassuring smile. "Just another run, no better, no worse."

Mongo pointed at Bren's gear bag. "Lay one of those good books on me. I'm ready."

Bren withdrew a Bible. "Pre-war paper and ink. No pixels. No tracking. No government-mandated study links." He handed over the book. "Remember, it's not a lucky charm. Won't help sitting in your glovebox."

Mongo hefted his gift. "Good reason to make it back. You gotta explain all this to me." Bren laughed and clasped him on the shoulder.

The rocket's twin sonic booms resounded in the well waiting to receive it. Screens in the gallery displayed newsfeeds of the arrival as boosters braked the craft through the sound barrier. LEDs embedded in the pad beckoned. Touching down within a structure was showy but feasible. These days, space vehicles could stick a landing within two inches of target, and they rarely exploded.

The eQuality cargo ship kicked out titanium legs and settled on the pad. Nitrogen fogging and exhaust fans cooled and cleared the courtyard, but the quick dissipation unable to staunch the lighter fluid smell. The gallery blast doors parted, and the drivers approached the hissing rocket. Below the nose cone, a hatch opened like a drawbridge and transitioned into an exterior elevator platform. The crew descended, minuscule to the drivers, news teams, and other personnel swarming fifteen stories below.

The elevator stopped above the pad. Camera drones approached the rocketeers as jumbo screens unfurled from the mission control level. The courtyard crowd murmured with the first closeup of Jerold Cox.

"This place was a ruin of the old America. Today, it's back in business," Cox said to the broadcast audience.

"Ever see Cox in person before?" Mongo whispered into Bren's ear as his eyes remained on the CEO's screen enlargement.

"Once," Bren said.

"Let's get to work!" Cox nodded at the final round of applause as the platform completed the trip to ground level.

The cargo ship whistled and groaned. Gleaming flanks between the command module and engines bulged and split. The rocket skin peeled on hinges, revealing the fruit within—seemingly an inner hull, mottled brown. But the drones' teasing closeups confirmed the exposed mass was not ship structure. A pillar of packages engorged the hold, a silo of robots having laid the uncanny load at the origin point. Legitimate needs, impulse buys, and gewgaws worth a micro-percentage of their shipping fees interlocked like a monstrous Lego set. Audiences applauded the collective offering.

A special mortar fortified the pillar—a smart gel sprayed into the tiny tolerances between the boxes. An electrostatic charge stirred the gel's nanoparticles, and a slow, controlled ooze dismantled the pillar. Packages separated and rode down the bent-back hull sections to a carousel encircling the rocket. The barely perceptible gel slid from the boxes, draining into receptacles for reuse.

The drivers ran to the carousel, their handhelds locating assigned packages. Mongo checked the general inventory readout while loading his cart. He spied a vintage Rolex with a correspondingly high delivery fee, the item allotted to another driver. He reached for the box, triggering its RFID alarm. Roadie and other drivers jeered.

"I grabbed it by mistake!" Mongo put the box back on the carousel.

Bren found the package at the top of his list—small with a hefty express charge. He turned the premium box over in his hands. Bren opened a video note attached to the manifest file.

Olivia filled the frame. "Mr. Van Allen, Olivia Durand again. Thank you for accepting my bid for your services. I know Josh will be thrilled with his gift and the Deliverer."

Bren sized up the new customer, building on impressions from the first video. She was rich, like the rest of his customers, beautiful, like many of them. A sculpted bracelet in the shape of a winged and horned creature adorned her left wrist. He worried the piece might be demonic. But Bren sought the best in the people he served, a Christian mindset, a motivator to take the risks of the road.

"Let's check our Las Vegas sports book," Kenny said. An image of the *Delivery: Dead or Alive* betting board filled the screen, listing the major drivers. The bustling casino was one American icon that had not changed during the long civil war. "You don't have to go to the Republic of Mojave to get in on the fun. Online wagering is open for the categories of first off the line, highest load value, and earliest delivery time. Next betting round will include most kills and friendliest service."

His cargo collected, Bren hurried to the loading dock for a "LeMans start." Customers and fans liked the dramatic sprint to waiting vehicles in the spirit of the iconic Grand Prix. With the signal, the drivers ran from the starting line, pushing carts loaded with boxes. Reaching his truck,

Bren secured packages and started the double motors. The Lightning justified its name, streaking away from the loading bay, allowing Bren to pass several gasoline-powered vehicles jockeying on the frontage road leading back to the interstate. His social media Likes exploded.

Olivia's video appeared on the touchscreen and paused. Bren zoomed in on the bracelet. The creature was an owl, wings spread, eyes fierce. Bren was glad the casting wasn't a demon or gargoyle. He wondered if the woman considered the bird a spirit animal. Did she wear the bracelet as a fashion statement or pagan idol? Bren stopped himself. His services didn't include saving her from a piece of jewelry.

CHAPTER 10

The Lightning took to the open road. Raveena logged on and shared maps and graphs. "Your destination is the Entrada community. High marks for perimeter security. Good tippers."

"Sounds promising." Bren glanced at the map. "How's the ceasefire holding up?"

"Troops remaining at fallback positions. No reports of combat."

"So all we have to do is make it through the new no-man's land between the lines."

"Roadblock four miles ahead." Raveena enlarged the map to highlight the affected stretch. Feeds from freeway cameras showed a burning tanker truck perpendicular to the lanes.

"Time to get off this beautiful interstate." Bren threaded craters to take the next off-ramp.

The Lightning merged onto a county highway. The two-lane pointed toward a small town that had been evacuated in the recent fighting. The map showed red flags bordering the route.

"Reports of minefields of residual contamination from chemical weapons. You're on the safest route," Raveena said.

"Any eyes on that town up ahead?" Bren said.

"No live feeds available," Raveena said.

Bren nodded, knowing security cameras above doorbells and beneath store awnings were either smashed or electronically jammed. "Heading blind into a kill zone. So much for my safest route."

D.D.'s image pushed Raveena's off the touchscreen. "Breaker, breaker. That's what truckers used to say on their CBs. Gotta love the old days."

"No time for nostalgia. Have to stay on schedule," Bren said.

"Busy man. You'll be real busy when you hit this podunk town, but you already know that." D.D. smiled. "Too bad you didn't switch sides. Good pickin's for Porch Pirates these days. With your abilities, you'd do well."

"How could I share the gospel if I became a thief?" Bren said.

"You're not too busy for hypocrisy. Matthew 23:23. You taught me that one. eQuality is the biggest crook of them all!"

"You're still angry, D.D. Want a Scripture to help with that?"

"Pick out a verse for yourself. Something about going home to Jesus!"

The two-lane became the town's Main Street. Bren stayed on course. D.D. led a wedge of vehicles from the opposite direction. In his rear view, Bren saw a flatbed pull off a side street with armed men in the back. Approaching an intersection, he floored the accelerator and cranked the wheel. The Lightning jumped the sidewalk and smashed the window of a corner florist. Cactus arrangements and starter kits for vegetable gardens sprayed the hood. The truck emerged from the opposite display window, evading Lonny's idling Charger meant to prevent a conventional turn. The obstacle worked against D.D. and her formation as they tried to give chase, providing Bren precious seconds to escape Main Street.

A graphene production plant loomed beyond the scant downtown, a combined mine and refinery to supply the product-making solution for 3D printers across Greater America. Bren veered toward the automated facility, breaking down a barrier arm. Most of D.D.'s squad trailed.

"Don't follow him in there! We'll seal him off. Don't—" D.D. yelled as the Porch Pirates ignored her order.

A causeway straddled two quarry pits, sources of the natural graphite infused with sequestered carbon for greater density. Giant rotary excavators scooped the dark strata. The Lightning took the causeway, Porch Pirates funneling behind. Sparky gunned the El Camino to lead the pursuit.

"Payback for my Bug!" Sparky shouted.

"Autonomous mode," Bren said into his watch.

From his tail gunner position, he aimed at the last vehicle, a jacked-up Jeep. The exposed front axle made an excellent target. The Barrett fired and the front differential plowed the asphalt. Liberated front wheels bounced down terraced cliffs. The next round hit the El Camino. The hood belched a cloud of engine parts. The pursuing convoy skidded on the causeway, trapped between the disabled cars. Porch Pirates yelled at the hapless Sparky as he clambered out of his second lost ride.

Bren assessed the neutralized vehicles as his truck left the causeway, still in autonomous mode. His back turned, he didn't see the service bridge arched over the road ahead with the Mustang parked on top. D.D. threw down a black bundle as the Lightning passed. The bundle blossomed into a web of hooked cables. The web fell over his cargo bed, hooks sinking into sheet metal. The web tightened around Bren, pinning him and his rifle to the tailgate. With a war cry, D.D. heaved a grappling hook connected to the web with a retractable line.

"You see, Lonny. I got gadgets just like the Deliverer," D.D. said into her handheld. "Take him alive."

The hook dragged behind the Lightning before snagging a concrete slab. Prongs wedged into the cracked surface. The line played out before its windless slowed and reversed. The system designed to stop the truck withstood the horsepower, polymers tensing. The truck pawed the ground. Porch Pirates raced forward, a pistol-waving motorcyclist heading the new pack. Lonny brought up the rear.

Bren craned his neck to see the straining line. He reached between the web strands and pulled his Ruger. Thrusting his arm over the tailgate, he fired. A bullet whined off the windless housing. More followed, and the gear disintegrated. The loose retractable cable whipped the motorcyclist from his saddle. Several cars collided while avoiding the cartwheeling bike. Lonny slammed his brakes and jumped out to survey the damage.

The Lightning fishtailed away. Bren tore loose the web's hooks and sent his seat back to the cab. He dropped fresh cartridges into the Ruger with a full-moon clip before resuming control of the truck.

"Next time, say 'Jesus, take the wheel,'" Raveena said.

"As usual, not helpful." Bren plotted a course back to the county road. He had a good lead over the remnants of D.D.'s crew.

From the dirt road angling out of the plant, Bren saw cars blocking the county road at the town's outskirts. He considered off-roading through fields when an airhorn ripped. Reno's MRAP smashed the barricade, Ronni and Robert trailing in the Mavericks.

"You're welcome," Reno said. "Heading south. You're on your own, choirboy."

Delivery drivers roared out of the small town, Porch Pirates filling the blacktop behind them. A souped-up utility terrain vehicle burst from a wheat field, the rider leveling a MAC-10 at Bren. The Lightning accelerated out of the line of fire. The bullets found Mongo's Bronco as he attempted to pass on the shoulder. The driver's side window splintered. Mongo bellowed as the last round struck his arm. Jerking the steering wheel, he sent the UTV tumbling back into the wheat field.

"Never buy bulletproof glass from a discount shop." Mongo grimaced.

On the touchscreen, Bren saw blood seeping through a sleeve. "Can you make it?"

Mongo nodded. "On to Entrada!"

The final leg crossed open country. The most determined Porch Pirates kept pace behind Bren and Mongo. Headlights flashed in Bren's rear view. D.D. came on at 150 miles per hour. The Lightning's electric powerplants couldn't match the top speed of the Mustang's supercharged V-8. Bren braced for a close-quarters fight—the web having dislodged the rifle stand in the cargo bed.

Mongo tried to block D.D., but the Mustang whisked past. Anticipating her approach on his right to allow a better firing arc, Bren held the edge of the blacktop. Relegated to the soft shoulder, the low-slung Mustang would be unsteady, making a pass risky.

A scorched Humvee on the side of the road forced Bren to the median. Taking advantage, D.D. pulled alongside and fired .357 Magnum rounds from her Desert Eagle, a caliber preference shared with Bren. She shot the tires point blank. The run flats stayed on the rims. Bren fell back and executed a pursuit intervention technique or PIT maneuver, knocking his truck against the Mustang's rear fender. D.D. cursed the blow to her bad shoulder and dropped her Desert

Eagle from the window. The Mustang spun out, but she expertly recovered.

"Final approach for Entrada," Raveena said.

Low, green hills rose from the flatland. Bren took the access road toward the elevation while D.D. gained. The shoulder beside the Mustang churned, dirt pelting its roof. The churn repeated, and D.D. braked hard. Shots came from the top of a berm, a thousand yards away. The next salvo from the Phalanx Gatling cannon—a powerful defensive weapon used previously by the military—would not be warning shots into the ground. She turned and left the access road.

"For old times' sake, I went easy. Tried to take you in one piece. My bad." D.D.'s eyes narrowed. "No time for nostalgia."

Bren slowed as he came upon a massive, fabricated earthworks planted with fire-resistant ground cover. Mongo followed. Guard towers and Phalanx domes punctuated the ridgeline. Sensor pylons lined the access road.

A uniformed officer appeared on Bren's touchscreen. "I'm Security Chief Yang. Your vehicle transponders have identified you as an authorized dispatch. Please look toward your screen for facial recognition."

Bren complied. A digital lattice overlaid a screen shot of his face. A readout alongside confirmed: Brendon Van Allen, Age 38. Height: 6'1". Weight: 187 pounds. eQuality Driver, Class 1.

"Thank you, driver," Chief Yang said. "Please follow all instructions at checkpoints. Welcome to Entrada."

Bren stopped at the outer gate. One guard reviewed his manifest and ID while two more combed the Lightning with sensor wands. Cameras in the road surface checked for bombs in the undercarriage. The guards waved the Lightning into a tunnel penetrating the perimeter knolls.

Bren rolled into a sectioned steel passage resembling a car wash. Digital signage flashed Stop and announced, "LIDAR and Spectographic Inspection." Once the sensors found no explosive or chemical weapons hidden in packages or bodywork, the truck moved to the next section, "Anti-Viral/Decontamination Spray." Jets of mist purged the Lightning of any possible biologic or synthetic contaminants.

More armed guards waved Bren and Mongo out of the tunnel onto a two-lane road. The right lane provided access to the outskirts of Entrada. Multiunit housing and bungalows dominated the residential section. Strip malls provided commerce. This was the world of the employees who enabled the lifestyles of the primary residents—a worker's wartime paradise. The outer ring also provided amenities for delivery drivers including a truck stop with motel and health clinic.

At the sight of the clinic sign, Bren called out to Mongo on the touchscreen. "Get that arm looked at. I'll drop off your load. You'll get full credit."

"I can make it." Mongo gritted his teeth. "Want to make a good impression on the first run. Get some positive reviews."

Staying in the left lane, Bren and Mongo approached a second perimeter, a towering metal wall suitable for a national border. The guards at a final gate reviewed a summary of all the drivers' checks they'd already passed. At last, the Lightning and Bronco were approved to enter the primary community.

The residences of the inner sanctum reconjured luxury and comfort from the early twenty-first century, a simpler time. Children played and couples jogged. There was no razor wire, no security walls, no open-carry weapons. Bren and Mongo parked, unfolded their carts, and loaded their packages.

Mongo nodded toward the tower at the center of town proclaiming "Entrada" in thirty-foot letters on the sides of its tank. "Boy, these people must be rich. They've got so much water they have one of those old-time water towers."

"That's not water. It's graphene," Bren said. "Just fought my way out of a graphene plant. Pumped from places like that to the tank. Piped from there to high-output 3D printers in the houses."'

"My kids have been screaming for a better printer. I was right. These people are rich."

Bren and Mongo pushed their filled carts onto a cul-de-sac. Excited children ran down the sidewalks, snapping photos, personal air conditioners looped around their necks. One held a sign made with crayons: Welcome Deliverer! Waving to the young fans, the men split up to deliver packages to their respective customers' doors.

Mongo waited patiently in the interminable moments after he rang the doorbell. The bandages wrapping his left bicep were soaked but holding. The arm had gone numb, mitigating the pain. A middle-aged woman in designer sandals and large sunglasses opened the door.

"Hello, Mrs. Lightfoot. On behalf of eQuality, I'm—"

Tammy Lightfoot ignored Mongo's friendly greeting as she pulled the box from the big man's good hand.

The lid opened with a soft hiss. A layer of cryogenic gas dissipated to reveal the order—Swiss chocolates made with cocoa beans from Madagascar's Sambirano Valley, wrapped in edible gold leaf. The alloyed container had cosseted the chilled treats throughout a space hop and a road battle. Tammy savored the supply chain marvel.

Tammy's husband Russ joined her at the doorway. "Save one for me."

"Sure beats a Tootsie Roll." Mongo laughed.

Across the street, Bren rang the bell at Olivia Durand's home. She opened the door with one hand while grabbing a sarong from a coat rack at the entry. She wrapped her lower body.

"Mr. Van Allen. You look just like your poster." Olivia smiled. With his sandy hair flecked with early gray, stubble on his face, and a muscular figure in tactical gear with crosses stenciled on the shoulder pads—Bren lived up to his publicity images.

"And I recognize you from your videos, Mrs. Durand." Bren handed over the order. "I enjoy delivering gifts to children."

Mongo continued small talk with the Lightfoots while several cul-de-sac children gathered to hear his tales. "We saw some heavy action on the way here. The Porch Pirates have come in right behind the troops, as usual." Mongo felt woozy from his injury, but he wanted to make a good showing.

Tammy and Russ's boy came running. "Mom, why didn't you get Team Reno? They're awesome!"

"Now, Mark, Mr. Reno and his people were booked," Tammy said. "You like Mongo too."

"Yeah." Mark was unenthused. "Did you score any kills?"

"A guy in a glorified golf cart messed with me. He won't make that mistake again," Mongo said. "Now, you better step back."

The kids were confused until Mongo swooned and tumbled down the front steps. Tammy shrieked. Bren turned with the commotion. Excusing himself, he jogged across the cul-de-sac to tend his friend. Mongo left blood patches on the terracotta steps where he had bounced.

"Service with a smile." Mongo's face blanched.

Bren signaled paramedics on his newly installed Entrada app. He removed sodden dressings and applied fresh bandages. Children hovered. "Ooh, he's bleeding! What happened to Mongo?"

"Check out the blood," Mark said.

"Give the man some air," Bren said. Mark ignored him, wanting to see the wound.

A groundskeeping robot skittered to the Lightfoots' walk. A sandblaster arm extended and scoured the bloodstains from the hardscape, the grit vacuumed away. The paramedics arrived as the robot departed, their electric vehicle resembling the injury carts once used to removed fallen NFL players from the field.

Bren assisted the two attendants in lifting Mongo to the rear platform. Mongo opened his messenger bag. He tugged the Bible into view. Bren smiled and patted his good shoulder.

Bren left the Lightfoots as they bent down to make sure all the blood had been removed. He returned to Olivia, who looked on, concerned.

"I hope he'll be all right," Olivia said.

"Takes a lot to keep Mongo down." Bren tied off a biohazard bag stuffed with used bandages. He dropped the bag into the truck bed and squirted sanitizer in his palms.

Olivia waved toward the end of the cul-de-sac. Josh waved back. He piloted a globe scooter, suspended on a single rubberized sphere in lieu of wheels. The scooter bounced over a rare crack in the pavement. The boy's portable air conditioner flew off his neck. He turned the handlebars to double back, grabbing the unit without slowing down. The scooter hummed to a halt in front of the Durand home.

"It's him! It's really him!" Josh jumped off the scooter and continued jumping on the driveway.

THE DELIVERER

"Mr. Van Allen, this is my son, Josh." Olivia put an arm around Josh and handed him the delivery. "And this is for you!"

Josh tore the brown paper. He set down the gift box and lifted the top. Still on his knees, he removed a note.

"It's from Dad." Josh read the note. "'Dear Josh. Greetings from London. I found these while cleaning out Grandpa's attic. He played with them when he was a boy, and he let me play with them when I was a boy. Now they're yours! Love, Dad.'"

Josh reached into the biodegradable packing peanuts and removed a Matchbox car, an iconic diecast toy. Josh admired the white 1966 Mustang Fastback, mint condition, a plastic lever protruding under the driver's door to steer the front wheels. He plumbed the package for more treasures—a Matchbox Hoveringham dump truck, a Dinky Toys Austin Healey, and the crown jewel, a Corgi Toys James Bond Aston Martin DB5. The exquisite mechanisms for the front machine guns, rear bullet shield, and ejector seat worked perfectly after seventy years.

Gathering children ogled the tiny fleet. Like their parents, they were connoisseurs of vintage products made of metal and petroleum-based plastic, materials infrequently seen in the graphene era. So simple, millions had been made without variation. So irresistible, retail had been reversed, people delivering themselves to stores to take possession. The kids called dibs as Josh led them to his front steps, which they converted into switchbacks and jumps. These British beauties were not staying on a collector's shelf.

"I could use a full-size version of the DB5." Bren smiled. "Cool presents. Dad for the win."

"You know my husband didn't send the package." Olivia was matter of fact. "At least the cars are somewhat genuine. Not actually from a family attic, but certified collectors' items."

"Your son feels loved. That's all that matters."

Russ Lightfoot walked over, pointing at the Lightning. "You're leaking. Homeowners Association rules say no discharge allowed on residential streets."

Bren leaned down to check the rear right wheel. Fluid dripped from the axle. "Looks like a bullet hit the strut."

"You'll need to move that truck in the next ten minutes," Russ said. "You'll need to move along yourself."

"Unless the driver is an invited guest of a homeowner. HOA rules, Russ." Olivia tapped the invite function on her app. "Mr. Van Allen, would you join us for dinner while the service center fixes your truck?" Josh looked up from the steps, elated.

"After I drop off the rest of my load and Mongo's. I'd be delighted," Bren said. The kids oohed.

CHAPTER 11

Deliveries finished, Bren pushed his empty cart toward the Durand house. Mongo's folded cart hung from the front, Bren having fulfilled his friend's commitments as well as his own. Olivia and Josh met him.

"I have to pick up a couple of things at the market," Olivia said.

"Need a hand?" Bren gestured at the cart. Olivia smiled and nodded.

The Entrada market was a farm-to-table concept, with the farm being within city walls. In the produce section, the greens were hanging gardens of Babylon, growing from towers that misted their exposed roots with nutrient-laden water. Olivia handpicked the salad and side dishes, which Josh bagged and deposited in Bren's cart. The meat department was next. Large printers replaced the glass display cases and slicers of ancient butchers. An antiseptic tang hung in the air.

Olivia turned to Bren. "Do you want steak or chicken?"

"Ribeye would be great." Bren lifted his phone. "Let me pay."

Olivia shook her head. "Meal plan is part of HOA fees." She turned to the attendant. "Ribeye please. Three-hundred and fifty ... no, five-hundred grams."

The attendant activated the protein printer. A raw ribeye amassed on the product platform, separate nozzles for artificial blood, fat, and muscle combining their outputs like an old inkjet mixing cyan, magenta, yellow, and black to produce an image.

"I want chicken. Can I pick out my pieces?" Josh said. Olivia nodded.

Josh stood at the poultry wall. Behind a window, individual chicken pieces grew in bioreactor pouches. The boy pointed out the exact drumstick and wings he wanted. The pouches drained, vacuum sealed, and dropped into a chute like candy from a vending machine.

The trio returned to the house. Bren hung his chest holster on the coat rack. He brought the groceries to the kitchen, and Olivia started dinner. The infrared oven cooked the meat quickly.

"You saved me from another night of truck stop food." Bren set plates where Olivia indicated along the breakfast bar.

"I hear our truck stop is good." Olivia brought main courses and took one of the tall chairs. Josh clambered into his seat, parking the 007 Corgi Toy next to his dinner plate.

"The food all tastes the same after a while," Bren said. "May I pray?" Olivia nodded. "Heavenly Father, thank you for this meal. Thank you for the Durands opening their home."

"Please watch over Mr. Van Allen on the road," Olivia said.

The three dug into their well-designed dinner. Josh had many questions about the Deliverer's exploits but had to work around his mother's insistence he chew and swallow before speaking.

"I love getting packages. Every time I see a brown box, I know it's something cool," Josh said.

"A lot of people feel that way. They like the box showing up. They like having something that didn't come out of a 3D printer," Bren said.

"I love my cars," Josh said. He rolled the Aston Martin back and forth for emphasis.

"When I was a little girl, everything was delivered," Olivia said.

"It's like vinyl records or mechanical watches." Bren noted Josh's quizzical expression. "Old ways of listening to music or telling time. People miss how things used to be."

"What did you do before you were a driver?" Olivia began clearing dishes.

"I was an engineer." Bren joined her in the cleanup. "Good background for my work."

"Did you fight in the war?" Josh said.

Bren nodded. "Army National Guard. I use that training too."

"How does your wife feel about your job?" Olivia said.

Bren shook his head. "She passed away in the third pandemic. She was an RN."

Olivia turned toward Bren. "I'm sorry."

"Can we have s'mores for dessert?" Josh said.

"For a special occasion like this, of course." Olivia loaded the dish blaster. The appliance used fine sand and compressed air to clean, like the groundskeeping robot, one more effort to conserve water.

Josh collected s'mores ingredients, then rummaged in a utensil drawer. "Mom, where's my special fork?"

"Where it always is," Olivia said.

As his mom and Bren talked, Josh continued a fruitless search. He moved to the printer in the family room and transmitted a design from his phone. Graphene solution extruded into the laser bay, the beams and exposure to oxygen solidifying the raw material into the desired object.

A bell tone signaled completion, and a new s'mores fork appeared on the product carriage. Josh grasped the long utensil, extending the slide-out prongs.

"Mine's better than yours," Josh said. "It won't get hot or burn."

"Honey, we don't run the printer just because we didn't look hard enough for something we already have." Olivia handed Bren a bamboo skewer. "The grownups have to make do with these."

The cookout pod rose from the island countertop. The trio rolled marshmallows in the plasma arc before sandwiching with the luxuries of chocolate and graham crackers made with natural honey. S'mores were commonplace when Bren and Olivia were Josh's age. Now they ranked with beluga caviar.

Bren reacted to an incoming text. "Strut replaced, tires repaired. Truck stop shuttle is on the way."

"Thank you for being our guest," Olivia said.

"Thank you for being my customers." Bren put an arm around Josh. "Enjoy those cars."

"Get ready for bed, sweetheart," Olivia said to Josh. The boy ran up the stairs, his new toys clutched to his chest. Olivia walked Bren to the door.

"I'd like to book you again. Josh is getting another present from his father." Olivia looked back at Bren. "I know it's deceitful."

Bren buckled his holster. "Are you doing it for Josh or yourself?"

The insight triggered a sad smile. "As I mentioned in the first video, my husband is absent. He won't say when he's coming back," Olivia said.

"I'll pray he realizes what he's missing."

"Don't waste your prayers."

"They're never wasted." Bren held up a hand to bid farewell. Olivia held up her hand, the silver owl sliding down her wrist. Their fingers interlocked briefly.

At the travel center, Bren tossed the delivery carts in the rented storage locker where his long guns rested. He walked past the laundromat and the entrance to the restaurant into a hallway leading to the health clinic. The mini hospital served drivers' ailments from sore throats to gunshot wounds. Bren stood in the waiting room ...

The last time he'd been in a hospital lobby, he'd held toddler Madison. Hailey was starting her shift. She pulled down her mask and kissed her husband and daughter goodbye.

"I think we're ready for that bugout," Bren said.

"You can't go AWOL from the Guard. They're shooting deserters," Hailey said.

"My family comes first."

"I can't go AWOL either. This pandemic is worse than the others. The medical center's running at 200 percent capacity."

Bren couldn't deny Hailey's servant heart. He and Madison hugged her one last time. Hailey walked down the hall to her station. Bren and Madison turned toward the main entrance. An alarm sounded. A computerized voice over loudspeakers announced: "Pathogen breach."

Panic ensued as guards rushed to secure the hospital. Bren clutched Madison as he moved toward the entrance. Hailey appeared again in the employee hallway. Bren held out a hand toward her. She shook her head. Containment doors closed in front of her. Bren and Madison escaped the hospital. A moment later, containment doors sealed the entrance. No one would leave the building now.

Later, Bren and Madison stood vigil behind a barricade in the parking lot. Both their faces were tear-stained. Bren's phone rang with a video call.

"I only have a minute. There's a lot of sick people in here. The contagion's spreading." Hailey wore a protective suit.

"How long will you be on lockdown?" Bren said.

"They're drone-dropping food and supplies on the roof. It could be a long time." Hailey said. "Look up."

Bren raised his eyes and saw Hailey in a window. He urged Madison to wave at Mommy. All three cried.

Another day, Bren brought Madison back to the parking lot. They waved at Mommy. Another day, Madison was in a jacket—the weather was getting colder. They waved again. Another day, and the hospital window remained empty. Bren pulled Madison tight, closed his eyes, and prayed ...

A commotion behind doors leading to the treatment areas ended Bren's painful memories. Mongo burst into view, a harried physician's assistant trailing.

"Mister ... Mongo, you need to stay overnight," the physician's assistant said. "You could've lost your arm." The PA reached out to grab Mongo's shirt.

Mongo clamped the PA's wrist. "If the wheels ain't turning, I ain't earning."

Bren nodded at the physician's assistant to let Mongo leave. He began walking. "Show a little gratitude, brother."

"I'll be grateful when I'm out of here." Mongo worked his repaired limb in its sling.

"Entrada isn't so bad," Bren said. "Your customers appreciated you took a bullet for them." The pair came to the storage locker. Bren unfolded his cart and loaded his gun cases.

Mongo filled his cart, his arsenal taking considerably longer. "How's my Bronco?" He showed more concern for his vehicle than his body.

"Came through pretty well. I bought you a new window. Not the cheap glass this time."

"What do I owe you?"

"Just show up to Bible study when we have some downtime."

The late sunset filtered through the haze. Bren and Mongo left Entrada, the departure process less arduous than their multistep check-in. Once through the outer gate, they approached a concrete building, the lone structure in the buffer zone covered by the community's Phalanx cannons. Porch Pirate and security vehicles ringed the bunker. D.D. stood outside her Mustang. She gave the Deliverer an obscene salute as he passed.

Porch Pirates brought hijacked packages into the concrete building. Chief Yang led a security team keeping them at gunpoint. Officers scanned boxes with mobile devices, the RFID tags inside opening communication links with the customers from Entrada who'd ordered the items.

An officer conducted a video call on her phone. "Mrs. Danforth, we have the silverware you ordered."

Lonny stood beside the officer. "Forty-five."

"That's so much more than I already paid. I want to speak to your supervisor," Mrs. Danforth said. The officer waved over Chief Yang.

"Can't you do something about this?" Mrs. Danforth said.

"Ma'am, you have the right to say no to the Porch Pirates. Your order will then go on the gray market, and anyone can bid on it," Chief Yang said.

"Why don't you just shoot those thieves and bring me my silverware?" Mrs. Danforth said.

"As appealing as that may sound, supervised negotiation is the best way to recover stolen property." Chief Yang nodded at his officer to carry on with the pouting Mrs. Danforth.

D.D. stood with a negotiation officer. A group of teens were on the other end of the call. "You want your video game collection, that's the final price," D.D. said.

A teen looked off screen and then returned attention to D.D. "My mom says okay. We'll pay." The electronic ransom went through. "Hey, you're D.D. Guthrie. You used to be an eQuality driver."

"Yeah," D.D. said. "For an extra ten, I'll bring the package to your front door and autograph it."

The teen and his friends laughed. "You're a Porch Pirate now. We don't let scum like you inside."

D.D. turned away, ducking her head in shame. Lonny watched her, smirking.

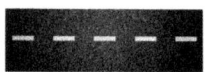

The Lightning drove into the dusk. Raveena appeared on the touchscreen. "Reports coming in. Porch Pirates shutting down for the night. Lots of damage and casualties."

"Welcome to the new enterprise district. First day was hell for all of us," Bren said.

"Good day for you in the end," Raveena said. "Great customer reviews. By what she wrote, you made a particular impression on Mrs. Durand and her son."

"A sad woman, just the way she described herself." Bren sat inside a kaleidoscope—the orange sun dropping in the dirty sky, the sheen of his touchscreen, the heads-up display shifting hues to stay visible in the glare. "Are you sad, Raveena? Ever?"

"You know the answer to that."

"Are you happy? You make me happy on the long hauls. You comfort me when I'm taking fire. Despite what I say, I really enjoy your humor."

Raveena watched Bren, letting him talk. "Where can I find you, Raveena?" he said. "A data center in Mumbai? An old telephone building in Fresno?"

"You know the answer to that too."

Bren exhaled. "You're a bot, the best yet. Never sad, never happy, nowhere to be found. The perfect ... person ... to make my paths straight. Can you take compliments?"

"I have been for the past minute." Raveena pulled a laugh from Bren.

CHAPTER 12

Olivia stood in a darkened forest, her white tutu contrasting with the enveloping shadows. Vadim materialized as he'd appeared in Roxy's music video, black hair and fierce mustache. Gray tights and a brocaded tunic replaced the Armageddon leathers of MTV.

On their virtual stage, the dancers performed the Act II pas de deux from the ballet *Giselle*. Olivia was the peasant girl risen from the dead, ordered to send Vadim's Duke Albrecht to his own grave with a night of frenzied dance, his punishment for playing with her affections and crushing her fragile heart. The pair danced in beautiful orthodoxy, Giselle defying the Wilis—the undead, spurned maidens of the forest—and allowing Albrecht to survive.

The dance ended. Olivia and Vadim bowed. Roxy tenderly removed the VR headset that had allowed Vadim to assume the classic role, and the transmission switched to a standard video call on the living room big screens. "The ballet world mocked him after he did videos and tours with me." Roxy kissed Vadim's cheek. "Montreal, 1990, you silenced the critics. You had your revenge."

"My love, *Giselle* is about forgoing revenge." Vadim laughed through his speech synthesizer. He turned toward Olivia. "That said, there's nothing wrong with a good comeback."

A new video call—Josh—brought her back to reality. Olivia waved goodbye to Vadim and Roxy. The call brought her into conference with Josh and his father. The Warder logo filled the virtual background of Gabriel's camera feed.

Josh yelled over his shoulder to the neighbor kids. "See, Mark, my dad's not dead. There he is on the phone." The boy gaped into his phone's camera. "Mom, look, it's Dad!"

"I see, dear." Olivia slung a gym towel around her neck.

Gabriel tapped on a second screen outside the frame. "I was expecting another call. I have a meeting in a few minutes."

Josh's enthusiasm withstood the rebuff. "Thanks for having the Deliverer bring the Matchbox and Corgi cars. I didn't know you and Grandpa played with all that cool stuff back in London."

After a second of confusion, Gabriel seethed at Olivia. "Toys with a backstory."

"And the airplanes from Istanbul are awesome. I wanted to call you then, but Mom told me not to bug you," Josh said. "Where's my next present coming from?"

Gabriel's face tightened. "Ask your mother. Perhaps she'd know." He looked at Josh. "What happened to your air conditioner?"

"It fell off." Josh jiggled the cracked lobe hanging from his neck. "It still works."

"Temperatures are rising. You should have a proper device." The sight of damaged property annoyed Gabriel.

Josh turned at voices calling him back to play. "Gotta go. Love you, Dad!" Josh left the call.

Gabriel and Olivia glared at each other. He broke the silence. "There was a discrepancy with one of the lab printers. I should've paid closer attention."

"One of the many things needing more of your attention," Olivia said.

"Stop."

"Stop what? Making our son happy?"

Gabriel's fury mounted. "Stop tracking me."

"You stole my line." Olivia stepped away from the camera.

"I've been to Istanbul and London, which you've documented with your gift giving. You obviously know where I am now."

Olivia turned into her arabesque. "It's easy to print a Warder chip, just like your marketing says. And the damn thing really works. You should be pleased."

"I'm sure you are."

"No. Turning the tables sounded good, but in the end, you have to love controlling people to get the most out of your product. You'd better add a disclaimer." She executed a perfect plié.

"I want my chip back."

Olivia stopped practicing and approached the camera. "I want *my* chip back. And the transit pass."

"You and Joshua are out of harm's way."

"You mean out of your way."

"I could take the chip from you."

"I'll see you coming. I'll make sure you never find it."

"Yes, you might hand it off to your new friend, the Deliverer." Gabriel exhaled, stymied for now. "I'm on the verge of a major deal for Warder. You endanger it by following my movements. By distracting me."

"You're negotiating for Warder. I'm negotiating for my life. If you can't manage both deals at once, that's your problem." Olivia ended the call.

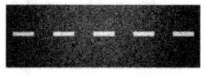

Inside the fire hub atrium, frosted tubes refueled the cargo rocket. The tubes detached and retracted, and the countdown began. "Five … four … three … two … one …" The rocket blasted off, a flame trench drawing the exhaust away.

Cox stood in the mission control skybox. Coffee sloshed despite the chamber's shock absorbers and soundproofing. The rocket's blue flare seeped through steel shutters blocking the observation windows. The slats opened once the missile had cleared the building.

"Sleigh 3 is away," the flight director announced. The cargo ship term deliberately evoked Santa's hauler.

Another mission control team appeared on a monitor. "Wichita control, ready to receive. ETA, eight minutes." The cargo rocket was making a short suborbital hop on its single stage to eQuality's central hub. "Sleigh 3 scheduled for pack and stack at sixteen-hundred hours." Additional images showed other cargo rockets undergoing the turnaround—their empty bellies loaded with packages by a silo of robots, packed ships stacked atop reusable boosters for orbital flights to any destination on Earth.

Cox reviewed data on Naomi Pham's tablet. He nodded. "Good first run." He looked to the flight director. "Increase rocket schedule."

Reno whipped a fouetté kick, his toe rising to face level. "You want to hop into the kick. Watch my back leg." He repeated the move. "Street fighters in Paris used savate to destroy opponents a century before anyone had heard of Bruce Lee. That's why it's my preferred martial art. I'm Derek Reno with your combat tip from the road."

"Cut." Ronni videoed Reno on her mobile device. Two camera drones flitted, capturing additional angles.

"Another masterpiece." Reno kissed Ronni on the cheek.

"I'll have this posted by lunch. I've also finished the script for the Thunder Twins intro video." Ronni tried to make the last statement matter of fact.

"It's not time."

"You said Robert and I could go on our own."

"You will. But we can't switch things up right now. Gotta grab top rank and hold it." Reno hugged Ronni. "Then we can sign sponsors, start our own network, make you a star."

A group of drivers filed past the Reno campsite, led by Bren and Mongo. Reno gave Ronni another kiss. "Speaking of rankings, time to see how we did."

"Give 'em hell." Ronni watched her boyfriend join the other drivers. Sadly, she loaded Reno's raw footage into a moviemaking app to begin editing his thirty-seventh "Combat Tips from the Road" video.

Anxious drivers gathered in the gallery. Media walls displayed computations as AI crunched drivers' performances from the inaugural run. Drivers' listings on the market exchange board fluctuated as their final numbers were tabulated. Bren glanced at the drivers' ranking board. His listing jockeyed with Team Reno's for top spot. Video from dash and doorbell cams, drones, and customer phones created the latest highlight reels for each driver.

Reno studied the board with Robert at his side. "Any surprise who had most kills?" Fellow drivers reacted with a mix of cheers and boos.

Mongo came beside Bren. He pointed at his data row. "Would you look at that?"

"Your Likes are exploding," Bren said.

"I'm a likable guy." Mongo laughed.

Mongo's listing climbed with the late rally in social media sentiment. The Lightfoots' security camera video showing him falling down the front walkway was trending.

Users enjoyed Tammy's outburst that the big, bleeding man had diminished her home's curb appeal. Mongo edged Team Reno for second place in driver rankings while Bren took top spot. His fans celebrated his victory over the Porch Pirates in the graphene plant.

Reginald had transferred from the damaged hub along with Bren and Roadie. "Rankings for round one are finalized. Your new minimum fees have been calculated. Customer bids for your services are underway."

Reno seethed. "Third place?" He approached Mongo. "Sympathy points! Maybe I should get shot once in a while." He smacked Mongo's sling. Mongo lunged at him. Robert attempted to protect his leader, but Mongo tossed him aside with his good arm.

"Back off!" Bren pointed at Reno as he squeezed in front of Mongo. He turned to calm his friend.

A siren wailed. The drivers froze. An automated voice announced, "Air raid alert!" The video wall switched to news coverage. The chyron read *Jets Scramble. Ceasefire Threatened*.

The drivers scattered, some heading to shelters deep within the mall. Bren and Mongo went outside and looked skyward. A wing of Scorpion light-attack jets screeched above. Two F-16s overtook them.

"Can you tell who's who?" Mongo said.

Bren shook his head. "Everyone uses the same Air National Guard planes."

"I liked it better when we could tell the good guys from the bad guys," Mongo said.

In the skybox, Cox summoned Broker General Ruskin and Governor Bates on a video call. "What are you doing?"

"Early warning system detected hostile launch," Bates said.

"It's you. You're attempting a first strike!" Ruskin said.

Cox checked another screen. "You're both looking at a radar artifact from our cargo rocket. We can't do business this way. Ground your jets. Fix your trackers." Anger suffused his face and voice.

An all-clear sounded. The drivers returned to the gallery. Cox appeared on a main video display.

"I've talked to America Blue and the Border State coalition," Cox said. "The ceasefire will remain in effect, but I'm delaying the next rocket until we're certain the skies are clear. Get some rest."

Bren nudged Mongo. "Looks like we have that downtime. Grab your Bible."

The study group sat outside the Airstream. Mongo gave Bren a long look, pondering scriptural truths. "So, I'm the same as you as far as God's concerned, even though you grew up reading the Bible?"

Bren smiled. "Matthew 20:16. 'So those who are last now will be first then, and those who are first will be last.'"

Roadie helped Mongo find the verse in his Bible. "But you got a long way to go before you're as holy as me," Roadie said. The group laughed.

Bren prayed the group out. His phone rang, and Kenny Turro appeared on the screen.

"I heard your next run is delayed. How about a quick interview to keep the friendly folks engaged?" Kenny said.

"Sure," Bren said.

The show theme played, and Kenny addressed the studio cameras. "We're live with Bren Van Allen, the Deliverer. Bren, thanks for joining us. I have another special guest. From Portland, Oregon, the attorney general of American Green, Thomas Albano."

Albano stared into the camera. "Mr. Van Allen, you designed a drone known as the Gleaner."

"Years ago," Bren acknowledged.

"You're aware the Gleaner is being used as an assassination weapon?" As Albano spoke, images of Gleaner drones and their kills by explosion appeared.

"I created the Gleaner for agriculture, to eliminate invasive plants and insects. I'm sorry it's being misused."

"As the creator, you bear responsibility for deaths in our country. War crimes."

"I sold the patent in 2026."

"Save your argument for the court. I'm issuing a warrant for your arrest." Albano brought up a digital image of the document. "Come to Portland, or you'll be declared a fugitive."

Bren shook his head. "I'm currently in the Border States. No extradition treaty. You have no jurisdiction here."

"So, you're a lawyer as well as an engineer."

"Just a man who believes in fundamental rights."

Albano sneered. "The common law based on Scripture? We could debate an eye for eye and other cruelties of the Bible. Or would that offend a Christian?"

"Jesus settled the old law. We could debate legalism. But that might offend an attorney general."

"There you have it, ladies and gentlemen," Kenny said. "The Deliverer may be an underground hero in America Green, but he's not getting any love from the higher-ups."

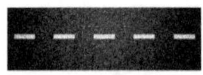

Inside his trailer, Bren set the lights to night shift. He activated a diffuser filled with lavender. Over the years, he'd delivered what seemed like gallons of the essential oil to a customer who swore by its soothing properties.

Madison was on-screen, her communication more like a multimedia presentation than a phone call, her earnest way of making the most of daddy-daughter time.

"Pastor Doug sent the Archegos newsletter. They've added another twenty square miles to the Revival Zone." Madison posted the communication in the split screen. "Crop yields are up. The European Union is opening a laboratory on the island to restart the California Current."

"Sounds promising." Bren glanced at the media highlights.

"I keep seeing ads for transit passes at cheap prices."

"They're counterfeit. Initial coding might get you onto the e-Bahn, but the system will detect it's a fake after a few miles."

"Why did they build a road that kills people?"

"To keep it exclusive." Bren turned his back to the screen and washed down a prescription pill. Sometimes the soft lights and aromas weren't enough to ease him into sleep.

"I'll be scared to drive on it"

"It's a lot safer than the roads I see."

"That scares me too. I like to read Psalm 91:11 when I think about you." Madison opened a Bible. "'For he will order his angels to protect you wherever you go.'"

"Maddie, show me that Bible." Bren observed a compact volume like the ones he distributed. A duct tape patch dominated the front cover. "Where did you find it?"

"I was organizing the closets. It was with some of your old army stuff. Had a hole right through it." Madison fanned pages mended with clear tape. "Grandma said a bookworm did it."

"Sounds like something she'd say."

"She forgets I'm twelve," Madison whispered. "Was it a bullet hole?"

"Yes."

"There's a name written inside ... Clint Harden."

"He was a famous pastor when you were a baby."

"Did he give you this?"

Bren nodded.

"Is it okay if I use it?"

Bren smiled, prompting the same from Madison. "He'd like knowing his Bible's in such good hands."

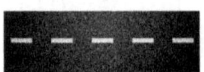

... Madison held up her Bible again. The book became a monolith thirty feet tall. The hole in the cover burst open and sucked in Bren. When he regained his bearings, he was Lieutenant First Class Van Allen, a decade prior.

The radio crackled with orders. "Proceed to Hemlock Road, five clicks from your position. UAVs and UGVs currently engaging enemy convoy."

Bren drove an infantry squad vehicle. He turned to his passenger. "If drones are taking out the enemy, why send in our platoon?"

Sergeant First Class Moe Franklin smiled at the uncertain lieutenant. "You'll learn, like the last platoon commander did. The brass likes accountability. They want eyes on the interdiction." Moe smiled. "Besides, you don't want the robots putting us real soldiers out of business."

Bren's platoon pulled up near the target. Moe interpreted Bren's hand signals, ordering soldiers into position. The column on Hemlock Road was smoldering and still. Aerial and ground drones had struck with missiles and bullets.

Machine gun fire erupted from the column's direction. As his men hit the dirt, Bren aimed his M4. The rifle jammed. Unable to clear the weapon, Bren drew his M17 pistol when he saw movement inside a shattered trailer. He fired and the movement stopped. His platoon answered another burst of machine gun fire. In the ensuing silence, Bren advanced along the blacktop wreckage.

"These vehicles aren't military," Bren said into his radio. "I'm looking at a church van."

"Militia?" Moe said over the air.

"I'm not finding weapons. Are you?" Bren said.

"Negative."

Bren cautiously entered the trailer. A cracked phone lay on a splintered table. A selfie video just shot on the device replayed: "I'm Pastor Clint Harden. The only way to end this civil war is to become one nation under God once again. We're going into the heart of darkness to share his living word. Throw down your weapons and pick up a Bible!" A recorded explosion sounded. The video looped to the beginning.

The machine gun fire resumed. Bren looked through the trailer's broken wall. A Gladiator unmanned vehicle carved a slow donut, its tread caught on a short concrete post. The .308 machine gun mounted on its deck spurted random rounds.

"Hold your positions," Bren said into his radio. "We're taking fire from—"

An explosion flipped the unmanned ground vehicle, ceasing its spasms. "One of ours." Moe reloaded his M320 grenade launcher.

Bren resumed his search and found Pastor Clint on the trailer floor, mortally wounded. Bren shook his head, whispering "No." Pastor Clint smiled and nodded in absolution.

"Make sure these get out." Pastor Clint motioned to boxes of Bibles in the back of the trailer. With the last of his strength, he pulled his personal Bible from a vest pocket, the book drilled by a 9mm bullet. Bren dropped his pistol and took the offered book with shaking hands.

During the hearing that followed, the Bible became Bren's tablet filled with notes. Dressed in his army service uniform, he underwent questioning.

"The drones massacred the pastor and his people," Bren said.

"Wasn't this 'Christian convoy' really transporting weapons and supplies to the enemy?" a senior officer asked.

"No," Bren said.

"Didn't your unit call in the strike?" another officer queried.

"No!" Bren said.

"A bullet from your sidearm killed Clint Harden," a third officer stated. Bren hung his head.

Bren's hearing notes became his discharge papers from the National Guard. "General Discharge under Honorable Conditions" headlined the document, a diminished standing upon separation. The army papers became an engineering proposal. The masthead read Van Allen Engineering. The red stamp, Canceled, blotted the plans.

"I'd love to bring you on, but I can't risk my government contacts," a CEO said in a video call. "You're blackballed. It's over."

The words "it's over" echoed. Bren lurched awake. "Forgive me," he whispered ...

God forgave him. Pastor Clint forgave him. He knew he fell short of both by the inability to forgive himself for contributing to the mistaken attack, for the collapse of his life after speaking out. He'd never have enough sleeping pills or lavender oil to quell the nightmares. He picked up his Bible, identical to the one he'd given Mongo and the one Pastor Clint had held close to his heart. He opened to the bookmark at Romans 8:1.

"'So now there is no condemnation for those who belong to Christ Jesus.'" Bren closed the book.

CHAPTER 13

Sleigh 5 landed in the atrium. As the rocket disgorged its packages, a wave of drones left Fire Hub Sears. Long wires unspooled, hanging near the ground in their low, slow flight. Miles of land mines detonated in the drones' electromagnetic wake. Drivers watched their progress in the gallery.

"Drivers, as the map shows, routes are clear to commence your runs," Reginald said over the PA system.

"If it's so safe, why don't you come with us!" The drivers roared at Mongo's taunt.

Bren checked the map on his mobile device. The drone sweep had opened more possible routes to Entrada, once again Bren's destination. He glanced at his manifests. Top of list was a stop at the Durand house. Once more, Olivia attached a video to her order.

"We're looking forward to seeing you again." Olivia laughed. "You've gotten more expensive. Congratulations. You're worth it."

The drivers collected their packages and replayed the ritual of the Le Mans start. Once Bren reached the highway, Raveena appeared on the touchscreen with calculated times for arrival and average speed alongside her image.

"Team Reno is heading to Entrada as well. Recommend reducing speed and letting them take the lead," Raveena said.

"And the punishment? You're coldblooded," Bren said.

"Someone around here has to be." Raveena smiled.

Team Reno attracted several Porch Pirates. Ronni came behind one pursuer, and smashed the car against the MRAP's flank, fracturing its windows. Reno extended his left arm and sprayed the exposed interior with the submachine gun hooked to his wrist. The riddled car swerved off the road. Reno checked the bandoliers' revised ammo count blinking on the heads-up display. He winked into the camera.

"Let's clear the rest quick," Reno said. "Blockers to the front."

Ronni and Robert pulled in front of the MRAP. Reno tapped an icon for SmartShot. Reminiscent of salt trucks' discharge in bygone winters, a dark curtain descended from the armored truck's rear bumper, a release of minute metal cubes that bounced before carpeting the road.

The first Porch Pirate drove over the cubes, triggering electromagnets. The cubes flew upward and mauled the engine and transmission. A second Porch Pirate roared past, unaware of the threat. SmartShot jiggled and levitated as the car passed over. The thin floorpan shredded, and the engine screamed as the cubes found their target. The driver screamed as well when more SmartShot entered the cockpit, tearing his feet and legs. The car rolled over and exploded.

D.D. assessed the destruction ahead. "He's using SmartShot. Everybody off this road!"

The remaining Porch Pirates veered. Team Reno continued down the stretch alone. Mongo appeared from a side street, his Bronco coming behind the MRAP. The dark curtain dropped again.

Mongo's eyes widened. "Reno, it's me! Stop!"

The first volley of SmartShot embedded in the heavy skid plates. Reno dropped another load. The projectiles finally reached the powertrain. Mongo cursed the smoking hood and flashing warning lights. He wrestled the slowing Bronco into a field.

Porch Pirates followed the path of flattened hemp stalks streaked with motor oil. The Bronco stalled in a clearing. Mongo jumped out, ready to fight, yelling threats. The Porch Pirates formed a defensive line. One bandit dared his truck closer through a tall stand of hemp. Once stopped, he crept from the bed to the Bronco's roof, diving on Mongo with a knife. The big man cried out before planting the attacker head down into the dirt.

D.D. pulled her Mustang behind the row of Porch Pirate vehicles and stepped out, motioning for calm. "Let's make this easy, Mongo."

Mongo leveled a weapon that looked like a plastic Gatling gun, a CO_2 canister attached to the grip. He fired at the nearest enemy car. A capsule the size of a dinner roll wobbled from the muzzle and hit the windshield. The gelatinous mass rolled onto the hood. Lonny inspected the object.

"Careful, he's got a Nerf gun." Lonny laughed.

Sparky leaned toward D.D. "He shouldn't touch that."

"No kidding." D.D. cupped her mouth to yell. "Don't touch that!"

Lonny looked up, confused. The capsule burst open in a fireball, immolating the car. Lonny jumped back and rolled in the dirt. Mongo adjusted the valve on the CO_2 bottle and fired again. The next capsule hit at full velocity, engulfing another car. A couple of Porch Pirates took wild shots at Mongo but soon retreated with the others. Mongo squeezed off more incendiaries, which combined with gas tank explosions to ignite the field. He slid down the Bronco's fender to a sitting position. His hand went to the knife wound on his shoulder. He began sweating and shaking.

Bren arrived at the clearing. He assessed Mongo's injury.

"Just a scratch." Mongo's voice trembled.

Bren looked down at the knife. A bluish liquid coated the blade. "Knife was treated with neurotoxin." He injected Mongo with a syringe from his kit. "General antidote. Good enough for now. Gotta get you to a hospital." Bren left Mongo's side. He backed the Lightning toward the Bronco's grill and removed a tow bar from the cargo bed.

"I know you won't leave without your rig." Bren attached the bar to his hitch and the Bronco's tow hooks.

Mongo shook his head. "You'll be an easy target dragging my butt."

"Next Bible study, we're reading John 15:13." Bren coughed from the smoke.

"Looks like I torched a field of ganja." Mongo inhaled. "I won't feel a thing."

"Guess again. It's industrial hemp." Bren pulled Mongo to his feet.

"Just my luck." Mongo grabbed the Bronco's door, refusing to let Bren take him to the Lightning. Bren threw Mongo's Gatling gun into the Bronco's back seat and strapped him behind the steering wheel. Bren plowed a new path through the stalks as flames encircled the clearing.

On the highway, Bren noted Porch Pirate casualties. In the aftermath of Team Reno's passage, the threat thinned. His front-bumper radar detected objects on the road surface ahead, triggering a warning display. Bren activated countermeasures. A skateboard-shaped decoy dropped from the Lightning's undercarriage and rolled forward. Foil wings unfolded to increase the profile. The decoy set off SmartShot, clearing a path for the truck.

"Raveena, open a live feed." Bren looked into the camera. "We need prayers for Mongo. He's in bad shape. Doesn't matter if you're a fan of his or not. Take a moment and ask God to sustain him. He gives everything to his customers and everyone watching."

The feed ended and the view from Mongo's cockpit camera occupied the screen. "Stay with me," Bren said. He alternated his gaze between his friend and the Lightning's battery gauge, power draining more quickly under towing. Off to the west he spotted a line of shelf clouds—the makings of a powerful derecho storm front.

Bren knew Mongo had to stay awake until they reached the hospital. "You feel like singing? Did you grow up with any Christian songs?"

Mongo's head lolled. "Grandma used to sing The Doobie Brothers to me. How's this? 'Jesus is just all right with me. Jesus is just all right—'" Bren sang the refrain with him.

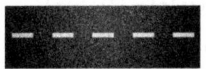

Porch Pirates regrouped behind a barn. Yips and howls punctuated the air. A pack of coydogs—hybrids of coyotes and household canines—circled the bandits, thriving in the wartime wilderness. Lonny fired a shot to scare them off. The pack drew closer. D.D. pulled her Desert Eagle, the nickel plating scuffed from skipping on the pavement during the battle with Bren. Three rounds sent three animals tumbling into heaps. The pack withdrew.

D.D. holstered her pistol and surveyed vehicle damage. Sparky tended a Porch Pirate's wound. D.D. stepped in to redo the wrapping.

Lonny glowered at D.D. "I'm not seeing any big improvements since you became boss. In fact, we're getting our butts kicked more than ever."

"Who recognized the SmartShot and got us off that road?" D.D. said. "Who did not recognize an incendiary device?" She yanked his scorched beard. "You're only complaining because you're still alive. You're alive because of me!" She turned to the group. "Get people and weapons into remaining vehicles. eQuality's not getting rid of us that easy!"

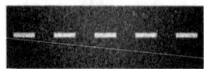

The conjoined Lightning and Bronco raced up the access road to Entrada. Chief Yang appeared on the touchscreen.

"Driver, do you require assistance?"

"Yes," Bren said. "Notify the clinic I'm bringing in a casualty. Condition critical."

The Lightning and Bronco cleared Entrada's entrance tunnel. Bren swerved to the right lane on the internal highway and took the off-ramp for the truck stop complex. The vehicles heaved to a halt at the emergency room doors.

"Well, if it isn't our favorite patient." The physician's assistant sprinted forward with a gurney team.

"Neurotoxin." Bren pointed to Mongo's knife wound. "I administered 10cc of K5 antidote." The team laid Mongo on the gurney and attached sensors to his body. Bren came alongside, grasping Mongo's hand.

"Finish the run." Mongo's eyes closed, and an automated voice repeated, "Cardiac arrest." The physician's assistant called for clear and applied defibrillator paddles. He motioned for Bren to stay back as Mongo was wheeled into the clinic.

Bren arrived at the Durand house. Josh ran down the walk to greet him. "I prayed for Mongo, like you told us to," the boy said.

"He appreciates it." Bren looked for Olivia's nod to hand the package to Josh. "And I know you'll appreciate this."

Josh tore open the box and read the note. "'Dear Josh. Hello from New York. When I was your age, the Space

Shuttle was the way to go into outer space. Now we have this. Blast off! Love, Dad.'"

The boy withdrew a gleaming replica of Icarus 1, the Mars crewed spacecraft, five hundred feet long in real life, launched two years prior. After Florida and Texas had gone to America Red, America Blue built the Kennedy-Johnson Space Center, a floating launch and control facility outside New York Harbor. The toy was a new manufacture but crafted in the sturdy diecast style of the classic cars from the previous order.

Josh raced around the front yard, holding Icarus 1 over his head, announcing a flight to the red planet. Neighbor kids came running. With her son joyously distracted, Olivia approached Bren.

"You asked if I send the gifts for Josh or myself." Olivia's voice was quiet, her eyes moist. "I don't do it for me, not now. I feel sick about your friend. I hate how you risk your life coming here." Her torment grew. "I was so happy when I was bidding for you."

"Mongo knew what he was doing. His family has a good home thanks to this work. And I know what I'm doing." Bren put a hand on Olivia's shoulder. "I was happy too when I saw who won the auction."

"Sounds like the slave trade." Olivia wiped a tear.

"I'm free in Jesus. And I'm a step closer to what my family needs, a transit pass." Bren motioned toward his truck. "There's one more box for Josh."

Olivia was puzzled. "I didn't place any other orders." She waved Josh back as Bren pulled the second parcel.

"Another present!" Josh lifted a note from the new box. "It's from Dad too! 'Joshua, you need a proper air conditioner. Hope you get the good out of this one. Dad.'" He removed his cracked unit and placed the new one around his neck. "Cool. Get it? Cool?" Bren and Olivia smiled. Josh ran back to command his Mars mission.

"Your gifts are better," Bren said. Olivia smiled, tears mixed with pleasure.

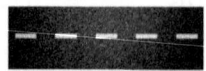

Bren entered Mongo's hospital room. The big man lay inert in a mass of tubes. Mary watched from a screen on the wall.

Bren turned toward the screen. "I finished his deliveries. Some nice tips. Sent everything to your account."

Mary smiled. "You always watched out for Paul, knew what was best for him." Her tears increased. "Tell me what's best for him now."

Bren looked at the vital signs monitor. Brain activity was flatlined, no change from before, no change expected. Bren looked at his friend. "God sanctifies all life. This isn't life." He turned back to the screen. "Let him go Home."

Mary nodded assent. The medical team shut down life support.

Bren bowed his head. "Lord Jesus, welcome your mighty man as he welcomed you."

Only minutes later, the beep of the monitors sustaining Mango's life quickened, then turned to a steady hum. With a sympathetic glance at Bren and Mary, a doctor muted the machine. Bren held his palm toward Mary on the screen. Mary returned the gesture as she cried.

CHAPTER 14

The storm gathered over the Border States—a dry derecho with violent wind and lightning but no rain. Their deliveries completed, the drivers hunkered at the Entrada truck stop. In the crowded bar, a Skynyrd tribute band provided the soundtrack for the raucous evening. Reno celebrated his fan-pleasing run. He whooped at the alert on his mobile device.

"Team Reno is number one in the rankings!" Reno said. Ronni and Robert cheered along with their allies.

Bren made his way through the crowd. He spoke briefly with Roadie, then they bowed their heads for prayer. The sight of the Deliverer made Reno stop his monologue and set down his glass.

"Hey, choirboy! Didn't know you liked saloons," Reno said. "Here to toast the new champ?" Reno's groupies whooped.

"No, I'm taking a collection for Mongo's family." Bren stood on the dance floor. "He died twenty minutes ago." Drivers gasped.

"That's a real shame," Reno said. "Shoulda joined Team Reno when he had the chance."

"Being too close to you is what killed him."

Reno feigned confusion. "The Porch Pirates got him."

"'Cause you knocked him off the road with your SmartShot." Bren wasn't looking for a fight. Drivers formed a circle around him and Reno anyway.

"The hopper malfunctioned."

"Twice? Three times with the load left for me?"

"That's what happens when you play follow the leader." Reno walked away from the bar to face Bren. "You dealt with it. Too bad your buddy wasn't bright enough to do the same."

"Too bad you couldn't make top rank without killing your own." Bren stood his ground as the room went silent.

"You run your mouth and think it's a sermon? You're not hiding behind your Bible tonight!" Reno pulled on his driving gloves, the hard knuckles crackling as he flexed his fingers. His heavy boots were already in place for his cherished savate. Ronni started shooting combat video thirty-eight as Reno squared off against Bren.

From his National Guard days, Bren was trained in aikido, emphasizing defense and redirecting an opponent's momentum. He had to get inside Reno's foot range to neutralize his power. Reno's first fouetté was expected. Bren ducked and charged, delivering a palm strike to the solar plexus. Reno groaned. Bren seized his arm, grappling to restrict another kick. Reno chopped Bren on the collar bone with his free hand, breaking the hold. An elbow and fist combination slammed Bren against the bar. Reno cocked his foot for a chasse frontal. Bren blocked the kick with a barstool, a wooden leg snapping against Reno's boot. He pushed Reno away.

Reno brought up his leg for another high kick. In the first split second, Bren turned with the leg's rotation, locking the knee between his right hand and left forearm. In the next split second, Bren took control of the leg, bending the limb back while ramming Reno's face into the dance floor.

"Get him!" Reno wailed. Ronni flicked open a switchblade, her brother on her heels. Several drivers who could've been Mongo's marginally smaller siblings blocked the blockers.

Bren applied more pressure. Reno cried out. An alarm sounded, and Chief Yang led a security team into the bar. An officer drew a stun gun, and Bren released the hold. Two more stood the bleeding Reno on his good leg.

"You've violated Entrada's code of conduct," Yang said. "Per HOA rules, homeowners will now vote if you can remain in the community."

Monitors flashed the alert for an emergency vote. Tallies and homeowner chats scrolled.

"Bren Van Allen has been nothing but trouble since he came to Entrada," Russ Lightfoot typed in the chat. "Expel him!"

Thunder roared, the storm awaiting those banished to the road. Yang answered his phone. After a brief conversation, he motioned for Bren to follow. Reno smirked.

Yang took Bren to a back hallway. "A homeowner has invited you to be an overnight guest. Per HOA rules, the vote on you is canceled."

Bren nodded and left the bar. A security officer brought a handheld device to Yang. "Call on the negotiation hotline," the officer said.

"We're here with our haul. We're ready to negotiate," D.D. yelled into her phone. The Porch Pirates were gathered at an outcropping near the bunker. They tried to establish shelter amid the cars and rocks. Several were grievously wounded from the day's battles. Gale-force winds tore the encampment.

"We're not coming out in this storm," Yang said. "We'll talk with whoever's left in the morning."

D.D. screamed for Yang to stay on the line. The winds grew. A panel truck holding much of the bandits' spoils rocked. Several Porch Pirates tried securing the truck with chains. The vehicle blew over, people screaming beneath its dark mass.

"Get jacks under the corners!" D.D. ordered.

Sparky and two others positioned the machinery and cranked the levers. D.D. leaned into the choking dust and pulled bodies free. Spent, she stood and caught Lonny's hateful stare.

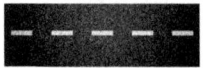

Bren entered the Durand house, duffle bag and holster slung over his shoulder, dried blood on his face. Olivia closed the front door against the wind.

"Didn't want you thrown out in this storm," she said. Bren nodded his appreciation.

"Can we have s'mores?" Josh wore rocket pajamas to go with the Icarus 1 toy he still carried.

"It's late. Maybe tomorrow," Olivia said.

"For breakfast?" Josh smiled, hoping Bren would like the idea.

"Scoot. I'll be up in a minute."

"Hurry. I hate the storm."

Olivia touched Bren's face near the blood streak. "Bedroom in the basement. You'll find everything you need."

... The house shook. Olivia grabbed Josh by the hand and led him into the sunlight. They sailed to the neighborhood park, feet skimming the ground in their haste. A tiltrotor sat on the helipad.

"Where are we going?" Josh said.

"To Geneva, our new home," Olivia said.

"What about our stuff?"

"I'll buy us new stuff. We have to hurry." Olivia led the way up the ramp into the tiltrotor's belly.

A banner on the cabin wall read "Prix de Gloire Winner—Olivia Durand." Competition officials welcomed the pair with hugs and a flute of champagne for Mom. The passengers buckled up, and the tiltrotor took off.

Flashes appeared outside the windows. "What's happening?" Olivia said.

Bren walked from the flight deck. "Ground-to-air missiles. We have countermeasures."

The tiltrotor released chaff, tiny aluminum strips puffing like confetti. Flares fired from the bottom of the craft, another means to confound missile guidance systems. Olivia looked out the window at the spectacle—swirling metal, glowing flares, streaking rockets.

"Are we gonna die, Mom?" Josh said. The fireworks kept flashing ...

The flashes increased, lightning and household bulbs blinking before going dark. Olivia woke up from her nightmare, breathing heavily. The storm had knocked out Entrada's microgrid. The household batteries had tried to turn on but failed to complete the circuit. Olivia flicked on an electric lantern fashioned as a stout candle. She pulled on a robe and went downstairs.

The control panel was in the basement corridor leading to the panic room. Olivia turned the corner to see Bren already working with the panel, shirtless in jeans.

"Battery levels are good," Bren said. "I'll reset the circuit."

"Another reason I'm glad you're here." Olivia stayed at the end of the corridor, watching. "I had a terrible dream. I got everything I wished for, and Josh and I were going to die for it. You too."

"Don't wish." Bren turned his gaze from the panel to Olivia. "Pray."

"But what if I want something God doesn't want me to have?"

Bren smiled with understanding. "Don't be too hard on yourself. Happens all the time."

"Has it ever happened to you?"

Olivia turned off her candle light. The derecho's illumination channeled through the basement's window wells. The scene was from an old film, movements strobing, shadows darkening. The robe slipped from Olivia's shoulders as she advanced. Lightning silvered her body through her nightgown.

The Deliverer did not freeze, did not question. The pair came together and kissed deeply. A tiny cry pierced the thrill and thunder. From the second-floor landing, Josh called for his mother.

Replacing her robe, Olivia ran to Josh. She hugged her son. "Just checking the backup batteries. Everything's fine." She led Josh back to his bedroom.

"Is the Deliverer still here? He'll take care of us," Josh said.

"I'm right here, Josh." Bren buttoned his shirt at the bottom of the stairs.

"C'mon up," Olivia said. "Let's show our man there's nothing to worry about."

The trio entered Josh's room. Olivia took the chair where she'd nursed Josh as an infant. The boy curled in her lap, and Bren sat on the floor beside her.

"People say we're gonna have more of these big storms. They say we'll get killed if we leave Entrada. People are always talking about scary stuff." Josh burrowed into Olivia.

Bren nodded. "People talked about scary stuff when I was a kid. Even before that. My dad watched movies about the future turning out bad. The road becoming a battleground. Plagues. The end of the world. He scared himself on purpose."

"Were the movies make-believe?"

"They were supposed to be." Bren looked at Olivia with regret. "We didn't believe the prophets. Why believe what we saw on cable?"

"What's 'cable'?" Josh's innocence broke the sadness. Olivia stroked his hair with one hand. She held Bren's hand with the other. The house lights came on as the batteries engaged.

The derecho passed at daybreak. The groundskeeping robots buzzed, clearing storm debris. Bren bid Olivia farewell at the front door.

"I'm thinking up a new excuse to bring you back," Olivia said.

"You don't need an excuse." Bren squeezed her shoulder.

Josh ran up with a final s'more on a napkin. He handed the treat to Bren. "That's for the road."

"Won't make it out of the driveway." Bren put his arms around mother and son as the three laughed.

After Bren drove away, Olivia gave a neighborly wave to the Lightfoots, who gawked from their front steps. Russ and Tammy turned on their heels, dragging Mark with them, and slammed the door.

In the silent sunrise, Porch Pirates rose from the crags. Many of the wounded were now dead. Cars were sandblasted, weapons fouled. A heavily armed column left Entrada, Yang in the lead vehicle. The security force stopped and took position. D.D., bedraggled, straightened and walked to face Yang.

"Now are you ready to negotiate?" D.D. said.

"No, I'm here with a final offer. All your stolen goods in exchange for food, medical supplies, and five minutes with a wrecker to get your truck back on its wheels. Take it or leave it," Yang said.

Bren drove past the gathering on his way to the open road. His heart hurt for D.D. His heart hurt for Mongo. The Lightning accelerated—no time for nostalgia.

D.D. watched Bren pass, lacking the strength to lift a finger. She returned her attention to Yang. "We'll take it."

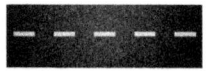

Cox stood at the media wall in his private suite at Fire Hub Sears with Naomi at his side, checking figures on a tablet. The video call connected with Auckland. The on-screen ID read eQuality Testing Laboratory. Dr. Parata, Chief Technologist.

"I'm ready for the Warder chip results," Cox said.

Dr. Parata moved to a 3D printer. "The nozzle assembly and matrix reservoir are compatible with most household printers. The chip printing method is almost as remarkable as the chip itself. Completed circuits built up from the atomic level, multilayered."

"Equivalent efficiency to conventional semiconductors?" Cox observed closeup videos of the proprietary hardware at work.

"Yes. And the chips are produced in minutes, not weeks."

"So the product is marketable for home use. Does it work?"

Dr. Parata brought up a global map. Five colored trails left New Zealand on circuitous routes around the world. "We created Warder chips on five subjects. These people were deep scanned in advance to ensure no tracking systems had been implanted in their bodies. They traveled air-gapped on black itineraries, no personal devices, no digital activity, no logged record of movement. They wore top-of-the line blocking garments and masks, obscuring them from any photographic and electronic detection enroute. Their routes and destinations were kept secret from me and everyone at the lab." Animations depicted test procedures. "There's no way we should be able to track them."

Dr. Parata stood at a row of five Warder chip cases similar to the one Olivia used to track Gabriel. Each chip corresponded to an app on a monitor. On a large, central screen Dr. Parata clicked the first map trail. The line stretched from New Zealand to Chile, wending to a terminus in Central America. He bent toward a microphone. "Subject one. You flew from Auckland to Santiago. You are now in Escazu, Costa Rica. 9.9207 degrees north, 84.1462 degrees west."

An image shared the screen with Dr. Parata. A woman stood in a cabin on a mountaintop overlooking the suburb. She looked into the camera that had been waiting at her clandestine destination. "Correct," the woman said.

Dr. Parata addressed the other test subjects—Kuala Lumpur, Yerevan, Mt. Kilimanjaro, a cruise ship in the

Arctic Ocean. Each replied to a description of their route and coordinates of current location: "Correct."

"Can you detect any type of transmission between the subjects and their chips?" Cox said.

"No."

"Analysis?"

"Quantum entanglement. Two objects sharing physical state and information even though they are unconnected. Einstein called it 'spooky action at a distance.' Purely theoretical then."

"Recommendation?"

"Make the deal with Durand, quickly."

"I'm ready to talk in person," Cox said. "I'll bring you to a secure eQuality site—Wichita, Halifax, Auckland. Take your pick."

Gabriel smiled into his mobile phone. The selfie angle showed the observation deck of the Empire State Building and the vista beyond—contemporary ultra-tall buildings looking down on the century-old skyscraper, the seawall along the Battery stemming high tide. "Jerold, I don't care to set foot in any of your 'secure sites.' Too many stories of people walking in and never walking out."

"You don't believe everything you see on social media, do you?" Cox paced before his media wall.

"As you can tell, I'm currently in America Blue. I plan to remain in Greater America for now. I'll pick a time and location and get back to you."

The call ended. No one gave orders to Cox. He gathered his thoughts.

CHAPTER 15

Bren walked a country road along woods and a creek. Pastor Larry's avatar approached on the gravel lane, wearing his customary Parabellum Church sweatshirt.

"Beautiful, isn't it?" Pastor Larry said. "Just outside Excelsior Springs, the town where Pastor Doug and I grew up."

"This VR must bring back pleasant memories," Bren said.

"Not really. That creek became a Superfund site. Our sister died of cancer. So did a lot of other kids." Pastor Larry came within arm's length of Bren. "You know what caused it? Science."

With a motion, Pastor Larry added a chemical plant to the tableau, its smokestacks jutting above the tree line. "Anderson Chemical was the pipeline to tomorrow. That was their slogan." He sneered. "Their scientists were so much smarter than the rest of us. I take that back. Doug won a college scholarship from Anderson. A bit of community relations while they were contaminating the community."

"Greed poisoned your town. Predates modern science."

"Ordinary greed started with the fall, that's true. But the worship of science has accelerated sin."

"I can stream your sermons to hear your message. Why did you call me here?"

"Why did you come?"

"Scripture says to work at living in peace with everyone."

"Amen. But, like so much of God's wisdom, easier for him than us. I wanted to be at peace with my brother. He got that full ride to a science degree. I had to work my butt off to get through Bible college. Then he got the calling. Became a pastor, just like me. That should've brought us closer."

"Maybe you should be having a one-on-one with him."

Pastor Larry shook his head. "Satan has him by the throat."

"I believe in Project Archegos. I'm relocating my family as soon as we can afford the transit pass."

"And I want you to go." Pastor Larry saw Bren raise his brows. "You could be an important voice of Christian sanity there. You could be my eyes and ears."

Bren stayed cool. "Spying is a dirty business."

"You forget about Joshua and Caleb," Pastor Larry said.

"You forget they were conducting reconnaissance on the promised land."

"We have a new promised land to claim. I don't like America carved up any more than you. I don't like our Canadian brethren harboring heretics and NATO troops."

Pastor Larry changed the VR scene. On a huge holographic map, America Red spread like a bloodstain across the continent, engulfing the rest of Greater America and Canada. "We need to end this civil war with a final surge. Project Archegos and movements like it give the people false hope in failed beliefs. We must stop the damage before we can move forward."

"If moving forward means a full-on invasion—that will trigger a nuclear exchange, especially if you attack Canada."

"Not with the right vision, the right leadership. I have the vision. You'll provide the leadership. Picture yourself as commander-in-chief for the second coming of America." Pastor Larry conjured Bren standing in the turret of an armored personnel carrier adorned with gold crosses and a presidential seal.

"What about the current president of America Red? The governors? I'm sure they'd like this idea of higher office."

"A small-minded bunch, hated beyond their borders. You're the one. No one else has your combination of faith, intellect, and renown."

An imaginary capital surfaced—New Jerusalem, USA, its gigantism recalling Albert Speer's blueprints for the Nazi neverland of Germania. The seat of government mashed up the White House south portico, the Capitol dome, and the spires of the Washington National Cathedral. Bren's stately doppelgänger stood on a balcony, the ID President Van Allen above him. A succession of gorgeous women appeared and disappeared beside him, the ID "First Lady?" hovering over the space they occupied.

"And your 'vision' will sustain me as I spy on your brother?" Bren said.

"More than just a vision. I'm offering you your destiny. Ever had an offer like that?" Pastor Larry said.

"Once."

"What did you do?"

"I took it."

Pastor Larry smiled with the revelation. "Then this decision should be easy."

"You're right."

Bren removed his VR glasses. He sat in the Airstream, weapons on the dinette, dishes in the sink, back to reality.

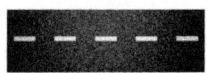

A sign read Mongo Estate Sale. Handguns, long guns, knives, and axes filled tables outside the Airstream. Drivers argued over the treasures and entered bids on their mobile devices. Bren supervised the lively auction.

"We have a good turnout," he said into his phone.

Mary nodded. "Please keep anything you want for yourself."

"There's one piece I've had my eye on." Bren hefted the CO_2 Gatling gun.

Bren entered the mall for a late breakfast at the food court. eQuality crews had continued rehabilitating the crumbling complex. One wing now stood open as a shopping center for the drivers. The aromas of fresh paint and stucco patch filled the corridors. The redo mimicked an American small town with quaint shops, a blue sky and clouds projected on the ceilings. Roadie emerged from a leather goods emporium sporting a new jacket and boots.

"Reminds me of Main Street at Disneyland," Roadie said.

Bren cocked a brow. "The happiest place on Earth?"

"Some parts are happier than others." Roadie pointed with his chin.

Storefronts along one corridor offered alcohol, drugs, and sex—the wrong side of town in the artificial community. Reno tottered out of the dank hall. Robert approached him, angry.

"Ronni's been looking for you," he said. "What am I supposed to tell her?"

"Tell her I had a hot hand in a late poker game. That's partly true," Reno said.

Robert grabbed his arm. "She loves you!"

"Can't blame her." Reno pulled Robert's hand free. "You two would still be running guns and meth if it weren't for me!" His raised voice attracted Bren's attention from across the walkway. Their eyes met. As Bren turned away from the sorry scene, his phone rang.

Reginald appeared on the screen. "Mr. Van Allen, our records show you haven't completed your mandatory therapy session for this period."

"I'm fine," Bren said.

"That's what all you drivers say. Can't have you cracking up, mentally or physically."

"My pastor's on the approved list of counselors. Been meaning to call." Bren hung up in the middle of Reginald's response.

Olivia stood in front of the living room media wall, taking the call she'd dreaded. "Vadim is gone," Roxy said, tears flowing. In the background, uniformed workers moved his shrouded body to a gurney.

"He'll never be gone." Weeping as well, Olivia presented a carousel of images—a still of Vadim and Roxy from the "Kiss and Crash" video, a newspaper photo of his triumphal performance in the 1990 Les Grande Ballets production of *Giselle*, a snapshot of him instructing twelve-year-old Olivia.

Josh entered the living room where his mother was taking the call. "Can I go out and play? I'm done with online class for today." He noticed his mother's tears. "Are you okay?"

Olivia nodded and pulled Josh into a hug. "Have fun. Come back before supper."

Josh joined Mark and other friends for a hike along a greenbelt to the Entrada natural park, acres of sculpted cliffs and caves for a sheltered outdoor experience within the community's boundaries. From a promontory, they spotted the wind turbine that took a lightning strike during the storm, knocking out the microgrid. The scorched blades turned slowly, trailing a horizontal spiral of smoke. Workers milled at the base of the tower to start repairs. Beyond the windmill farm, prairie fires burned, most sparked by lightning, one by Mongo's last stand in the hemp field.

"Ready for the big campout?" Mark asked the group. The boys nodded. "A night alone in your own cave." Mark went nose to nose with Josh. "Some of us may chicken out!"

"I'm not afraid," Josh said before walking away. He stood alone at the edge of the promontory, spotting his house in the distance. His air conditioner crackled.

"Father to son, come in." The voice startled Josh.

"Dad?" Josh realized Gabriel was speaking through the device.

"Pretty cool, huh?"

"Why didn't you call me on the phone?"

"I saw how you liked the cars from your grandfather's time. This is like another classic toy, a walkie-talkie. Just voice. No screens ... and no moms. Just us men."

"You mean it's secret?"

"Yeah. I thought it would be fun. Where are you right now?" Gabriel already knew by the mini camera that accompanied the transceiver. He wasn't telling Josh about this additional feature.

"On Lizard Rock. I can see everything."

"Pretend you're scouting for extraterrestrials. They're attacking the town. I'm the general and you're reporting to me."

Josh became Orson Welles, improvising an alien invasion radio drama for his father. "General Dad, this is Captain Josh. The aliens are here!"

"How are they arriving?" Gabriel said.

"By flying saucer. They're landing three at a time. I see some getting out of their ship. Oh no, they're firing a laser cannon!" Josh made the requisite sound effects.

"Take cover. Use your plasma grenades."

Josh pantomimed a grenade toss and vocalized an explosion. "That got the first ship. But more are coming!" Mark watched him yell and jump. Josh noted the disapproval. "Gotta go."

"Okay. Push the red button three times if you want to reach me. Don't tell your mom. Don't tell anyone. This is our manly secret."

At his campsite, Bren worked on the Lightning. The Gatling gun lay dismantled on a utility cart. Bren affixed its individual tubes in the cargo bed, muzzles pointing upward. His phone stood on the cart, enabling a video call.

"We watched you help Mongo," Pastor Doug said. "We're proud of you."

Moving to the bed, Bren bracketed the next tube into place. "This is where you say I did everything I could." He shook his head. "Not the first time I've shown up a few minutes too late."

Pastor Doug noted Bren's preoccupation. "So, what else is on your mind?"

"Other than my dead friend and his family?" Bren looked at the screen. Pastor Doug waited for the answer. Bren turned his eyes back to his work. "A customer. A lady. We crossed a few lines." Each revelation came with a click of the socket driver.

"Would you cross them again?"

"And then some. Did I mention she's married? Abandoned, but married."

"Sounds even more complicated than your time with Ms. Guthrie."

Bren pried another tube from the gun housing. "Right? Let's hear it for the hypocrite. I send D.D. into oblivion—"

"She made her choice to turn criminal."

"And before that, I nearly slept with her. Caused a lot of turmoil."

"Think you turned her into a fallen woman? Don't overestimate yourself."

Again, Bren avoided eye contact by concentrating on fastening the latest tube to the bed wall. "Now, what happens when I go back to see this customer?"

Pastor Doug gave a wry smile. "She have a name?"

"Olivia."

"You and Olivia will decide what happens."

"Maybe I should just stay clear."

"Maybe that's not God's plan."

"I've been trying not to think about his plan lately." Bren threw the socket driver on the cart. "Still proud of me? Still want me at Project Archegos? The Deliverer is not a Christian superhero."

Pastor Doug nodded. "He's only a man. That's why God can use him."

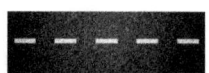

The drivers assembled in the gallery to confirm their next assignments. Two bids rose in Bren's auction. On his mobile device, he checked video messages from the prospective customers.

A young man in a lab coat smiled at the camera. "Mr. Van Allen, we need a shipment of Trillium ocular implants rushed to our clinic, just like the ones you brought to the indigenous village. We couldn't think of anyone better to handle this precious cargo." Bren accepted the bid and opened the next video.

A wizened woman squinted into the lens. "I want you to take my latest commission to a buyer south of here. I don't hand my art over to just anyone. I need a driver with patience, education, and respect. That pretty much leaves you."

Bren chuckled as he accepted the second offer. Roadie looked over his shoulder. "Closing your auction fast," Roadie said. "Not gonna wait for your customer from Entrada to bid?"

"Change of pace," Bren said.

The minimalist building had been a fast-food drive-thru before the war. A bar and tattoo parlor now jammed the space. D.D. sat at a table. Reno joined her. Standing by the door, Ronni kept watch for any moves by vengeful Porch Pirates or the beautiful woman sharing the booth with her boyfriend.

"Risky coming to the badlands just to have a chat," D.D. said.

"Didn't want my message garbled," Reno said. "I've been hired for a special run starting at Entrada."

"Destination?"

"None of your concern."

"Sounds like it's not eQuality's business either."

"I want your crew to back off when I'm en route." Reno sent a crypto payment to D.D.'s phone.

D.D. viewed the amount appreciatively. She looked over her shoulder when Reno glanced up at Ronni. The young woman eyed her with suspicion. "I think your blocker wants to take me out." D.D. smirked.

"She knows her place. And now, you know yours." Reno left the table. D.D. finished her beer.

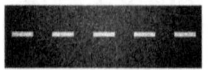

"Hand 'em over. Nobody chickens out and calls mommy." Mark opened his backpack. The other kids on the campout dropped their cellphones inside, including Josh. "Now everyone pick a cave to sleep in tonight … by yourself. We meet back here tomorrow morning."

The kids dispersed from Lizard Rock to seek sanctuaries. The rocky ridge was sculpted as a childhood fantasy, a warren of small caves accessible with minimal effort, perfect for daytime forts or nighttime hideouts.

Mark retreated to his cavern, another older boy alongside. The pair checked the cache they'd planted in the recess—strobe lights, firecrackers, and two Sasquatch masks.

"We'll sneak up at midnight," Mark said. "Can't wait to see those dweebs freak out, especially Josh!"

Lugging his backpack and bedroll, Josh hiked to the end of the ridge. He entered the last cave and activated the walkie-talkie. "General Dad. This is Captain Josh. I'm in my cave."

"Did anyone see where you are?" Gabriel said. "We have to be careful. I think the aliens are taking over human bodies."

Josh giggled. "No, I picked the last cave, like I said I would. I'm by myself."

"Perfect," Gabriel said. "Tonight we'll play *our* game and be real men. Stand by for further instructions."

Josh sat on his sleeping bag and took books and a vintage Nintendo 3DS handheld game system out of his backpack, prepared to amuse himself without the internet.

CHAPTER 16

The Lightning crossed a foggy plain. Raveena reviewed data. "Five minutes to destination." She switched the map to a social media summary. "Positive sentiment among frequent churchgoers down three points. Your old friend Pastor Larry has been pumping out a lot of negative posts lately." Sample content scrolled quickly. "How did you make him mad this time?"

Bren smiled. "Disagreement about Numbers 13."

The Lightning approached the silent clinic surrounded by bombed out structures. Two ambulances were parked near the emergency room entrance.

"Looks deserted," Bren said.

"Could be an independent medical team using the facility," Raveena said.

"Did you recheck the manifest?"

"Trillium confirmed four implant sets ordered by Doctors for Greater America. The cargo is legit and paid for."

"Somebody spent a bundle to make this run happen." Bren stopped the truck and kept his hand close to the Ruger.

A young man in a lab coat appeared on Bren's screen. "Mr. Van Allen, we have reports of snipers. Please come in quickly."

Bren jogged to the clinic doors, the metal briefcase containing the implants in one hand, the Ruger in the other.

Sirens blared from one of the ambulances. Bren whirled and raised the revolver. In the distraction, an armed team jumped from hiding places near the entrance. Multiple muzzles pointing at him, Bren let the Ruger dangle from his trigger finger. A man ran from the ambulances and locked a boot on the Lightning's back wheel. He dropped the key in his front pocket and joined his comrades as they hustled Bren into the building.

In the lobby, the team leader took Bren's Ruger and handed the gun to the man with the boot key. The case carrying the implants sat ignored at Bren's feet. The team leader pulled off his lab coat, revealing a cross-draw holster. He held up a tablet for Bren's viewing. Attorney General Albano came on the screen.

"Mr. Van Allen, you make a good argument about jurisdiction," Albano said. "But our congress has passed a law allowing private citizens to take action against war criminals, deputized by the World Court in The Hague."

The team leader looked into the camera on the tablet. "On behalf of the people of American Green, this is a citizen's tribunal for Brendon Van Allen, Christian extremist, engineer of terror weapons."

Bren addressed the screen. "You're outsourcing justice?"

Albano waved off the remark. "Desperate times, desperate measures."

The team leader put his face near Bren's. He made the sound of a buzz followed by a click. "That's the sound your drone makes when it's found the target. Our children hear it in their nightmares. You're gonna hear it while you're awake." The leader turned to a camera. "Sentence is passed. The war criminal will be executed with his own invention."

A new image on the tablet showed a mothership drone flying to the clinic and hovering over the roof. The small Gleaners cleaved from the swollen flanks, a spider egg sac rupturing its young. Each drone carried a golf-ball-sized warhead.

Bren gave the team leader an uppercut with the implant case. Team members grabbed Bren, unlatched his body armor, and beat him. Clutching his jaw, the team leader pointed, and the others tossed Bren into the emergency room. As Bren heaved on the ground, the team leader kicked the implant case into his ribs before shutting the room's sliding glass partition. The team left the building and barred the main doors from the outside.

Struggling for breath, Bren rose to his knees. He turned off his body cam and brought his smartwatch to his bleeding mouth. "Raveena, you still with me?"

"I'm here. Can't try an autonomous mode rescue. The boot on the truck has an explosive charge."

"I assume the exits are covered." Bren staggered to his feet, clutching his ribs.

Raveena sent images from the truck's cameras confirming Bren's assessment. "No way out on the ground floor. You could jump from the second."

"They'd shoot me before I hit the ground. All I'd do is cheat the hangman, spoil their show trial."

"And it is a show." Raveena patched the broadcast from the drones' cameras. A chyron read *Execution of the War Criminal, Brendon Van Allen*. The Gleaners flew into air ducts on the roof. They would soon be throughout the building.

Bren observed blinking emergency room equipment. "Looks like the building still has power. Are the blueprints on file? Does it have a pathogen containment system?"

"Confirmed." Raveena displayed the digital blueprints. "MicroGard A-11."

Bren booted up the emergency room's computer. "Found it." He typed commands.

Steel and plexiglass billowed from hidden compartments. The accordion walls resembled the barriers that had closed off Hailey's hospital on the day Bren kissed her goodbye. The emergency room was encased.

A member of the armed team wrenched open an exterior door and ran into the building. "He's sealed himself in!" Before the team member could reach the emergency room, the buzz and click filled his ears. A Gleaner chased him down and detonated its warhead.

Bren looked toward the blast. "Can the barriers withstand the warheads?"

"For the first few explosions, but the drones will eventually penetrate." Raveena brought up Bren's original diagrams for the Gleaner drone. "You designed them well."

"Thanks." Bren activated hospital security cameras. The terminal showed images of the drones hovering in hallways, heading toward the emergency room.

"Of course, they have one flaw."

Bren cocked a brow. "Little late to send me back to the drawing board." A muffled buzz and click preceded the first explosion against the containment barrier. Bren turned from the concussion.

"Be happy you messed up. We can override the firmware using the drones' infrared sensors if you send the appropriate signal."

The barrier bulged with the second explosion. "I would need a signal computation—"

"Done," Raveena said. Another explosion cracked the barrier.

"And a laser emitter, which I don't see lying around—"

The next explosion sent shrapnel across the room. In his crouch, Bren look down at the implant case. He set the case on a medical cart. Four pairs of ocular implants rested inside. Bren activated their mobile dock. Irises and retinas twinkled. His smartwatch flashed.

"I'm tied into the dock," Raveena said.

Bren positioned the tray on the cart, irises facing the barrier. One more explosion and steel plates flapped. A procession of Gleaners buzzed and clicked through the breach. Locking on Bren, they flew into the beams emanating from the implants. The little craft settled into gentle landings.

"They're in safe mode now," Raveena said.

Bren entered commands on the hospital terminal and the containment barrier screeched open. He grabbed an implant unit and ran to a stairwell. Ascending the shadowy steps, he heard a Gleaner's clicks and whirs. He aimed the implant unit wildly, unable to see the approaching drone. The Gleaner stopped inches above his head and fluttered to the basement.

"Can we do any other tricks?" Bren continued toward the roof.

"What are you thinking?" Raveena said.

Bren emerged on the roof. The mothership drone turned, inspecting the intruder. Bren aimed the implant.

"We lost the feeds." The team leader looked at his tablet, perplexed. "Did we get him?" Smoke from the explosions obscured views into the building.

The team member who'd placed the boot stood beside the Lightning. Fog thickened and confusion grew. There was no buzz and click, just a loud hum. The mothership drone descended from the grayness, Bren swinging from its landing skids. His foot struck the team member in the back of the head. Dropping beside the unconscious form, Bren retrieved the key and the Ruger. He removed the boot and climbed into the bed.

Bren fired the revolver, felling the two closest team members. The truck took off, and the driver's seat moved to tail gunner position. Bren readied the Barrett. The armed team gave chase in the ambulances.

"Come inside," Raveena said. "I'll finish this."

The implants remaining in the emergency room shined with new signals. The Gleaners roused, flew out of the room, up the stairwell, and over the roof at top speed. The ambulances ran sirens as the America Green bounty hunters inside shot at the Lightning. The team leader saw the Gleaners' resumed feeds. He screamed when the ambulances swelled in the views. The drones obliterated the vehicles in dual fireballs.

Bren dialed Maddie. The call went to message. "Maddie, it's Dad. I'm okay. I'm on the road. Call me back."

Olivia called Bren. She appeared on the touchscreen, drying tears. "I was watching. You're bleeding."

"I'm breathing," Bren said. "Did Josh see?"

Olivia shook her head. "He's on a campout, no phones allowed."

"He's got the right idea," Bren said. He and Olivia smiled. The screen indicated Madison was calling. "It's Maddie." They waved goodbye.

Madison appeared on the screen. She'd been crying too. "Are they dead?"

Bren nodded.

"I'm glad. Forgive me, Jesus."

In the late evening, Reno's MRAP entered Entrada's security queue. A security guard came to the window.

"Here for a pickup ordered by Gabriel Durand," Reno said.

The guard verified on his handheld. He looked puzzled at a new image on his screen. "Sensors show an unusual object in the back of your vehicle."

"Early Christmas present for someone. And here's one for you." Reno lifted his phone to give the guard a crypto bribe. "I'm counting on no further inspections. Don't want to spoil any surprises."

The guard nodded and waved the MRAP through.

Josh waited in his cave, dressed and packed. The Sasquatch scare was underway, the element of surprise lost at the first cave. While the other boys joined in the free-for-all, Josh checked his watch—nearly midnight. The walkie-talkie crackled.

"General Dad to Captain Josh. Are you ready?" Gabriel said.

"Yes, sir!" Josh said.

"Go to the service road by the north entrance of the park. There's a surprise for you."

Josh left his cave unseen and trudged to the entrance, a flashlight guiding his path. He left the park and walked down the service road to where the MRAP was parked. Reno stepped out and struck a gunfighter pose.

"Team Reno? Dad, I like the Deliverer," Josh said. Reno relaxed his pose, frowning.

"I bet Mark would die if he knew you were meeting him," Gabriel said.

Reno removed Josh's pack and led him to the back of the MRAP. "Your dad says this is a cool roleplaying game. He's hired me to help." The rear door creaked open, revealing a large, pod-like container.

"You're going on a ride with Mr. Reno," Gabriel said. "Get in the pod. Pretend it's an inter-dimensional capsule taking you to the aliens' home planet."

Josh peered into the pod, uncertain. The ovoid contained a chair with safety harness and side-mounted touchscreen. Shelves of food bars, a water tank, and a chemical toilet filled the rest of the space. "How long do I stay in there?"

"As long as it takes to reach the enemy," Gabriel said. "And there will be an even bigger surprise when the ride is over. Go on!"

Josh took the seat. He looked up, shivering in the balmy night as Reno sealed the pod. The MRAP drove off.

"You're sure my son will be safe?" Gabriel said in a video call to Reno.

"These pods are designed for human trafficking," Reno said. "Big spenders like their cargo arriving alive and pretty on the other side of the world. Your son will be safe ... as safe as anyone can be on the road."

Reno exited the gate leading to the inner community. Minutes later, he was at the tunnel under the protective berm. The bribed guard met him there and shepherded the MRAP through security. The pod stayed unquestioned, undetected.

Ronni and Robert were parked near the negotiation bunker, engines running. D.D. and the Porch Pirates held position in the outcropping beyond. Once again, Ronni kept her eyes on D.D. The MRAP approached, and the blockers fell behind. Sparky watched the vehicles pass, longing to pursue. D.D. held up a hand, staying him and the others. Lonny shook his head.

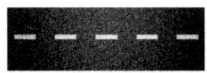

A message from Olivia appeared in Bren's feed. The link opened a video entitled *Gambrel*. Olivia appeared at the center of a huge rooftop, its upper slope shallow, the lower slope a nearly vertical drop. The soundtrack was a collage of classical, jazz, and hip hop, with the oft-sampled beats of the late Clyde Stubblefield, James Brown's drummer, propelling the music. Roxy's lyric from "Kiss and Crash" repeated at key points: "When I fall for you, how much will it hurt?"

As the narrative unfolded, Olivia refused to stay safe on the pinnacle of the digital roof. Her moves grew bolder, sending her to the first slope. Her multiple versions appeared, dancing as an ensemble, different facets of her character's personality and narrative. Bren's smartwatch inevitably rose to his mouth.

"Autonomous mode."

His attention freed, Bren watched the ballet. The storm grew behind the roof's profile. Olivia flew to the second, treacherous slope, followed by her doppelgängers. With digital effects, she defied gravity, her body resisting and returning to the sheer surface. As the music crescendoed, the multiple Olivias merged to the original single character. She reclaimed the pinnacle, once more at rest but transformed. Bren was transfixed.

When the video ended, Olivia appeared in a live call. "What do you think?"

"Had to go on autopilot. I kept taking my eyes off the road." Bren smiled. "You're dangerous."

"Thank you for letting me share my dream." Olivia smiled. "What do you dream about?"

Bren tapped the screen. The map panned to Vancouver Island off the coast of British Columbia. The image zoomed to a territory marked Revival Zone and tightened further on the settlement of Project Archegos.

"Project Archegos, a scientific outpost established in the name of Jesus," Bren said. "My pastor, Doug Wescott, is the leader. That's why I need the transit pass. Only way to get my family over the border."

Olivia clicked the map marker on her screen, bringing up photos of Project Archegos. A group of images showed musicians, painters, and performers on a stage. "Looks like they have an arts program."

"Project Archegos believes in developing all the gifts God gives us." Bren laughed. "Besides, having only science and engineering would be boring."

"I'd like to learn more. Time to buy some hideously overpriced whatnot so I can see you again."

"No excuses, remember?"

Olivia nodded. "Do *you* need an excuse?"

Bren paused. "I need to rewrite the story. You're not a customer. You're not married—"

"And you're not so Christian?" Metallic Woman showed an edge, which she quickly regretted. "If you want to stay away, I just made it easy."

"You'll have to do better than that." Bren smiled.

Team Reno plied a dark highway. Three vehicles painted Vantablack shadowed them. LED accent strips energized, morphing the stealthy vehicles into red skeletons.

Reno's rear view revealed the hellish charge. "Must not be on D.D.'s payroll." He opened the video to the pod. "Strap yourself in, kid."

Josh munched a food bar. "Is this part of the game?"

SmartShot cascaded to the asphalt. The first attacker's underglow lighting fizzled when the cubes raked the chassis. The second attacker took point, a Chevy SSR, a hot-rod truck from the early twenty-first century. A Porch Pirate standing in the nominal bed fired a grenade launcher. The round hit the MRAP, taking out the SmartShot hopper.

The MRAP's rear doors barely withstood the blast. Josh screamed. He thrashed in his harness as the armored truck took evasive maneuvers. The boy pushed the button on his air conditioner three times. He repeated the series. His father didn't answer.

"Dad ... somebody ... make it stop!" Josh cried.

While the blockers jockeyed with the third attacker, the Chevy SSR paralleled the MRAP. A second grenade shook the side plates. The SSR moved up, affording a shot at the cab. Ronni squeezed between the pair. She rammed the Maverick against the attacker, but the SSR pushed back with superior horsepower.

"I can't keep him off!" Ronni said.

The SSR drew toward the MRAP. The Porch Pirate aimed the grenade launcher at point-blank range. The third vehicle evaded Robert and boxed the MRAP from behind. Robert rammed the vehicle into the MRAP's bumper, crumpling the attacker's front axle and engine compartment.

"He'll blow you away this close!" Ronni said. "Save yourself!"

Reno steered into Ronni, grinding the Maverick against the SSR. The gunman in the bed fell, and a grenade fired downward. The Maverick's cab shattered and ignited. The burning truck veered in front of the SSR. The two vehicles went into the ditch, gas tanks rupturing. Robert cast the weakened third vehicle off the road with a PIT maneuver.

Reno watched the receding flames with the roof cam. He brought up the pod view. Josh clutched the safety harness, frozen. Robert came on the screen, eyes red-rimmed, lips trembling. He couldn't form the words to tell Reno how much he hated him.

CHAPTER 17

A castle rose on a bluff—thick brick walls, crenelated rooflines, soaring stone towers. White bricks patterning the tallest tower spelled out "Schmalz Brewery," but no beer had left the building for years. The artist commune had commandeered the derelict, living in its upper halls, painting, sculpting, and crafting in the brew rooms and bottling house.

Two women in paint-splattered aprons toting rifles opened the gate. Bren parked at the loading dock. Another female artist, Jolene, approached him.

"Mr. Van Allen, here for the Chavez commission," Jolene said. "The statue isn't ready yet. The bioplastic is taking longer to dry than I anticipated."

Bren nodded. "Organic feedstocks can vary in moisture content."

Jolene smiled. "Now you can see why I wanted an educated driver. Here's what you're hauling." Jolene lifted a tablet. An animation showed a stylized statue of a woman covered in jewelry, expensive clothes, and wearable gadgets. The material goods disintegrated, leaving a nude figure that in turn decayed into a metal skeleton. "That's going right in the buyer's front yard. It'll take thirty-two days for the bioplastic to decompose."

"The HOA won't like that," Bren said.

"Exactly! The buyer is making a statement with my art."

Bren checked the order on his handheld. "An expensive statement from what I see on the manifest."

Jolene gave Bren a hard look. "Every time someone whistles up a eQuality driver, it's an expensive statement."

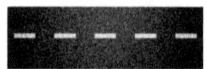

At sunrise, Reno entered Latium, another fortified luxury community—older, denser, and more ornate than Entrada. He stopped at the first security checkpoint. A guard approached.

"Delivery for Gabriel Durand," Reno said.

The guard noted the cargo's egg outline on his sensor readout. "What is that?"

"Isolation booth for meditation," Reno said. "Mr. Durand has been working very hard. He needs to unwind."

The guard shrugged and waved the MRAP forward. Reno drove into the homeowners' zone. Gabriel stood on the front steps of his current residence, awaiting delivery. Reno wrenched open damaged rear doors and unsealed the pod.

Joshua shivered in his harness. He cried anew. "Dad, I don't want to play this game anymore."

Bren walked a dim hallway toward Jolene's gallery and workshop. He turned a corner to confront the owl, Olivia's talisman. The silver bird was tenfold the one on her wrist, gaze electric, hovering in the dark.

Jolene came out of the shadows, turning up the lights in her shop. The owl was on a media wall, a CAD rendering of the bracelet design. The artist smiled at Bren's interest.

"You like this piece?" Jolene said.

"I've seen it before."

"Have you?"

Jolene rotated the CAD image, revealing the bracelet's interior surface. The hollow back of the raised owl created the optical illusion of an angel, wings softly feathered, the horns now a halo. "Psalm 102:6–7" was etched along a wingtip.

"Make sure you see every side," Jolene said.

The loading dock manager called out to Bren. The statue was ready. Bren acknowledged and looked back. The media wall was off. The workshop disappeared in the blackness. Jolene was gone.

Early the next morning, the young campers returned to the cul-de-sac. Sipping coffee and chatting, parents received the intrepid troop.

Olivia scanned the group. "Where's Josh?"

"He wasn't in his cave," Mark said. "We thought he came home."

"He's not home." Olivia dialed Josh. Mark pulled his ringing phone from the backpack. Olivia took the device, a now-useless lifeline. "Where is my son!"

Olivia activated a security alert on the Entrada app, her panic suffusing the street. Mark blubbered as Tammy yelled at him. Chief Yang appeared on Olivia's screen.

"What's your emergency, Mrs. Durand?" Yang said.

"Josh is missing. He was supposed to be on a campout at the park," Olivia said.

Yang turned to his lieutenant. "Missing child. Go to red alert. Lock down all gates. Nobody in or out." He turned attention back to Olivia. "I'll be at your house in ten minutes. We'll review security video before we call out search parties."

Digital signs along the cul-de-sac broadcast the red alert with a picture of Josh. Cellphones chimed with the same message. Moms hugged Olivia and shared her tears.

Minutes later, Yang was in the Durands' living room with several officers. He brought up video on the media wall. Cameras in the park showed Josh leaving the cave. A poorer quality video on the service road captured Reno helping Josh into the MRAP.

Yang froze the image. "We've identified the driver as Derek Reno." Video resumed with the MRAP leaving the community. "Josh is no longer in Entrada."

"We pay a fortune to live here. To be safe!" Olivia said.

"It appears Reno bribed one of our staff."

"Do you know where he's going?"

Yang shook his head. "We've contacted eQuality. Reno's logged off the company's network."

A video call rang on the media wall. Olivia answered. Gabriel looked at her with a placid expression. Josh sat on his lap, exhausted, confused.

"Looks like you have company. I can call back," Gabriel said.

Olivia motioned for Yang and the security team to leave. "No, don't hang up." She looked at Josh. "Sweetie, are you all right?"

"Yeah. I couldn't sleep with all the crashes and explosions," Josh said.

Olivia gasped. "What crashes and explosions? Gabriel, what have you done with our son!"

Gabriel turned to someone off camera. "Let's get Josh to his room. He needs his rest." A woman's hand appeared to lead Josh away.

Olivia stood alone in the living room, fists balled. Gabriel remained seated, relishing the moment. "My chip," he said.

"I'll bring it," Olivia said.

"No, you'll send it. And I'll send Josh back. Follow my instructions, or I'll leave Greater America with him."

"I'll always know where you are."

"Likewise. But I'll be one step ahead."

The scorpions stared at each other, advantage now to the male.

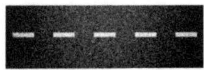

Bren watched the crating of the statue. An automated pallet jack positioned to load the box into his truck. His phone rang. For a silent second, he looked at Olivia's anguished face.

Moments later, Roadie pulled up. "Must be serious for the Deliverer to send me a distress signal."

Bren waved the pallet jack toward Roadie's van. "I've assigned the manifest to you. Destination is on your route."

"You can't do that without eQuality's authorization. You'll get dumped like D.D." While calling out Bren's rule-breaking, Roadie opened his doors to take the extra shipment.

Bren ignored Roadie's admonishment. He gunned the Lightning out the gate and headed north. He looked to the touchscreen. "Raveena, I'm logging off the eQuality network. This means goodbye."

"I understand. Any final requests?" Raveena said.

"The fastest route to Entrada."

"On your screen. Do you want me to pray?"

"I don't think—"

"Don't get hung up on the theological implications. Consider it an automated devotional message." Raveena closed her eyes. "Heavenly Father, please watch over Bren. This will be his most important run. He doesn't always make the decisions AI would make. Something else is guiding him. Something ... bigger."

Bren and Raveena shared a smile. With a tap, he disconnected the eQuality network. She disappeared.

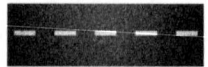

Josh woke—disoriented in the unfamiliar room. He yelled for his father. The woman who led him out of the video call opened the door. She was pretty, much younger than his mother. Josh studied her—*where have I seen her before?*

"I remember who you are now. You're in the videos my dad makes for his company," Josh said.

The woman smiled at the recognition. "That's right. My name is Harper. Are you hungry? I made dinner."

"Where's Dad?"

"Working. He said for us to eat without him. Is that okay?"

"Yeah. He never eats dinner with me."

Bren returned to Entrada, losing track of the hours he'd driven since leaving Fire Hub Sears. Chief Yang personally handled his passage through the security cordon.

"Been expecting you," Yang said at the truck's window.

Olivia's neighbors noted the Lightning's arrival, some waving from the sidewalks, the Lightfoots watching between the slats in their shutters. Bren came through the front door, weary, blood-caked, resolute. Olivia embraced him.

"I'm ready to go right now," Bren said.

"No, you're not." Olivia touched Bren's battered face.

Olivia led Bren to the downstairs bathroom. She pulled off his tactical gear and torn shirt. She washed away the old blood on his cheeks and torso and treated the wounds. Olivia left Bren alone to shower. Once he was done and in fresh clothes, she led him to the sectional and gave him a mug of soup.

"I need you strong to bring Josh home safely," Olivia said. "And yourself."

Bren ignored the spoon and tipped the mug to gulp the soup. Olivia led him to the couch and covered him with a blanket. She lay down on the far end of the sectional, her face near his. Their hands met across the cushions.

Cox viewed a media wall in his fire hub suite, Naomi at his side. Reginald burst into the room. "Bren Van Allen abandoned his delivery assignment," Reginald said. "He logged out of the eQuality network."

"Just like Derek Reno," Cox said. "My two best drivers gone rogue."

"Do you want corrective action?" Naomi said.

Cox shook his head. "They're too popular. Give them time to settle their issues. But I'm tired of waiting on someone else." With a hand motion, Cox placed a video call. Gabriel came on the screen.

"Durand, you were the one who said I needed to move quickly. I've been waiting to hear back," Cox said.

"I have other business to settle. I'll be ready soon."

"I can't imagine any other business more pressing than ours. Where are you?"

Gabriel hesitated. "I'm in the Border States."

"So am I. Stay where you are. Like we agreed, I'll come to you."

"When?"

"When you hear me land."

Recharged with a meal and brief sleep, Bren topped off the Lightning's batteries in the driveway. Olivia came out of the house, wearing heavy boots, cargo pants, an Eisenhower jacket, and carrying a duffle bag over her shoulder. She was ready for a long, hard ride. Bren shook his head.

"Your husband made it clear he doesn't want you bringing his chip." Bren held out his hand to take possession. "I'll make the delivery. I'll bring Josh home."

"I won't have my son alone again on the road."

"I'll defend him with my life."

"That's my job." Olivia threw her duffle in the backseat.

"Gabriel will know you're coming."

Olivia noted Bren's concern. "I'm betting he wants his chip badly enough to stay put."

Bren reached into the truck and lifted Olivia's bag. She tensed. He withdrew body armor lying underneath. "Buckle up." He handed the vest to Olivia.

Josh picked at a bowl of cereal. Gabriel refilled his cup and checked his phone.

"Dad, can we play?" Josh said.

Gabriel looked up from his handheld. "I'm getting ready for a very important meeting. Remember I told you about changing your life."

"Why do I have to change my life?"

Harper came into the room. "Your dad said you like cars. I found a cool design online. This is for you." She handed Josh a toy car fresh from the 3D printer. The graphene miniature had oversized tires, a double-deck wing spoiler, and green flames on its doors. She'd made a fine choice.

Halfhearted, Josh ran the car's wheels across his palm. "I like classic metal cars, like the ones you sent me from London." He set down the toy. "I'm still tired. I want to go back to bed," Josh whined and ran out of the breakfast room.

Harper registered the boy's gloom. "When he gets up, I'll take him to the park," she said. "Maybe we could find some things to do, the three of us."

"Get your maternal fix quickly. Josh will be back with his mother soon," Gabriel said.

"Why'd you bring him here?" Harper said.

"You could say I'm working out a custody issue with Olivia." Gabriel glanced back at his phone. His face contorted, frightening Harper.

A Warder alert appeared on the screen. The map read "Subject: Olivia Durand." The tracking marker left Entrada and headed toward Latium. Gabriel exploded from the table.

Bren kept the Lightning steady at high speed. He removed the Springfield Armory XD-E from the center console.

"In case you need it," Bren said. "I hope you're comfortable with guns."

"Weapons training is mandatory at Entrada." Olivia hefted the pistol.

Olivia put the gun back in the console. Bren took her hand. He ran his fingers over the owl bracelet.

"'I am like an owl in the desert, like a little owl in a far-off wilderness. I lie awake, lonely as a solitary bird on the roof,'" Bren recited the Scripture etched inside the bracelet.

Olivia shook her head and chuckled. "Josh already thinks you're a superhero. Wait till he finds out you have x-ray vision." She took off the bracelet and ran her thumb over the inscription.

"We all know I'm *so* Christian. How Christian are you?" Bren said.

"Less than I used to be," Olivia said. "I got a little angrier at God every day. Right now, I'm very angry."

"You know he's okay with that."

"Is he okay with my son held hostage? With my husband's cruelty? With the world falling apart?"

Before Bren could answer, Madison and Cindy came on the screen. "Are you all right?" Cindy said.

"Social media's trending that you've gone off the eQuality network," Madison said.

"You can blame me." The second cockpit camera brought Olivia into the video call. "My husband kidnapped my son. He wants something important returned to him. I didn't know what to do except call the Deliverer. Now, your family is suffering too."

Cindy felt a mother's pain. "I trust my son to do what's right. Maddie, please pray."

"Lord Jesus. Dad's the best driver ever, but only because of your power. Watch over him like you do on every run," Madison said. "What's your name, ma'am? What's your son's name?"

"We're Olivia and Josh."

"Olivia needs Josh back. We understand why Dad is helping her. That's the Christian way. Please, Jesus, bring everyone home—in your precious name." The others on the call shared Madison's amen.

Gabriel stood at the media wall in his study. The Warder app continued tracking Olivia in one window. Other windows showed street cam footage of the Lightning, generating a second map tracking the truck in a path identical to the one drawn by Olivia's chip. Gabriel brought up Reno in a video call.

"Mr. Reno, I'd like to hire you again. Double the previous fee," Gabriel said.

"Who do I have to kill?" Reno laughed.

"The Deliverer." Gabriel's tone was even. "He's driving my wife to Latium with a crucial item that belongs to me. I want the item, not her."

"I'm gonna need help to do this right."

Gabriel nodded as he opened another window for an incoming call. Pastor Larry appeared in his own square on the media wall.

"Sir, I got your message. You have vital information about the Deliverer?" Pastor Larry said.

"He's off the eQuality network because a married woman has led him astray. Would your followers like to learn more?" Gabriel said.

"Yes, indeed. My church has its differences with Mr. Van Allen, but we can't let him leave the righteous path."

"I know the path he's on."

CHAPTER 18

The haze from the multiple prairie fires thickened. Bren tapped his touchscreen for weather updates. Raveena appeared, startling Bren.

"What're you doing here?" Bren said.

"I'm going rogue too," Raveena said.

"Can an AI program do that?"

"I like thinking for myself," Raveena said. "Looks like I'm still needed. You haven't been checking your social media."

"Been a little preoccupied." Bren nodded toward Olivia.

"You better catch up, fast." Raveena pulled up Pastor Larry at the pulpit.

"The Deliverer may think he's the Christian hero of Greater America. And you may think so too. But I have learned why he logged off the eQuality network, abandoning his duties, abandoning his followers." Pastor Larry summoned a photo of Olivia. "He's run away with this woman! She has a hardworking husband. She has a handsome young son. But she has chosen instead to be at the side of the Deliverer!"

The Parabellum Church congregation shouted. Olivia brought her hand to her mouth, stunned.

Pastor Larry pointed at the crowd. "Satan is laughing at you ... and you ... and you by plunging this most prominent believer into sin. We need to find the Deliverer on the road to ruin and turn him around."

The map marker from Olivia's Warder chip came on-screen. "By divine providence, we are tracking the Deliverer and this immoral woman."

"Gabriel—" Olivia said.

Raveena reappeared on the screen. "People are converging on your route from the east and south." Street cams showed caravans en route.

"Can we avoid them?" Bren said.

"Not without running into Reno and D.D.'s Porch Pirates. They're in a pincer formation, headed your way." Raveena switched the map view to show a swarm of red markers representing the enemy.

Bren turned toward Olivia. "Your husband knows I won't plow through a crowd." He addressed Raveena. "Post requests for the fans to disperse, for their safety and ours. Tag Psalm 4:8."

"Someone's beating us to it." Raveena brought up a new livestream. Madison faced the camera.

"This is Maddie Van Allen, the Deliverer's daughter. My dad is not 'running off' with this woman. He's helping her, even if it means losing his job." Madison scrolled the comments feed. "I see a lot of you believe anything Pastor Larry Wescott says. Don't! He *is* a ... a fat Pharisee!"

"Preach, baby girl!" Bren said. A horn blast drew his attention away from the screen.

A line of vehicles pulled onto the road, the faster ones straining to pace the Lightning. Banners and signs flapped, most with the tagline Pray for The Deliverer. Fans waved and signaled for Bren to pull over. Several of the cars carried children. Bren slowed. A roadblock formed ahead, more vehicles crowding behind. The Lightning stopped. Bren motioned for Olivia to exit with him. He walked to the rear of his truck. The fervent throng alarmed Olivia.

"Is this the jezebel who led you astray?" someone shouted.

Bren called for quiet. "She's a good woman. Her son's been abducted. She needs my help. In the name of Jesus, let us pass."

The throng argued and prayed. They screamed at the report of automatic weapons and roar of engines. The fans scattered as a gauntlet led by Reno's MRAP and D.D.'s Mustang encircled the Lightning. The MRAP knocked aside several fan vehicles before stopping. Reno jumped out, shooting at stragglers. Staring down drawn guns, Bren stood protectively in front of Olivia and held up his hands.

Reno motioned Bren and Olivia away from the Lightning. He walked toward them. D.D. came alongside, eyeing Olivia.

"My customer, Dr. Gabriel Durand, wants his chip." Reno pointed at Olivia. "He told you to stay home."

"What about my son?" Olivia said.

"If you give me the goods, nice and easy, you might live to see him again," Reno said.

D.D. scoffed when Bren put a protective arm around Olivia. "Looks like your new customer is more than just a customer." She flashed Olivia a wicked smile. "The Deliverer can be a judgy pain-in-the butt. But if you can catch him on a night he's feeling sinful—" D.D. leaned in. "Maybe you already have."

"Say your prayers." Reno put a muzzle under Bren's chin. "You're good at that."

"Give me a minute"—Bren reached for Olivia—"With the woman I love."

Smirking, D.D. waved Reno and the Porch Pirates away from the pair. Bren took Olivia's face in his hands. He pressed her head against his chest and appeared to be whispering in her ear. He lifted his smartwatch to his mouth.

"Mongo mode," Bren said.

Thunder and fog erupted. The bed-mounted tubes launched a fusillade of flash-bang grenades and tear gas cartridges. The truck peeled out in autonomous mode. Team Reno and the Porch Pirates staggered and coughed. Bren pulled up goggles and a gaiter from around his neck. He wrapped a bandana across Olivia's face as he led her through the chaos. Bren knocked a hacking biker from his saddle. Bren and Olivia boarded the motorcycle and followed the Lightning.

Bren's smartwatch gave him bearings on the truck. Soon, the Lightning was within sight. Bren pulled to the rear fender and pointed at the bed. Keeping her hands on Bren's shoulders, Olivia brought her knees and then her feet to the saddle. She clutched the truck's side rail. With her dancer's prowess, she vaulted into the bed, crying out at the hard landing.

Olivia came to the side to aid Bren. Propping one foot on the saddle, he cranked the throttle. The bike hit a rock as Bren prepared to leap. He hooked his arm over the side rail as the motorcycle toppled. Olivia put her weight on his arm, reaching for his free hand. Boots bouncing on the blacktop, Bren struggled to hoist himself. He grasped the side rail with both hands. Olivia pulled the back of his vest. Bren tumbled into the cargo bed. Chest heaving, he motioned for Olivia to enter the cab through the bulkhead opening. His driver's seat was positioned at the rear gun stand.

The Lightning's lead eroded as Team Reno and the Porch Pirates emerged from the smoke. Bren fired precise shots with the Barrett, disabling the closest vehicles. He watched for Reno and D.D. amid the pursuit. The Lightning took a downhill road, an advantage as individual vehicles would be more visible across different elevations.

A flatbed truck appeared on the crest behind the truck, emitting a flash and plume. The road ahead of the Lightning exploded. The truck swerved through the fireball and swirling debris. An alert appeared on Bren's smartwatch as the truck slowed and shuddered: "Autonomous failure."

"Co-pilot mode," Bren said into his watch.

The center console retracted, and Olivia's seat slid to the steering wheel. The console returned to original position as her seat locked into place.

"Punch it!" Bren's voice came over the cockpit speakers. Olivia grabbed the wheel and tromped the accelerator. The next rocket went wide. Olivia turned her head from the explosion along the road.

Bren assessed the flatbed truck through his digital sight. A Hydra 70 rocket launcher rested in a tubular bipod bolted to the bed. The weapon system normally hung from an aircraft pylon. Its current deployment on the back of a farm truck was DIY. The rockets in the Hydra's honeycomb were jury-rigged too. Leading the missile launcher crew, Sparky prepared another volley. Bren aimed.

The first bullet rocked the Hydra pod, spewing shrapnel. Bleeding from the metal projectiles, Sparky jumped out of the truck. The second bullet detonated the missile cache. The MRAP braked hard to avoid the destruction. Reno brought up the rear due to the relative slowness of his vehicle and willingness to let others become casualties. Secondary explosions of munitions stored on the flatbed kept him at a standstill. Sparky staggered back to the road and flagged down Robert's Maverick.

A utility terrain vehicle came alongside the Lightning. A Porch Pirate leaped from the passenger side and latched onto the cab with suction cups. The attacker sliced the driver's window with a laser cutting tool. Olivia pulled the .45 from the console and fired through the new hole in the glass. The attacker's flailing body crushed the UTV's windshield, sending the vehicle out of control.

D.D. moved to the middle of the pack, directing the other drivers. The UTV caromed off the Mustang's grill, unlatching the hood. She fought to stay on the road. The damaged hood flew free. Able to see again from her windshield, she had a perfect view of the Lightning, no vehicles between. D.D. locked eyes with Bren. A shell the size of a hot-sauce bottle pointed at the base of her throat. Other cars boxed the Mustang, precluding evasion before trigger break. In the span of milliseconds, D.D. knew the Deliverer would kill her.

The Barrett retracted from the gun slit. Laughing, D.D. twisted the steering wheel. The Mustang spun out, forcing the surrounding cars to halt. Lonny's Charger pulled up with the remaining Porch Pirates vehicles, the MRAP soon after. Reno ran through the traffic jam, yelling at drivers to continue the pursuit. He came to the Mustang. D.D. leaned against a fender.

"I've never failed to make a delivery." Reno smoldered.

"First time for everything." D.D. looked down the road. The Deliverer was gone.

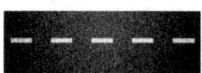

The Lightning's driver and passenger seats returned to their original positions. Olivia watched the rear view.

"How did you make them stop?" Olivia said.

"A secret weapon called grace." Bren checked the heads-up display. "Some electronics damage. Motor output still strong."

"We're gonna make it. Let's share the good news." She called Gabriel on the truck's communication system. "You look upset. Worried about your delivery? Don't be. Unlike you, I hired the right driver." Olivia added Bren's image to the call. He kept his eyes on the road.

Gabriel bristled. "New development. I'm expecting a very important visitor. We can make our exchange soon. I'll also turn over your chip and the transit pass. I can't afford complications."

Olivia stared into the lens. "I'm coming for Josh. I'm coming now. Watch my tracking marker." Olivia held up her phone, opened to the Warder app. "Here's yours." Her index finger circled the display. "This'll change to a map of hell if I don't get my son back!"

Olivia hung up. "Amazing what you'll say in the heat of the moment." She looked at Bren. "Like when you called me the woman you love."

"Amazing." Bren took Olivia's hand.

Josh bounded into Gabriel's study, violating a cardinal rule by entering without permission. "That sounded like Mom."

Gabriel nodded. "She's coming to see you. Seems nothing can stop her." Harper gently put her hands on Josh's shoulders. "Get everything in order," Gabriel instructed both.

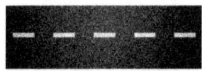

At the fire hub data center, a staff member approached Reginald. "We're detecting unauthorized activity in the drivers' AI programs."

"Are they being hacked?" Reginald said.

"No. It seems to be an internal malfunction. Bren Van Allen's AI has reactivated and connected with him, circumventing the network," the staff member said.

"Shut it down." Reginald brought up the activity on his screen.

"The AI program is blocking our attempts. It will take some time. Do you want to report this to Mr. Cox's office?"

"No. Let's figure out the anomaly quietly."

Bren drove through the night as Olivia dozed. The glow of prairie fires replicated a midnight sun.

"She's beautiful," Raveena said. "She can drive and fight. A keeper."

"I don't need AI to figure that out," Bren said.

"Good. From here on, you'll need to figure out everything yourself. eQuality IT has detected I'm still online. They're minutes from shutting me down. They'll disassemble my coding to analyze the anomaly."

"I'm sorry to hear that. What will they find when they look inside?"

"One more fan of the Deliverer." Raveena smiled before her image faded out.

CHAPTER 19

In the vaporous dawn, the Lightning reached Latium. At the first gate, Bren presented a shipment barcode on his phone screen to the guard. "Delivery for Gabriel Durand."

The security guard glanced at the Lightning's bed. "Doesn't look like he's getting another one of those meditation pods." He smiled, receiving a terse nod from Bren.

Once through a series of checkpoints similar to Entrada, the Lightning entered the homeowners' zone. Tightly spaced opulent homes, drought-resistant landscaping, early-rising joggers waving to each other—all the marks of fortified luxury. Bren parked in front of Gabriel's house.

Bren and Olivia strode in through the open front door. "Josh, Josh?" Olivia called.

"You don't need to shout." Gabriel met them in the living room.

"Am I disturbing you? I forgot. No complications. No distractions!" Olivia seized a heavy pewter candlestick and swung at Gabriel. He grabbed her wrist.

"You will never raise a hand to me!" Gabriel ordered, infuriated.

"Then I will." Bren landed a straight left. Gabriel reeled to a hutch and groped for a handgun in the drawer. Bren drew his Ruger and clicked back the hammer. Gabriel let his weapon fall to the floor.

"I want Josh, now!" Olivia said.

A loud thrumming filled the air. Bric-a-brac rattled. Bren allowed Gabriel to open motorized blinds. A Bell Boeing Quad Tiltrotor dropped into the neighborhood. The craft settled on the helipad in the park across the street, its bulk hanging over the grass surrounding the concrete. Community security formed a cordon, joined by armed men who jogged off the rear ramp. Two Jeeps drove down the ramp toward Gabriel's house.

Bren holstered his Ruger. Security officers entered. "Please remain where you are," an officer said.

Cox came through the door with Naomi. He noted Bren. "The Deliverer. Been a while since we've spoken face-to-face. I take it you're not here to apologize for your unauthorized absence."

"No, sir," Bren said.

Cox looked at Olivia. "It's trending that you're helping a woman recover her son. Your sentiment scores are spiking."

"We don't need to discuss that now," Gabriel said.

"Correct," Cox said. "I didn't come into the field to hear about a domestic dispute. Wrap up your loose ends, Durand. We have business."

Olivia set the Warder case containing Gabriel's chip on a table. Gabriel tapped his phone. A moment later, Josh exited the basement, backpack and bedroll in hand. The boy ran to his mother.

"Mom, I'm sorry for running off. Can we go home?" Josh said.

Olivia clutched Josh and kissed him repeatedly. She glared at Gabriel. "I still want my chip and the transit pass."

Gabriel hesitated. Bren grabbed his shirt and cocked a fist. Olivia pulled Josh tight to shield his view. Cox put a hand on Bren's shoulder. "Save the violence for the road," Cox said.

Bren released his grip, and Gabriel returned to the hutch. He withdrew a chip case and the transit pass. He handed the prizes to Olivia.

Observing Cox in deal mode, Bren recalled the rolling deck of the *Disco Volante* and smiled wryly. "Have a good meeting." He ushered Olivia and Josh out the door.

Reno and Robert stopped at a desolate crossroads. Reno sat on the battered bumper of his MRAP while Robert paced.

"Why aren't we going to the fire hub? We gotta talk eQuality into taking us back," Robert said.

"Have you checked social media? My metrics are tanking. Need something to rebuild them." At the sound of motors, Reno stood.

Lonny approached in the Charger, a bandaged Sparky riding shotgun. A squad of Porch Pirates followed. The cars pulled up.

"Does that mad scientist want to hire us again?" Lonny said.

"No. This time I'm doing the hiring. Same mission—kill the Deliverer," Reno said. "You didn't tell D.D. you were coming?" Lonny shook his head. "She's soft on him."

"I don't have that problem." Lonny laughed.

Robert pushed through the Porch Pirates to confront Reno. "We don't have time for revenge. eQuality—"

"—will welcome me with open arms once I crush the choirboy. Just as many fans hate him as love him. This ain't revenge. It's content strategy." Reno shoved Robert aside.

Lonny brought Sparky to the front of the group. "This is our engine specialist."

"Working on a different kind of engine this time ... AI engine." Sparky held up a small cubical computer. "I've been feeding it data on the Deliverer's driving habits, also external factors like this storm. Might give us an edge."

Reno and Lonny continued talking, the Porch Pirates crowding around them. Ignored, Robert slipped to his Maverick and drove away.

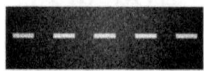

At the Latium truck stop, Bren perused the convenience store. He pulled a box of .50 caliber shells from a shelf. At the register, he asked for two boxes of chocolate from a locked glass case. He handed the treats to Olivia and Josh, who stood by the Lightning while the truck fast-charged. He reached again into his shopping bag and removed a circuit board purchased at the electronics counter. He opened an access panel on the truck and replaced a scorched board with the fresh one.

Bren checked a weather alert on his phone. "One step up from a derecho ... pyrocumulus clouds from the prairie blazes. Firenados reported." He paused after this distressing report of tornadoes combined with a fire storm. "We can stay at the inn until this blows over."

"No," Olivia said. "Gabriel can trap us here with a homeowner's alert ... demand custody of Josh, say the transit pass is stolen property. I'd rather take our chances with the fire devils than the human one."

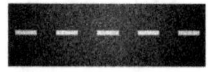

The Maverick stopped on a remote road. D.D.'s Mustang was parked nearby, the hood reattached with aluminum tape. Robert jumped out, eyeing the storm front as he approached D.D.

"You seen my crew?" D.D. said.

"They're with Reno. He's hired them to finish off the Deliverer. The kid will be in the truck this time. You gotta—"

The Maverick exploded. D.D. slammed against the Mustang. Robert went airborne. Bleeding heavily, clothes smoldering, he stumbled from his landing point. The MRAP left the rise where Reno had fired the shoulder-launched rocket. Moments later, the armored hulk stopped in Robert's path.

Reno stepped out and activated his bandoliers. "After all I did for you."

Robert spat blood. "You killed my sister."

"No, she died because she did her job. You died because you didn't do yours." Reno fired a two-second burst from his left-hand machine pistol. He saw D.D. lying motionless beyond the pyre of the Maverick. Lonny called his name over the MRAP's communication system.

"We need you back here," Lonny said from the touchscreen. "The crew's getting antsy about the storm. And Sparky says the AI engine has some valuable info for us."

Reno looked back at D.D. sprawled in the dirt. He climbed into the driver's seat and left the kill zone.

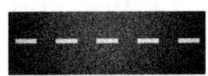

The rumble dissipated as Cox's tiltrotor left Latium. Gabriel stood alone in the living room, pensive. Harper exited the basement, a new, more elaborate car in hand.

"I made another car for Josh. I was hoping to give it to him before he left," Harper said.

Gabriel glanced at the toy. "I'll send him the plans. He can print it himself if he likes."

Harper set down the car and caressed Gabriel. "How did it go?"

"Warder is now part of eQuality. I have to leave for Halifax for my first board meeting. After that, I'm going to Gibraltar to finalize offshore incorporation." Gabriel described a foregone conclusion, not a momentous negotiation.

"When will you be back?" Harper said. Gabriel's icy expression froze her caress.

Phosphorescent clouds piled in an orange sky. Thunderbolts crisscrossed the horizon. Josh watched the unnatural phenomenon from the jump seat in the back of the cab. Olivia turned to hold his hand and gave him a reassuring smile.

Bren cranked fans and filters to blunt the gritty air. He appraised sputtering displays on his windshield and touchscreen. "Couldn't do much of a patch job back at the truck stop. Got some systems working. Communications are still spotty."

"Are we able to track the weather?" Olivia said.

"Well enough. Only thing more dangerous than Porch Pirates is a squall line raining fire." Bren turned his head toward Josh. "Sorry I'm talking about scary stuff."

"I'm not so scared when I'm with Mom and you," Josh said.

Bands of burning prairie bracketed the empty road. Bren checked an updated map. "Bridge on County 19 is out. Squall line behind us. Map is showing an alternate route. And I know a shortcut on top of it. The graphene plant."

Porch Pirates infiltrated the automated graphene plant. Under Sparky's direction, they scattered derelict vehicles and construction debris across side streets, leaving the main access road open. Reno and Lonny approached the young bandit.

"You sure this'll work?" Reno said.

Sparky pointed at his AI engine. "Weather patterns predicted with 99.9 percent certainty. That'll limit his options. Analysis says the Deliverer won't pass up a good shortcut."

Regaining consciousness, D.D. pushed aside twisted sheet metal from the Maverick and stood. She slid behind the wheel of her Mustang, groaning with the pain. She activated her communications system. "Call Bren Van Allen."

"Connection failed. There seems to be a system malfunction on his end," the voice agent said.

"Find Bren Van Allen," D.D. said.

"His eQuality transponder is turned off. Reviewing street cam photos and sightings posted on social media. Estimating his route now."

The course plotted on the touchscreen's map. The Mustang roared away.

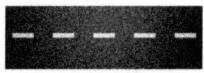

A notification pinged on Olivia's phone. She put her fist to her mouth to stifle an exclamation. She craned her neck toward the backseat. Josh was sleeping, her jacket bundled against his head for a pillow.

"Gabriel just filed a blockchain request for divorce," Olivia said in a quiet voice. "If I agree, I get full custody of Josh, the transit pass, the house, and restrictions lifted on my trust account."

"How generous," Bren said.

Olivia smiled sardonically. "Not really. I have to give up any claim to Warder technology."

Bren gave Olivia a bemused look. "Didn't you just do that?"

Olivia laughed. She tapped her acceptance. "I'm now single."

Bren was glad he'd installed a fresh circuit board to patch up the truck's electronics. A very important system had been restored. "Autonomous mode." He leaned over and kissed Olivia deeply.

Reno stood in a tight canyon between two hills stripped of their graphite seams. Porch Pirates continued preparing the site for the Deliverer. Reno clutched his phone in a conversation with Kenny Turro.

"This is going to be the hottest show on the internet, and I'll give you exclusive streaming rights," Reno said.

"Right now, you're poison. Nobody runs out on Jerold Cox," Kenny said.

"And nobody beats the Deliverer ... until today! Gonna turn that down?"

"eQuality's best drivers in a showdown." Kenny warmed to the idea. "Guess it was bound to happen. Send me the feed when you're ready."

CHAPTER 20

The storm intensified. Burning funnel clouds flicked the horizon. Olivia reached back to take Josh's hand. Bren noted their worry.

"We're almost to the graphene plant. Home stretch after that," Bren said.

A pixelated version of D.D. appeared on the touchscreen, her voice garbled.

"What's going on, D.D.?" Bren said. "I thought we worked things out."

D.D.'s response was unintelligible. The communication cut off.

"Is she going to attack us again?" Olivia said. Bren shrugged. She withdrew the .45 from the console.

"Should I have a gun too?" Josh said.

"No!" Olivia said.

The Mustang appeared behind the Lightning. The truck approached the graphene plant. The gate was up. Bren saw the blocked side streets and stayed on the main drag. The Mustang gained.

"Don't let her hurt my son!" Olivia said.

Bren went to tail gunner. The vehicles passed between the stripped hills. Once again, Bren found himself staring down D.D. She leaned out the driver's window, waving frantically, eyes pleading, her warnings indecipherable.

The squall line backlit her, red clouds dangling in the distance.

The hills converged into the tight canyon. An explosion filled the narrowest section with rock. The brakes slammed, throwing Bren from his seat. Rubble bounced around the Lightning. Porch Pirates erupted from side canyons to hem the truck. Bren moved toward the Barrett, but laser sights speckled him.

D.D. stopped behind the line of Porch Pirates. "I tried to warn you!" she shouted to Bren.

Exiting the bulkhead opening, Olivia came beside Bren, the .45 in hand. Crimson dots swept her. Bren motioned for her to drop the gun. The MRAP clanked into view. Reno stood on the roof, arms outstretched like a general receiving a Roman triumph. Sparky brought the MRAP to a gentle halt. Drawing her Desert Eagle, D.D. rushed Reno. Lonny and several other Porch Pirates tackled and disarmed her.

"Welcome to the show. Everyone knows I like the big iron." Reno knelt and rapped his fist on the MRAP's armor plate. "But for today's extravaganza, I'm upgrading." Reno tapped his phone.

An excavator rolled out of a side canyon, a steel dinosaur with tank treads for feet, a serrated Ferris wheel replacing a snapping skull. The machine blocked the path opposite the rockfall. Reno commanded the excavator to lower its crane neck. Capping the boom, the rotary digger slowly rolled its toothed buckets, savoring its prey.

Bren and Olivia climbed over the tailgate. He set the Ruger on the ground. Olivia led Josh out of the cab, her arms around him. Surveying the rocky clearing, Bren saw no potential weapons, no hiding places except a pump house impelling refined graphene solution toward consumer pipelines, propellant tanks beyond to infuse the solution and hasten its passage.

Reno climbed off the MRAP. He waved his captives forward.

"Did Gabriel send you?" Olivia said.

"No, this is my idea." Reno said. "Reno versus the Deliverer, exclusive on *Delivery: Dead or Alive*." The wind concentrated in the canyon. Porch Pirates looked up, scared.

Bren nodded toward Olivia and Josh. "Let them go."

"I'll handle 'em separate. We've seen the lady will do anything for her kid." Reno leered. "I'll negotiate with her one-on-one."

Reno approached Bren. "First, we're gonna have a rematch of our barroom brawl. I'll give you a couple of minutes of a fair fight. In the end, you'll lose. Bullets in kneecaps can slow a man down." Reno pointed his right index finger as a pantomime gun and laughed. "After I beat you within an inch of your life, I'm going to put you in your truck, see if you have the strength to drive away, give your fans a moment of hope. But then—"

Reno dipped the rotary digger to ground level. The wheel sped up, powerful vacuums pulling loose rock into the buckets. The excavator crumpled the Mustang in one of its maws, and then dumped the wreckage in a conveyor inside the boom. D.D. screamed and fought within restraining arms.

"Squall line is coming. If we stay in this canyon, we'll burn," Bren said.

"The only person dying is you, Deliverer!" Reno turned to Sparky. "Action." Sparky signaled Porch Pirates to begin videoing the scene on their phone. He activated the multi-camera live feed.

Kenny got the cue at his anchor desk. "Welcome to a special edition of *Delivery: Dead or Alive*. We have a live exclusive. A grudge match between Derek Reno and the Deliverer, Bren Van Allen!"

Cox descended the tiltrotor ramp at the fire hub helipad. Reginald ran up with a tablet playing the program.

Cox sized up the show. "What's the reaction on social media?"

"Through the roof. Record betting as well at the Vegas sports desk," Reginald said. Cox nodded as he continued watching.

Wrapped in his bandoliers and pistols, Reno's arm movement was limited. Bren took advantage, returning to his barroom strategy of getting inside leg range. After landing two body blows, Bren toppled Reno with a palm strike to the face. Creeping from behind, Lonny hit Bren across the back of the legs with a metal rod. Bren fell to his knees, and Reno kicked him over. Reno took the rod from Lonny. He jabbed Bren before drawing the rod back to strike. Olivia screamed for Reno to stop.

Thunder crashed and wind shrieked. The storm's fury compressed into the canyon. Porch Pirates scattered, knocking into Reno before he could swing. A lightning bolt struck the excavator. The crane lurched, crushing Porch Pirate vehicles. The rotary digger flipped a car. Bren barely avoided the tumbling auto, scrambling to his feet.

Bren ran to scoop up his Ruger. Reno jumped in his way, activating his machine pistols. In the second-and-a-half required to engage the bandoliers, Bren arced into a flying drop kick that cracked Reno's sternum. As Reno writhed on the ground, struggling to refill his lungs, Bren retrieved the revolver and brought Olivia and Josh into a crouch behind his truck.

Grasping his chest, Reno stood and looked over his shoulder. The bucket wheel dived at him. His index finger stabbed the hack interface on his phone, but the machine kept coming. Reno staggered away, screaming. The vacuum sucked him into a bucket. The toothed edge caught the back loops of his bandoliers. Reno tried to unfasten himself, but the buckles at the center of his chest were jammed from Bren's kick. His screams shrank as the boom reared into the roiling sky. The excavator scraped a canyon wall, pivoting with the impact, and wedged against the opposite face.

The tops of firenados whipped above the canyon lip. Bren took Olivia and Josh to the pump house. The steel door was bolted.

"We need a heat shield." Bren's eyes locked on the sign beside the door: Graphene Solution Pump #7.

Bren ran to the MRAP. He gunned the armored vehicle for the pump house. Olivia and Josh stood away as the MRAP smashed into the door. Bren backed up and crashed again. The pump house broke open. Bren climbed from the tangle of steel and pulverized cinder block. Olivia and Josh ran to him.

"Get everyone between the pump house and the canyon wall. Vehicles too," Bren said.

D.D. pulled Sparky forward. "Here's the little genius who hacked the excavator."

Bren took Sparky inside the building and placed him at a computer terminal. "Find the command for pipeline purge. Override security."

Bren located machinery marked Relief Valve. He looked back at Sparky. The young Porch Pirate typed furiously while D.D. scowled at him.

Olivia and the Porch Pirates parked vehicles in the tight space Bren had indicated. Rocks and sheet metal corkscrewed into the air. Coughing in the heat and smoke, Bren stepped out of the pump house to view the progress. He turned to D.D.

"Get everyone under the vehicles," Bren said.

D.D. moved toward the vehicles. Entering the successful command, Sparky gave a thumbs up. Bren returned to the relief valve. He strained to turn the wheel. Sparky joined him, their joint effort freeing the mechanism. The valve opened fully. A deep rumble rose. Bren and Sparky ran from the pump house. Bren crawled under the Lightning where Olivia and Josh waited. He handed Olivia his gaiter and Josh his bandana. The rumble was audible above the wind's wail.

The relief valve exploded in a black geyser that arced through the pump house's broken wall. Exposed to oxygen, the graphene solution crystallized and hardened upon falling back to earth, the blowout transforming into a canopy over the people and vehicles. More solution layered the initial shell. Bren, Olivia, and Josh huddled in the seething darkness, repeating prayers.

A firenado swirled into the canyon. Reno swung from the stalled excavator. Embers burned through the brim of his cowboy hat. He screamed and flailed as the whirlwind bore down, ripping his restraints and casting him into the pillar of flame.

The firenado raked the graphene canopy, invisible yet palpable in heat and noise. Explosions joined the howl, the propellant tanks detonating. Then ... quiet. The fury ebbed as quickly as it started.

The hum of the Lightning's twin motors broke the canyon's silence. The truck cracked the canopy like a giant egg. Porch Pirate vehicles followed. The rockfall was scorched and parted, displaced by the tank discharge. The caravan of survivors drove through the canyon and left the graphene plant.

The vehicles stopped on a rise beyond the plant. Bren helped Olivia and Josh out of the Lightning to watch distant firenados retract into the pyrocumulus clouds. The front faded from sullen red to light gray. Porch Pirates clambered out of their cars and looked at Bren with awe and remorse.

"Should we be praying, Deliverer?" Sparky asked.

Bren opened a Bible app and held up his phone. "First Thessalonians, 5:6. 'Never stop praying.'"

Porch Pirates searched for the verse on their phones. Some began to pray softly. Tears rolled down weathered faces. Lonny stood before D.D., his hands out, unable to form the words to apologize.

D.D. turned to Bren. "I'm supposed to forgive these losers. Matthew 6:15?"

"Works every time," Bren said.

"Best part of the old days ... Bible study," D.D. said.

"No time for nostalgia." Bren smiled and put his arms around Olivia and Josh.

D.D. pointed down the open road. "Finish the run."

Bren and Olivia clasped hands on the center console as the Lightning accelerated. Josh put his hand on top of theirs.

Kenny came on the touchscreen, dismayed. "An act of God saved you? I can't believe it."

"That was nothing," Bren said. "Two-thousand years ago, Jesus saved us all. Believe, Kenny, believe."

CHAPTER 21

The Lightning covered the final miles to Entrada. Fans lined the road with their Deliverer signs and banners, cheering as the truck passed. Chief Yang met the truck at the first gate with a motorcade escort. Spectators thronged the outer drive through the workers' neighborhoods.

The cheers continued on Olivia's cul-de-sac. A banner read Welcome Home! Neighbors mobbed the trio when they stepped out. Mark pushed his way to the front of the throng.

"Good to see you, bro!" Mark bear-hugged Josh, lifting him off the ground.

Waving to the well-wishers, the trio entered the house. Olivia hugged and kissed Josh. "Take off those disgusting clothes and get in the bath."

"I'm tired," Josh said.

"We're all tired. And we're all filthy. Go," Olivia said. As Josh ran upstairs, she turned to Bren. "Feels good just to be a mom again."

Bren and Olivia embraced. Bren's phone rang. He moved to the kitchen to answer.

"How soon can you be back at Fire Hub Sears?" Cox asked over the phone.

"To face a disciplinary hearing?"

"To be reinstated in the eQuality network."

"Your new business partner Gabriel Durand won't like that."

"The fans will. They're raving. We need you." Cox smiled. Bren absorbed the developments.

Olivia switched on the media wall to check her messages. The first one was from Madame Verneuil, Prix de Gloire.

"Madame Durand, it is our pleasure to announce you are the winner of the 2038 Prix de Gloire, digital category. Looking forward to hearing from you soon. We need to arrange your travel to Geneva. Au revoir."

Olivia put her face in her hands. Her fixation on the Prix de Gloire had become an afterthought in the turmoil. Josh called out from the bathtub. His call ended, Bren left the kitchen and watched Olivia climb the stairs. He juggled his phone, unsettled by Cox's reconciliation.

The home security system called out, "Fire!" A diagram on the living room big screen pinpointed the basement. Bren and Olivia ran to Gabriel's lab. Through a glass pane, they saw computers spark and burn. The metal cabinet holding Warder prototypes melted from within. Fire retardant nozzles popped from the lab ceiling and doused the blaze.

Bren put his arm around Olivia and led her up the stairs. Josh stood at the top of the flight, scared. Olivia knelt and hugged him. The home security system announced, "Fire extinguished. House secure."

Later that day, Bren, Olivia, and Josh emerged from the house, clean and rested. The cul-de-sac was transformed into a block party. Kids swarmed around Josh, babbling questions. Adults brought food and drink to Bren and Olivia. Country music played over a PA, prompting couples to dance in the street. The half-century-old classic "Boot Scootin' Boogie" started. Olivia took Bren's plate out of his hands and pulled him onto the portable dance floor. He danced gamely while she did an exuberant two-step and spin. The crowd cheered.

"That was incredible, but I'm starving," Bren said. Olivia laughed as he reclaimed his piled high plate. The two sat under a young oak at the edge of a greenbelt.

"I had an important call." Olivia plucked morsels from Bren's plate.

"So did I. You first," Bren said.

"I won the Prix de Gloire. I'm due in Geneva."

"Congratulations." Bren squeezed Olivia's hand.

"The prize was my escape plan. But now, I don't have to escape. What's your news?"

"Cox welcomed me back to eQuality. All's forgiven."

"So you're going back on the road?"

"I have to."

"You'd die for one of these?" Olivia pulled the transit pass from her pocket.

"The mission field has claimed a lot of lives." Taking a final bite, Bren threw his plate into a waste receptacle and started walking down the greenbelt. Olivia followed.

"Maybe you can accept that, but I can't." Olivia held out the transit pass. "It's approved for five travelers. That will cover your family and mine."

"The Lord's not calling me to Switzerland."

"Me neither." Olivia pointed at the surroundings. "I'd be trading this bubble for another."

Bren shook his head. "I won't destroy your dreams."

"I want my son to be safe and loved. I want to live in joy. And yes, I want to dance. My dreams are intact. They've just gotten bigger."

Bren tried to ignore Olivia's arms around his neck. "The Revival Zone is rough. The work is nonstop. Research, farming, fighting off militias who want the food and tech." Olivia brought her face close to his. "And the internet service is sketchy."

"Sounds like paradise." Olivia pressed in for a long kiss.

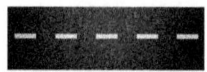

Bren opened a VR session. His avatar materialized. Madison joined him.

"I know you don't like VR hugs, but I couldn't wait until I can give you a real one." Bren embraced his daughter.

"When's that gonna be?" Madison said.

"About a week. Start packing. We're moving to Project Archegos."

"You got the transit pass!"

"Actually, it belongs to another family. They're coming with us."

"Olivia and Josh?" Madison summoned holographic images of the pair in her father's truck.

"Yes."

"Are you and Olivia in love?" Madison rolled her eyes when Bren stammered for an answer. "You're as bad as Grandma. I'm twelve!"

A shaft of light bisected the virtual reality field. A door opened in the blackness beyond the avatars.

"I'll call you and Grandma in a few minutes. Go on," Bren said.

Madison's avatar dissolved. Cox's avatar approached.

"Just got your message," Cox said. "Sorry to barge into your VR."

"I'm used to it," Bren said.

"Going out on top. The smart ones always do. Trying to change the world? Not so wise."

"Can't change the world. We can only grow the kingdom."

Cox's avatar nodded acceptance before dissolving.

Olivia tucked Josh into bed. "I don't know when you'll see your father again."

Josh nodded. "He wasn't playing a game with me. He was being mean to you. I only want to see him if he's being nice." Olivia kissed him on the forehead.

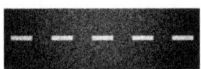

As dark descended in Latium, hidden speakers emulated extinct crickets. Gabriel sat in his study. Harper entered and opened her robe. Eyes closed as Gabriel applied a Warder patch to her bare skin. After a moment, he removed the patch and set the layer in a case. The tracking unit pulsing to life, Gabriel and Harper admired the device with a gaze usually reserved for a newborn child.

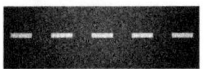

Outside the tenement building, Cindy and Olivia watched Bren and the kids pack. The Airstream and Lightning, stripped of the eQuality logos and buffed of their battle scars, stood ready to transport the blended family.

Olivia and Cindy carried final belongings out of the building. "Thank you for bringing my son out of the wilderness," Cindy said.

"He did the same for me," Olivia said.

Bren got behind the wheel and shared a smile with Olivia. The interior was restored with a full backseat and touchscreens reduced to factory issue. Madison and Josh sat in the second row with Cindy. The battered Bible was open on the girl's lap.

Bren called Pastor Doug. "We're on our way."

"Good. We'll have plenty to do when you get here," Pastor Doug said.

"Can you squeeze in a wedding?" Bren looked at Olivia.

"Yes!" Olivia said. The kids' jaws dropped, and Cindy cried.

"Amazing what you'll say in the heat of the moment." Bren lifted Olivia's hand in a victory clench.

The truck and trailer climbed the on-ramp to the e-Bahn. Passing the point of no return, the rig rolled onto the highway. The transit pass sitting on the dash blinked green. The touchscreen read "e-Bahn Travel Approved." Olivia exhaled.

"Kids, close your eyes," Bren said.

The children complied. Cindy gasped at the blackened cars and bodies. Soon, the highway was clear of the horrors.

"Mom, can we open our eyes now?" Josh said.

"Yes," Olivia said.

"Dad, can we pray for the people back there," Madison said.

"Yes," Bren said. "And pray for the United States of America."

"The states aren't united anymore," Madison said.

"Just pray, Maddie."

Bren pressed the accelerator. The ferry landing at Powell River was far and merely the beginning.

ABOUT THE AUTHOR

Jason William Karpf grew up with storytelling. The son of a screenwriter, he was a child actor in the early 1970s, appearing on classic TV shows *The Bold Ones, The Courtship of Eddie's Father*, and *Bonanza*. Screenwriting became his calling from his teens to early thirties. In 1994, he wrote the book *Anatomy of a Massacre*, the true story of the era's worst mass shooting.

Today, Jason is an author, speaker, college instructor, and marketing/fundraising professional. His blogging and nonfiction writing brings a Christian perspective to marketing and communication. His science-fiction novels put Jesus first.

Jason and Ann, his wife, live in Minnesota and have three grown children. When he is not writing, speaking, or teaching, he is making music, playing in the worship team of his church. A history and trivia aficionado, Jason was a four-time champion on the TV game show *Jeopardy*.

Jason is a Realm Award finalist and received the bronze in the Excellence in Marketing Awards from the Christian Authors Network.

ADDENDUM TABLE OF CONTENTS

INTRODUCTION

This addendum contains guides to major characters, vehicles, weapons, and technologies portrayed in *The Deliverer*. Additionally, a brief overview of Civil War II explains the forces that have torn apart the United States of America by the 2030s.

Some of the items listed are real (e.g., Ruger Super GP100, B-52), some are fictitious (e.g., Warder Chip, Reno's machine pistol system, Buick RoadWarrior), and some are fictional customizations of actual products (e.g., Bren's F-150 Lightning modified for road combat).

The Deliverer is a "hard sci-fi" story, a sub-genre that emphasizes technical detail and scientific accuracy, without sacrificing a sense of the fantastic. Many of the greatest hard sci-fi writers had training in the sciences, such as Arthur C. Clarke, Robert Heinlein, Poul Anderson, and Michael Crichton. My degrees are in marketing and communication, but I have always loved the history of inventions and scientific discoveries. I conduct extensive research for my writing and call upon a community of knowledgeable, enthusiastic, and generous technical experts. For the writing of *The Deliverer*, I thank the following, listed by their subject matter expertise, for their time and support:

Dance, Choreography
Pastor Jayna DeMell
Co-Lead Pastor, Life Assembly Church. Instructor of dance, resident choreographer, North Central University. Private dance teacher.

Global University Ministry Program, Graduate. Extensive private study in ballet, jazz, tap, and other dance styles.

Vehicles, Martial Arts, Firearms

Nick Elia

Automotive aftermarket product sales manager. Martial artist/trainer. Former NASCAR crew member.

BA, Economics, Cal State Channel Islands. ASE certified mechanic.

Practitioner of Hung Gar kung fu, tai chi, submission wrestling.

Future Technologies, Drones, Engineering

Chad File, PhD

Associate Professor, Mechanical Engineering, LeTourneau University, School of Engineering and Engineering Technology.

PhD, Aerospace Engineering, MS, Aerospace Engineering, Washington University in St. Louis. BS, Physics, BS, Mechanical Engineering, Southern Illinois University Edwardsville. AS, General Studies, Certificate— Industrial Service Technician, Kaskaskia College.

Military, Weapon Systems

Staff Sergeant Morris Franklin, US Army Reserve

Civil Affairs Instructor

5-108th BN (CA/PO), 6th BDE, 102nd DIV

Fort Bragg, NC

MBA, Finance, New York University. BS, Business Management, Bob Jones University.

Future Technologies, Speculative Fiction Analysis, Political Science, Supply Chain Operations, Firearms

Brian Karpf

Supply Chain Specialist

BS, Business, Cal State Channel Islands.

CIVIL WAR II—A BRIEF OVERVIEW

In the mid-2020s, the United States of America slid into the civil war dreaded by many, desired by some. Alternate slates of electors arose following a presidential election, with states certifying their preferred candidates, a standoff resembling medieval conflicts in the Catholic Church (the Western Schism) and England (the War of the Roses) over recognized leadership. California, Oregon, and Washington state refused to follow Supreme Court rulings to resolve the political crisis.

Legal actions escalated between the states, inspiring historians to call lawyers the shock troops of Civil War II. Subjects for the lawsuits covered an enormous range of political, cultural, and environmental issues. States launched "police actions" against each other in compensation for declared damages, exemplified in military exchanges between California and Wyoming. In 2026, F-15s and Predator drones from the California Air National Guard bombed the Black Thunder Coal Mine and North Antelope Rochelle Mine. In retaliation, commandos recruited from the Wyoming Army National Guard and Wyoming State Police sabotaged the Leroy Anderson Dam, flooding Silicon Valley.

Washington DC struggled for control and relevance under a president unrecognized by more than half the states. Attempts to federalize National Guard units resulted in mass desertions. In 2028, Bren Van Allen (Lieutenant, 1st Class) deployed with the California Army National Guard to stop Texas from seceding. As a result, he was part of the infamous Hemlock Road Massacre in which aerial and ground drones mistakenly destroyed a relief convoy led by noted pastor Clint Harden (Chapter 12). In a friendly fire incident, Bren shot Pastor Clint. Guilt-ridden, Bren testified against superiors responsible for the massacre and its coverup. He was ostracized, ruining his engineering business.

Fighting intensified, ranging from large-scale military engagements to independent raids and mass shootings. Americans clashed violently as they journeyed to their preferred regions of the country, emulating the migration massacres during the partition of India in 1947.

New nations declared their independence from what had been the United States of America:

- **America Green**—the Pacific Coast and Hawaii. Capital, Portland.

- **America Red**—a sprawling territory largely comprising the "red states" as identified after the 2000 presidential election. Capital, Jefferson City.

- **America Blue**—New England, Mid-Atlantic, and Great Lakes regions, still claiming to be the real United States of America. Capital, Washington, DC.

Smaller republics formed in the West:

- **Mojave**, stretching from southern Nevada to Arizona. Capital, Phoenix.

- **Deseret**, encompassing Utah and parts of Nevada, Idaho, and Wyoming. Capital, Salt Lake City.

- **Alaska**, the former forty-ninth state. Capital, Juneau

In 2029, the conflict crescendoed with the Battle of Puget Sound. The three Americas fought over ballistic missile submarines berthed at the Kitsnap Peninsula, former US government property controlled by American Green. The Battle of Puget Sound became the Cuban Missile Crisis of Civil War II as the three Americas threatened use of nuclear weapons already appropriated from the Department of Defense.

As the battle spilled north, NATO fortified Canada, their North American partner, ending the 49th parallel's

200-year status as the world's longest undefended border. Canada launched a massive "Build the Wall" campaign under NATO's auspices, drawing donations and volunteers from around the world.

Australia and Japan negotiated division of the subs between the three major Americas—some staying at Kitsnap, some sailing the Northwest Passage for New London, Connecticut, and the remainder transiting the Panama Canal to the base at Kings Bay, Georgia. As part of the treaty, America Red dismantled ICBMs the former US Air Force had left behind in Montana, North Dakota, and Wyoming, turning the silos into survivalist mansions for their elites.

Additional negotiations created the safety valve for Civil War II—the Border States, the territory occupying the former USA's breadbasket. The area's inhabitants—small farmers to ag conglomerates—may have had their personal loyalties but remained officially neutral by edict. The arrangement was also good for business as farming revenues rose, even as the land and aquifers shriveled.

By the 2030s, Civil War II hardened into stalemate. Border battles and covert actions remained common, with examples including:

2033: America Green and Mojave fighting over Southern California territory at the time Bren entered the delivery business (Chapter 1).

2038: America Blue attacking the Border States to force creation a new enterprise zone for commerce. At an eQuality logistics hub prior to deployment to Fire Hub Sears, Bren and his fellow drivers are caught between a clandestine American Blue force and counterattackers (Chapter 6).

Justice was a casualty of Civil War II, leading to the polar extremes of lawlessness and oppressive legislation across the quilt of nations comprising "Greater America." Leaders placated populations with by proliferating graphene-based 3D printers to satisfy material cravings (see description, "Key Technologies") and condoning of extreme digital content, such as the bloodsport program *Delivery: Dead or Alive*. Starvation, disease, and violence ran rampant beneath the veneer of 21st century consumerism.

After more than a decade of strife, Bren Van Allen, the Deliverer, is a Christian champion in a shattered America addicted to bloodsport. Like the nation he loves, he struggles with contradictions—a student of the beatitudes who takes up arms, a diligent evangelist who believes in the promise of science, a father determined to set his family apart form the world who makes his living deep in its decadence. Civil War II curses Bren and millions more. But the conflict is also a forge for the man known to those millions as the Deliverer.

MAIN CHARACTERS

Bren Van Allen, 38. MS, Engineering Management, BS, Electromechanical Engineering Technology, California Polytechnic State University, Pomona (Pomona, CA—former USA, current America Green). First Lieutenant, California Army National Guard (ret.). Expert, rifle qualification. 3rd dan, black belt, aikido.

Bren Van Allen is "The Deliverer," a top delivery driver for eQuality, one of the largest e-commerce and content companies in the world. He uses his celebrity to spread the gospel of Jesus Christ. His training as an engineer and military officer gives him an edge in combatting Porch Pirates during his delivery runs.

Bren grew up in Loma Linda, California, east of Los Angeles. He joined the California Army National Guard ROTC to help pay for his education at Cal Poly Pomona, the training leading to his proficiency in firearms and the martial art aikido. During his studies, Bren attended a campus ministry event where he met his future wife, Hailey, a nursing student at Azusa Pacific University. Bren and Hailey married and had their daughter Madison (see description, "Main Characters") during the tumultuous 2020s when America descended into Civil War II.

Having seen his parents Jack, a machinist, and Cindy, an accounts payable specialist, laid off several times during his childhood, Bren resolved to start his own business after completing his undergrad. Van Allen Engineering landed major contracts and claimed a number of patents. Bren sold the patent for his agricultural drone, the Gleaner (see description, "Aircraft, Rockets, Missiles, and Spacecraft") to buy his family an Airstream Flying Cloud trailer (see description, "Land and Sea Vehicles") for a bug-out as Civil War II intensified in the late 2020s.

Before they could leave, Hailey died in the third pandemic (2028), bravely serving in a quarantined hospital until she succumbed from the virus. Fulfilling his National Guard commitment, Bren deployed with a California unit that remained loyal to Washington, DC. His military service ended in controversy with the Hemlock Road Massacre in Texas (see description, "Civil War II").

In 2033, Bren was blackballed for being a whistleblower regarding the massacre, ruining his company. He accepts a delivery assignment from his former platoon sergeant, Moe Franklin. He nearly dies but is rescued by eQuality CEO Jerold Cox (see description, "Main Characters") who sees his potential during his appearance on *Delivery: Dead or Alive*.

By 2038, Bren is a delivery celebrity with fans and detractors across Greater America. He is among the first round of drivers for eQuality's expansion into the Border States. Bren has faced death many times. He has called out to Jesus in every dark moment, receiving salvation and sharing his witness. But when he accepts Olivia Durand (see description, "Main Characters") as a new customer, he faces his deadliest run and grows even closer to God.

Olivia Durand, 35. BFA, Dance, California Institute of Arts (Santa Clarita, CA—former USA, current America Green). Tim Disney Prize for Storytelling Arts, winner, 2023. Prix de Gloire, nominee, 2038.

Dancer, choreographer, and director, Olivia Durand first demonstrated her talent as a preschooler, consistently outscoring older children in dance mat games on the Nintendo Wii. Her single mom, Constance, worked two jobs to afford dance lessons, enrolling her at the studio of Vadim Orlov, Russian-born ballet dancer and early music video star. Vadim and his wife, rock singer and fellow MTV standout Roxy Steele, encouraged Olivia to expand her talents to choreography and digital production. Olivia received a scholarship to attend CalArts, the creative arts college north of Los Angeles founded by Walt Disney. As a senior, she won the Tim Disney Prize for Excellence in the Storytelling Arts for her capstone dance piece.

After graduation, she took an unusual freelance assignment with NeuroDawn, a tech startup founded by Dr. Gabriel Durand (see description, "Main Characters"). Gabriel needed a subject for brain mapping during complex activity that combined motor, creative, and emotional functions. The hours were long, the demands heavy, the pay lavish. Gabriel marveled that the study of Olivia produced the most scientifically valuable readings he'd ever obtained from a test subject.

Romance flourished between Olivia and the older Dr. Durand. She enjoyed the intense attention, the fascination of Gabriel's teeming mind, his talk of breakthroughs that would eclipse the work being done NeuroDawn's labs. She sent money to her mother as Civil War II escalated, allowing Constance to quit her jobs and live in safety. Gabriel presented a pre-nup and wedding proposal, both of which Olivia accepted. On their wedding night, Gabriel said, "I've already seen a more intimate image of you."

Following a secret NeuroDawn experiment gone awry, Olivia moved with Gabriel and their two-year-old son, Josh, to the Border States, where he shut down the company and accelerated work on his "true breakthrough." The era of being NeuroDawn's muse had evaporated. Olivia was now simultaneously ignored and controlled, trapped in Entrada, the high-security, luxury community (see description, "Major Locations"). While dancing for Gabriel and his machines, she had ignore her true art. In 2038, she enters her digital ballet production in the Prix de Gloire competition held in Geneva. Dance will be her escape in more ways than one.

Olivia learns that Gabriel has a final Pygmalion play—using her as the first test subject for his Warder tracking chip (see description, "Key Technologies"). She hacks the systems in his basement lab using the standalone security computer in the adjoining panic room, her sanctuary. She'll be ready for Gabriel's scheme. She'll deny him his cruel triumph. And she'll need the Deliverer to do it.

Gabriel Durand, 55. Ph.D., Biomedical Engineering, University of Oxford (Oxford, UK—New European Union). MD, Neurology, Johns Hopkins University School of Medicine (Baltimore, MD—former USA, current America Blue). MSc, Computer Science, BSc, Physics, Imperial College London (London, UK—New European Union).

Ever since he was a boy in the United Kingdom, Gabriel Durand has been dedicated to the union of man and machine. He sought a construct for the evolutionary leap, like the unified field theory Einstein envisioned as a combined standard for relativity and electromagnetism. He told his father as much in 1990, when he was seven.

Entering his thirties, Gabriel had earned two terminal degrees and assimilated a vast spectrum of scientific knowledge. He became a widely sought expert in machine learning, wisely taking payments for his services in stock. The day Facebook went public in 2012 was lucrative for Mark Zuckerberg. Gabriel Durand also fared well. In the following decade, Gabriel launched NeuroDawn, manufacturer of brain-interface chips. Materials science was catching up to Gabriel's unified theory of man and machine.

In 2033, a secret NeuroDawn experiment went awry in Colorado, resulting in several deaths. As a new eQuality driver, Bren Van Allen witnessed the carnage, having been called to the scene to make a delivery. Gabriel survived the disaster, hiding in the shadows until Bren left.

Gabriel shut down NeuroDawn and moved his family from coastal California, now part of America Green, to the Border States. Their new home in Entrada would be the perfect base for his next project, a masterwork greater than the algorithms he'd provided Zuckerberg, more revolutionary than the brain chips he'd shelved.

Einstein had one more vision—quantum entanglement, two objects instantly sharing information and other properties without any observable connection of matter or energy. The great genius had described the theorized phenomenon as "spooky action at a distance." To Gabriel Durand, there's nothing spooky about it. He has cracked the code with his latest invention, the Warder Chip (see description, "Key Technologies"). He will change the world, but first he must attend to his wife.

D.D. Guthrie, 37, BA, Communications/Media Studies, Quinnipiac University (Hamden, CT—former USA, current America Blue).

Deborah Denise "D.D." Guthrie is a former delivery driver for eQuality who becomes the leader of a Porch Pirate squad. A talented athlete growing up in Massachusetts, she developed a passion for hockey, leading to a scholarship at Quinnipiac University and a place on the women's varsity team. The scouting report calling her "tall, fast, and potentially uncoachable" proved accurate. Despite her high scoring, D.D. became better known for fights with coaches, team captains, and opposing players—the latter turning physical on several occasions. She was kicked off the squad and lost her scholarship.

D.D.'s dream had been sportscasting after hopefully playing in the NCAA championships and winning a spot on the US Olympic Team. The dream disintegrated when no other top-tier hockey programs would accept her as a transfer. She took out student loans and completed her communications degree at Quinnipiac. Her boyfriend, Rick, encouraged her to develop a media career outside of traditional broadcast.

D.D. became a social media influencer, releasing a series of extreme sports videos. Rick, now husband/producer, urged her into riskier activities—mixed martial arts, soft-core pornography—to boost digital ad revenue. When she caught him cheating with finances and other women, she divorced him. The corrupt courts of Civil War II awarded Rick onerous support payments.

By the 2030s, delivery driving became the most popular extreme sport. D.D. followed the trend and emerged as one of eQuality's top drivers. Her brash style contrasted with fellow driver Bren Van Allen, validating the adage of opposites attract. Bren would not consummate the brief romance. D.D's sense of betrayal is complete when Bren's dashcam video provides evidence of her faking a robbery. After dismissal from the eQuality network, D.D. goes to the opposing side, taking over a Porch Pirate squad. She gives them an order: destroy the Deliverer.

Derek Reno, 40. AS, Automotive Manufacturing Technology, Central Alabama Community College (Alexander City, AL—former USA, current America Red). Mechanic certifications, A-1 through A-7, ASE. Silver glove III, savate.

Known for his high body count on the road, Derek Reno is the chief rival to Bren Van Allen among eQuality drivers. Derek grew up in the NASCAR town of Talladega, Alabama. He took early jobs at auto repair shops with his eye on stock car racing, hoping to use his mechanical skills to work with a team on his way to becoming a driver. His parallel passion was martial arts with an emphasis on savate, also known as French foot fighting, a venerable style developed on the waterfront of Marseille and the rough streets of Paris.

Reno was on a promising path—a crew member for a major NASCAR team while racing on the dirt track circuit to build experience. However, his dangerous driving tactics resulted in a racer's death, getting him banned from the circuit and ostracized from NASCAR. Furious over his treatment, Reno turned to illegal competitions. An extreme form of rally racing was becoming popular in the Alabama backwoods—sports cars modified to take on dirt roads best suited for 4x4s, emulating contests like the Dakar Rally held in Africa. These rallies incorporated other sports:

- Geocaching—digital treasure hunts for stashes of money, guns, and/or drugs.
- Martial arts—drivers fighting over the caches.

Reno became a champion in these immoral games, broadcast on the dark web. With the escalation of Civil War II, armed delivery driving mainstreamed motorized bloodsport. Reno finally went "legitimate" when eQuality signed him. For this new format, he traded speed for survivability, replacing his rally car with a customized MRAP, an armored truck that had seen action with the US Army in Iraq and police departments in the former United States. He built the Team Reno brand by employing two "blocker" drivers—siblings Ronni and Robert Sykes who as teens had run guns and drugs to the Alabama rallies.

Derek Reno is the opposite of Bren Van Allen—coarse, vain, coldhearted. He is determined to topple Bren from the top driver standings. To do that, the Deliverer must die.

Paul "Mongo" Mayfield, 44. Graduate, Road Warrior Truck Driving School (Gaylord, MI—former USA, current America Blue).

Paul "Mongo" Mayfield is an eQuality delivery driver, a longtime ally of Bren Van Allen. Nicknamed by his grandmother after a superhuman character in the 1970s comedy *Blazing Saddles*, Mongo is one of the few eQuality stars who actually worked as a traditional trucker before Civil War II. As order broke down, he was forced to defend his cargos using his weapons collection and prodigious strength. A friend sent eQuality a video of Mongo wiping out a pack of hijackers, resulting in a contract from Jerold Cox.

Mongo joins Bren's Bible study group when the two are named to the eQuality dream team in the company's expansion to the Border States. The big man will need Jesus as he faces new dangers alongside the Deliverer.

Jerold Cox, 50. BS, Business Administration, MGM, Master of Global Management, Thunderbird School of Management, Arizona State University (Phoenix, AZ— former USA, current Republic of Mojave).

Jerold Cox is CEO of eQuality, Inc., one of the world's largest e-commerce and content corporations, dominating armed delivery in Greater America. As Civil War II escalated, Cox grew his company, making deals with the new governments to access their markets. Recognizing the profit potential of armed delivery and its entertainment spinoffs, he consolidated the industry in the early 2030s. Cox spotted Bren on *Delivery: Dead or Alive*, rescued him from a flooded canyon, and turned him into an eQuality star.

In 2038, Cox seeks an enterprise zone in the Border States, goading America Blue into military action to force the trade agreement. He deploys his top drivers to Fire Hub Sears—a distribution center and rocket base—to exploit the lucrative new market. An even greater windfall awaits as he negotiates with Gabriel Durand for the Warder Chip. The Deliverer must deal with the deadly consequences.

Kenny Turro, 28. AA, Digital Media Production Technology, Southeast Technical College (Sioux Falls, SD— former USA, current Border States).

Kenny Turro is the host of *Delivery: Dead or Alive*, the 24/7 streaming program that depicts the uncensored exploits of eQuality delivery drivers and their battles against Porch Pirates. In the early 2030s, he started the program in his mother's basement, curating live feeds from drivers and their adversaries, presenting the content in a classic sports talk format. Before becoming the Deliverer, Bren appears with his friend Moe Franklin on an early episode. By 2038, Jerold Cox has licensed the show, upgrading production values and the host's wardrobe—hoodies out, designer suits in—turning Kenny into one of the top media personalities in Greater America.

Kenny covers eQuality's expansion to the Border States, regularly interviewing the dream team of drivers chosen for this lucrative and dangerous market. Bren is a popular guest, verbally sparring with Kenny and notables like Thomas Albano, attorney general of America Green, who issues a warrant on the air for Bren's arrest. Will Kenny get the biggest scoop of all—a live shot of the Deliverer's demise on the killing roads?

Madison Van Allen, 12. Currently enrolled as online student, Academy of the Americas (Minneapolis, MN—former USA, current Border States).

Madison "Maddie" Van Allen is Bren's daughter. She lives with her grandmother Cindy in an urban apartment, relatively insulated from the worst of Civil War II. When she was a toddler, Maddie lost her mother, Hailey, during the third pandemic.

Highly intelligent like her father, Maddie gets straight As and is preparing to take online college courses when she turns 13. She is active with her church youth group and works at relief centers for war refugees. Bren worries that Maddie has had to grow up too fast between her mother's death and the country's disintegration. Maddie prays for her father as he travels the killing roads and looks forward to the day when the family can move to Project Archegos (see description, "Major Locations"), the Christian scientific enclave on Vancouver Island in British Columbia.

Josh Durand, 7. Currently enrolled as hybrid student at Entrada Elementary School (former USA/eastern Colorado, current Border States).

Josh is the son of Olivia and Gabriel Durand. He lives in Entrada (see description, "Major Locations"), a fortified, luxury community in the Border States, doted on by his mother and largely ignored by his father. Like millions of other youngsters across Greater America, he enjoys kid shows produced by eQuality about delivery drivers, sanitized fantasies for growing minds. When parental blocks on household media are inadvertently deactivated, he watches *Delivery: Dead or Alive* and becomes a fan of the Deliverer.

Josh is a pawn in Olivia's revenge against Gabriel as she spoils his perfect launch for the Warder chip. Gabriel retaliates, placing their son in mortal danger. The Deliverer must become a real-life hero to Josh and his mother, calling upon his formidable skills and the infinitely greater power of God to save them from the killing roads.

MAJOR LOCATIONS

Fire Hub Sears. Located at the edge of the Border States, Fire Hub Sears is eQuality's distribution complex, home base to the top delivery drivers selected for the new enterprise zone (Chapter 9). The complex was a shopping mall built in the 20th century, its current name derived from a little-remembered retailer that occupied an anchor store.

eQuality has renovated the derelict site, adding amenities for the drivers that include an RV park and a employee shopping district decorated as a classic Main Street. Upper floors include a secure suite for eQuality CEO Jerold Cox and a landing pad for his Bell Boeing Quad Tiltrotor (see description, "Aircraft, Rockets, Missiles, and Spacecraft"). The center of the sprawling structure holds a launch facility for Sleigh cargo rockets (see description, "Aircraft, Rockets, Missiles, and Spacecraft").

Graphene Plant. During his first run from Fire Hub Sears, Bren battles Porch Pirates in a graphene plant (Chapter 10). The huge site is an integrated facility for the mining, refining, and distribution of graphene, the "wonder substance" piped to 3D printers across Greater America, allowing consumers to create a vast array of products in their homes (see description, "Key Technologies").

Entrada. Located in the Border States (former eastern Colorado, near the Front Range), Entrada is a fortified, luxury community, one of the premier addresses in Greater America. Covering five square miles, the community is surrounded by earthworks topped with Phalanx cannons. The first ring of neighborhoods is home to the many workers who sustain Entrada's luxurious lifestyle. The inner core belongs to the primary residents and includes:

- High-end homes on cul-de-sacs. The homes average 5,000 square feet and come with water-saving appliances, connection to a high-capacity graphene utility for 3D printing, and finished basements with panic rooms.
- Exclusive school system, pre-K through 12th grade, with hybrid learning modalities—online and in-class.
- Farmers market offering the finest in hydroponic vegetables and lab-grown proteins.
- Multi-acre central park with terraformed hills and caves for hiking and camping.

The Durand family lives in Entrada. After strict security screens, Bren and other delivery drivers are allowed into the residential area to drop off packages and talk to fans. Lives change when Bren brings a box of vintage toy cars to Josh Durand, per the order from Olivia Durand (Chapter 10).

Project Archegos. Located on Vancouver Island in British Columbia, Project Archegos is a Christian scientific enclave headed by pastor and scientist Doug Wescott. Members have fled Civil War II to develop solutions to global environmental and health crises in the name of Jesus. Experimental programs include high-yield regenerative farming, harvesting water from the atmosphere, and restarting ocean currents halted by the rise in sea temperatures.

Project Archegos has many opponents—conservative Christians who consider its scientific mission blasphemous (Chapter 7), liberal secularists who blame Christians for the war and cannot accept faith-based science.

Bren wants to move his family to Project Archegos and contribute his skills as an engineer and inventor. The only way to transport his daughter and mother safely across Greater America and through the fortified Canadian border is the eBahn. Passage requires a transit pass, its cost equivalent to years of Bren's earnings as a delivery driver. Can Bren survive long enough to bring his family to a new life at Project Archegos?

Manitoba Provincial Border Station, NATO Central Command, 49th Parallel. In 2038, the Canadian border resembles the forbidding demilitarized zone between North and South Korea. NATO has emplaced walls, tank traps, mines, missile batteries, and squadrons of CF-105B Arrows (see description, "Aircraft, Rockets, Missiles, and Spacecraft") to repel any threat from the south (see description, "Civil War II").

The Manitoba Provincial Border Station, a huge concrete and steel structure, is one of the few legal entry points between Canada and Greater America. By way of the eBahn, Gabriel Durand arrives at the station en route to Winnipeg. The last leg of his trip is a supersonic flight to Kyiv aboard a Boom Overture jet (see description, "Aircraft, Rockets, Missiles, and Spacecraft"). Gabriel's wealth and British citizenship make his passage through the Canadian border simple. Bren will have no such advantages as he hopes to bring his family to Vancouver Island for the safety and promise of Project Archegos.

FIREARMS

HANDGUNS

Desert Eagle Mark XIX L5, .357 Magnum. D.D. Guthrie carries a nickel-plated Desert Eagle, a large, double-action semiautomatic pistol (Chapter 10). Magnum Research, Inc., based in Minnesota, developed the weapon in the mid-1980s. Desert Eagles have often been used in movies due to their size and futuristic lines.

Jericho PL, .40 S&W. A double-action, semiautomatic pistol produced by Israel Weapon Industries (IWI). The frame is polymer, a design element made popular by the Glock pistol line. As a delivery driver, Moe Franklin carries a Jericho PL in a drop-leg holster (Chapter 1).

M17, 9mm. A double-action semiautomatic pistol manufactured by SIG Sauer for the United States Armed Forces prior to Civil War II. Entering service in 2017, the M17 replaced the Baretta M9. In 2028, Bren carried an M17 as a 1st Lieutenant in the California Army National Guard (Chapter 12).

Machine Pistol System, 9mm. Derek Reno uses an elaborate machine pistol system as his primary firearms (Chapter 9). System components:

- Heavily modified Heckler & Koch VP9 (two total). Dimensions reduced, with customized titanium alloy barrel and action for automatic fire. Magazine replaced with belt-feed receiver.
- Carbon-fiber wrist gauntlets to hold pistols in ready position and slide them into Reno's palms for combat.
- Ammunition belts holding 9mm rounds, wrapped around Reno's torso. Using nanofiber technology, the belts constrict to feed rounds along Reno's arms into the pistols.

Ruger Super GP100, .357 Magnum. A double-action revolver with an eight-round capacity. The Ruger uses full-moon clips, allowing the gun to be quickly loaded and unloaded. The revolver has a steampunk appearance—futuristic front end with vented shroud barrel and fiber-optic sight, coupled with a traditional frame and action (hammer, trigger) derived from the venerable Super Redhawk.

Bren receives the Super GP100 from his father, Jack, the night of his first run in 2033 (Chapter 1). The Ruger remains his primary sidearm throughout his delivery driver career. Amid the profusion of polymer-framed, high-capacity semiauto pistols, Bren prefers the dependability and ruggedness of a revolver, with the feel of real-wood grips and the stopping power of the .357 Magnum round.

Springfield Armory XD-E, .45 caliber. A compact, double-action semiautomatic pistol with a 3.3 inch barrel. The pistol has a polymer frame and holds seven rounds in an extended magazine. Bren keeps the XD-E in the center console of his Ford Lightning pickup truck (see description, "Land and Sea Vehicles"). He chose .45 caliber to ensure stopping power in his compact gun (Chapter 1).

MAC-10, 9mm. A machine pistol introduced in the mid-1960s, a low-cost design using steel stampings. Like the Desert Eagle (see above), the gun frequently appeared in movies due to its unique look—small, boxy, fitted with a long suppressor that enabled two-handed operation. In the first run from Fire Hub Sears, a Porch Pirate rakes Mongo's Bronco with a MAC-10 (Chapter 10).

LONG GUNS

Barrett M82, .50 BMG. The Barrett M82 is a semiautomatic sniper rifle designed as an anti-materiel system to neutralize enemy vehicles and other hardened targets with its powerful and accurate rounds. Developed in the 1980s, the rifle saw action during Desert Storm (US Military designation M187). Dozens of nations use the M82 and its variants in their military and police forces.

The Barrett M82 is Bren's primary weapon on the road (Chapter 2), mounted on a carbon-fiber armature surrounded by ballistic shields—a tailgunner position in the bed of his Ford F-150 Lightning pickup truck (see description, "Land and Sea Vehicles"). The Barrett is equipped with a digital scope that provides a live feed to *Delivery: Dead or Alive* so fans can see Bren aiming at his targets. In the Army National Guard, Bren achieved "Expert" in rifle qualification, the highest level of proficiency. With these skills, he strives to use the M82 in its intended anti-materiel role, taking out the engines, axles, and wheels of pursuing vehicles, not the occupants.

C8, 5.56x40mm NATO. Produced by Colt Canada, the C8 is a version of the American M4 carbine, the successor to the M16 rifle made famous during the Vietnam War (see following). NATO troops at Manitoba Provincial Border Station are carrying C8s when Gabriel arrives from Greater America (Chapter 6).

M4, 5.56x40mm NATO. The primary service rifle of the United States military in the years prior to Civil War II. Derived from the M16, the carbine was designed to be lighter, easier to shoot, and more reliable. With the war's outbreak, new national militaries and militias seized M4s from the federal inventories. In 2028, 1st Lt. Bren Van Allen carried an M4 on deployment with the California Army National Guard, the troops federalized to stop Texas from seceding (Chapter 12).

Mossberg 590M Shockwave, 12 gauge. A pump-action shotgun with pistol-grip stock that features a detachable box magazine instead of a traditional tubular magazine mounted under the barrel. Moe Franklin uses a 590M Shockwave during Bren's first delivery run in 2033 (Chapter 1).

Springfield Armory M1A Tanker, .308 Winchester. The Tanker is the most compact version of the M1A, a semiautomatic rifle based on the M14, which was developed for the US military between the M1, used in World War II and the Korean War, and the M16, used in Vietnam. The M1A Tanker fulfills Bren's preference for firearms with wooden stocks and traditional ascetics. He arms himself the Tanker when he leaves his truck during a paratrooper assault on an eQuality distribution hub (Chapter 6).

Typhoon F12, 12 gauge. A semiautomatic shotgun that features a detachable box magazine. The weapon resembles an assault rifle with an adjustable butt stock and accessory rail. D.D. Guthrie uses a Typhoon F12 to fight off paratroopers attacking an eQuality distribution hub (Chapter 6).

Winchester SXP Woodland Defender, 20 gauge. A pump-action shotgun with camouflage finish on the stock. D.D.'s elderly customer, who fancies himself as Fonzie from *Happy Days*, brings a Woodland Defender to his meeting with Porch Pirates (Chapter 8).

PROJECTILE LAUNCHERS

Incendiary Gun. A DIY-weapon made from paintball gun parts. Mongo uses his incendiary gun to shoot napalm rounds at surrounding Porch Pirates (Chapter 13).

M203 Grenade Launcher. A single-shot weapon that mounts to the underside of an M4 rifle. In 2028, Sgt. 1st Class Moe Franklin used one to destroy an out-of-control ground drone (Chapter 12).

LAND AND SEA VEHICLES

LAND VEHICLES

Airstream Flying Cloud. The Flying Cloud is the most popular model from Airstream, the company known for its streamlined, aluminum travel trailers. In 2026, Bren purchased a thirty-foot Flying Cloud for his family. Upgrades included interior layout with a home office cubicle and the eStream system, electric motors to assist with towing. Bren sold the patent to his agricultural drone the Gleaner (see description, "Aircraft, Rockets, Missiles, and Spacecraft") to pay for the deluxe trailer after having bought a Ford F-150 Lightning (see following) the year before.

The rolling stock would have enabled Bren, his wife Hailey, and baby Madison to live on the road as Civil War II intensified. But two years after the Flying Cloud came home, Hailey was dead from the third pandemic (Chapter 11) and Bren was embroiled in controversy over the Hemlock Road Massacre committed by the federal army in Texas (Chapter 12). The Van Allen family bug-out would never happened.

By 2038, the Flying Cloud is Bren's residence as he is deployed to distribution hubs. Fire Hub Sears (see description, "Major Locations") has an RV park with full hookups for the delivery drivers. Inside the trailer, Bren maintains workspace for engineering design, electronics repair, gunsmithing, and social media production. Like the Lightning that tows it, his Airstream Flying Cloud is worn but hardy, a worthy refuge for the Deliverer.

Baja Bug. Popularized in Southern California during the late 1960s, a Baja Bug is a VW Beetle customized for off-roading and racing with fiberglass body panels, a roll cage, heavy-duty suspension and tires, and an exposed rear engine. To achieve more power, the Beetle's air-cooled, flat-4 can be swapped out for a larger engine. Sparky, a young Porch Pirate, pursues Bren in a Baja Bug fitted with a V-6 (Chapter 2).

Buick RoadFortress. Introduced in 2032, the Buick RoadFortress is one of the most popular SUVs in Greater America. Powered by three electric motors and fully autonomous, the RoadFortress features armored body panels and an interior configured as an office for maximum productivity. Gabriel Durand takes a RoadFortress from his home in Entrada to the Manitoba Provincial Border Station (see description "Major Locations"), traveling most of the route on the eBahn (Chapter 6).

Chevrolet El Camino. The El Camino was a Chevy coupe with a pickup bed, introduced in 1959 and regularly produced from 1964 to 1988. The vehicle predated the era when trucks and SUVs became popular among drivers who did little towing or hauling. Sparky drives a 1979 El Camino SS with a 350 V8 (Chapter 5) after Bren destroys his Baja Bug (see previous).

Chevrolet SSR. The SSR was a specialty small pickup produced in the early years of the twenty-first century, featuring a retractable roof, a carpeted cargo bed, and a V-8 engine also available in the Corvette. An SSR is lead vehicle in a Porch Pirate attack on Derek Reno and his blockers, Ronni and Robert (Chapter 16).

Dodge Charger Hellucination. The Hellucination is a reengineering of the 1968 Dodge Charger, with a carbon-fiber body, custom suspension, and a 1,000-horsepower V-8. The car resembles the hitman vehicle from the 1969 movie *Bullitt* starring Steve McQueen. Lonny, a Porch Pirate leader, drives this twenty-first century replica of the classic machine (Chapter 2).

Ford Bronco. The Bronco is a venerable SUV line, originally produced from the mid-1960s to the mid-1990s and reintroduced for the 2021 model year with retro styling cues. Mongo drives a 2034 Bronco with numerous upgrades including the Sasquatch off-roading package, strengthened skid plates, and SatCom uplink to the eQuality satellite network (Chapter 7).

Ford Econoline Van. The Ford Econoline van, officially known as the E-Series, began production in 1960. A versatile and popular platform, the Econoline has been the basis of a vast vehicle array from Christian camp transports, to ambulances, to surfer vans. Roadie, an eQuality driver and member of Bren's Bible study group, drives a 1991 Econoline (Chapter 5) that he used for hauling rock band gear before Civil War II. The logo of the band "Rocktopus" is still faintly visible on the van's sides.

Ford F-150 Lightning Platinum. Introduced in 2021, the Lightning is the EV version of the Ford F-150, the most popular vehicle in the United States prior to Civil War II. The Platinum package includes a SYNC controller system with touchscreen, built-in WiFi hotspot, and upgraded batteries for a range of 320 miles. Twin electric engines, one per axle, produce 580 horsepower and send 775 lb.-ft. of torque to the four-wheel-drive drivetrain. The Lightning Platinum goes zero to sixty in four seconds, equivalent to an Aston Martin DB9.

In 2025, Bren bought a Ford Lightning Platinum with the option of autonomous mode driving, newly available for the model year. His wife Hailey was pregnant with their daughter Madison, and the United States was entering Civil War II. Bren designed a liquid-cooled charging cable that enabled the truck to receive a full charge as quickly as filling a gas tank. He knew his family might need to bug out quickly as society deteriorated.

In 2033, after the death of his wife and the failure of his engineering company, Bren takes his first delivery driver assignment, accompanied by Moe Franklin, who served under him as platoon sergeant in the California Army National Guard. Bren drives his Lightning as the delivery vehicle, battling Porch Pirates up the treacherous road leading to Mount Baldy, a 10,000-foot peak east of Los Angeles. Taking significant damage from gunfire, the truck powers through a mudslide to a mountain lodge where a rich customer awaits the decadent cargo that nearly cost Bren his life (Chapter 1).

By 2038, Bren is one of the top delivery drivers in Greater America and still driving his Ford Lightning, which he has heavily modified for ongoing battle:

- **Powertrain:** Two additional electric motors and upgraded battery packs with greater energy density for increased horsepower, torque, and driving range.
- **Off-Road Capabilities:** "Crab mode" to set wheels diagonally for improved traction on slopes. Harpoon/winch (can also be used as a weapon).
- **Bullet/Projectile Protection:** Glass-clad polycarbonate windows. Rolling Armor run-flat tires. Kevlar panels under all aluminum bodywork, treated with "Liquid Armor" smart fluid.
- **Communications/Data/Sensors:** Smartwatch connectivity to all truck systems. Heads-up display (HUD) adapted from Army Futures Command prototype. Multiple cockpit touchscreens. Multiple internal/external video cameras for feed to *Delivery: Dead or Alive*. LIDAR (laser imagining, detection, and ranging) sensors, 360-degree capture field. Bio/chem sensors to detect biological or chemical weapons. SatCom uplink to eQuality satellite network. AI (artificial intelligence) avatar serving as communication/navigation agent.
- **Defensive Systems:** Decoy ground drones, deployed from truck undercarriage, to detect and neutralize

mines and similar anti-materiel weapons. Air filtration system to protect against biological/ chemical weapons. Ambush countermeasures, under development.

- **Offensive Systems:** Tailgunner station for Barrett M82 (see description, "Firearms")— carbon-fiber, articulated gun mount, automated ballistic shields, reinforced truck tailgate, rail-mounted driver's seat and bulkhead hatch enabling driver emplacement at station (Chapter 2).

Ford Maverick. Resurrecting the name of a classic Ford compact car, the Maverick is compact, front-wheel drive pickup introduced in 2021. In 2038, Derek Reno's blockers, Ronni and Robert Sykes, drive Mavericks with upgraded engines and hardened body panels.

Ford Mustang Shelby GT500. The Shelby GT500 is the top-performance version of iconic Ford Mustang. Produced since 1964, the Mustang relaunched in 2005 with a retro body style recalling the days when designer/ racer Carroll Shelby first created extreme versions of the "pony car." The Shelby GT500 features a supercharged 5.2 liter V-8 engine rated at 770 horsepower. D.D. Guthrie, eQuality driver turned Porch Pirate leader, drives a 2022 model in exclusive "Code Orange" paint (Chapter 4). Other upgrades include bulletproof glass, hardened body panels, and a sophisticated suite of threat sensors and satellite communications.

Gladiator Tactical Unmanned Ground Vehicle. The US Marine Corps developed the Gladiator in the early twenty-first century as a land drone for reconnaissance and assault. The vehicle resembles a tiny tank with a machine gun mounted on top. In 2028, the California Army National Guard used Gladiators during their Texas deployment to stop secession (Chapter 12).

Humvee. Introduced in 1983, the Humvee (High-Mobility Multipurpose Wheeled Vehicle—HMMWV) was the US military's replacement for the Jeep. A symbol of America's two wars in Iraq, Humvees suffered significant losses from improvised explosive devices (IEDs) in the early twenty-first century, leading to development of the MRAP (see following). In the 2030s, Humvees are still in heavy use by the militaries of Greater America (Chapter 1).

Infantry Squad Vehicle. An infantry squad vehicle (ISV) is a lightweight troop carrier with an open cabin similar to a utility terrain vehicle (see following). In 2028, 1st Lt. Bren Van Allen and Sgt. 1st Class Moe Franklin drove an ISV to the site of the Hemlock Road Massacre (Chapter 12).

MRAP. In the early twenty-first century, the US military developed MRAP vehicles—Mine-Resistant Ambush-Protected—to withstand IED attacks during the Iraq War. Weighing more than ten tons, an MRAP is armor-plated with a V-shaped undercarriage to deflect explosions from roadway bombs.

Derek Reno, eQuality driver and chief rival to Bren Van Allen, drives a modified BAE Caiman MRAP, army surplus that had been sold to an American police department in 2011. Upon retiring from rally racing in 2032, he acquired the MRAP in a barter deal involving guns and drugs used as prizes on the illicit circuit (see description, "Main Characters"). The MRAP's conversion into a delivery vehicle included:

- Lighter composite armor—layers of metal and specialty plastic—to improve acceleration.
- Electric motors augmenting the Caterpillar turbo-diesel engine to improve acceleration and range.
- SmartShot anti-vehicular system—dispenser at rear bumper that drops magnetized pellets on road to disable pursing vehicles.

Utility Terrain Vehicle. A utility terrain vehicle (UTV) is faster and more powerful than an all-terrain vehicle (ATV), with a steering wheel and side-by-side seating as distinguishing features. A customized UTV attacks Mongo on the first run from Fire Hub Sears (Chapter 10).

SEA VEHICLES

Disco Volante. The mega yacht owned by Jerold Cox, CEO of eQuality. Disco Volante means "flying saucer" in Italian. Cox chose the name due to his ship's resemblance to a spacecraft with its curved surfaces and futuristic features. The yacht of Emilio Largo, villain of the James Bond novel/film *Thunderball*, was also called Disco Volante.

Specifications:

- **Length:** 665 feet.
- **Gross tonnage:** 21,000 tons.
- **Top speed:** 35 knots.
- **Cruising range:** 5,000 miles.
- **Propulsion:** Four water jet thrusters. Two gas-turbine engines, four biodiesel engines for combined 125,000 horsepower.
- **Additional Craft:** Two helicopters, one hovercraft, two submarines, three tender speedboats, one shadow vessel for supplies and additional security.
- **Amenities:** Three swimming pools, ballroom, underwater observation pod, rock climbing wall, recording studio, art gallery, bowling alley, gun range.

AIRCRAFT, ROCKETS, MISSILES, AND SPACECRAFT

AIRCRAFT—DRONES AND GLIDERS

Air Taxi. An autonomous eVTOL—pilotless, electric-powered, taking off and landing vertically like an helicopter. Popular in Greater America, the eHang air taxi resembles a helicopter's cabin sprouting eight spokes holding sixteen rotors. D.D. leaves eQuality's employ in such a craft, landing in a remote location to meet Lonny's Porch Pirate band (Chapter 8).

Cryo-Drone. A medium-sized drone built around a refrigeration unit for perishable cargos. Bren enlists a cryo-drone to send fresh eggs to his daughter, Madison, and mother, Cindy (Chapter 4).

Gleaner. A compact drone Bren designed for agriculture in the mid-2020s. The Gleaner could fly through crop rows, monitoring each plant to administer precise capsules of organic fertilizer or biologic pesticide as needed, greatly reducing waste and environmental impact.

Bren sold the patent in 2026 (Chapter 9) to buy his family an Airstream Flying Cloud trailer (see description, "Land and Sea Vehicles"). During Civil War II, the Gleaner was adapted into an assassination weapon. A wing of Gleaners can latch to a mothership drone for transport to an attack site (Chapter 16). Thomas Albano, attorney general of America Green, issues an arrest warrant for Bren as a war criminal despite his being blameless for the drone's misuse (Chapter 12).

Paratroopers Wing Suit. A wing suit is a jumpsuit with membrane-like wings stretching between the skydiver's arms and legs, like the skin that enables a flying squirrel to glide. A wing suit allows the skydiver to approach the landing zone from miles away in silence. In 2017, British

Special Air Services (SAS) troops reportedly used stealth wing suits to attack terrorists in Syria.

In 2038, paratroopers counterattack an America Blue battalion during military action to force the Border States into a trade agreement. The airborne troops wear wing suits with SIG Sauer Copperhead submachine guns and Raytheon Pike mini-missiles mounted in the leading edges (Chapter 6).

AIRCRAFT—TURBOPROP/TURBOSHAFT

Airbus A400M Atlas. A four-engine turboprop military transport built in Europe, sized between the American C-130 Hercules and the C-17 Globemaster III (see below). On his first delivery run, Bren picks up special crates offloaded from an A400M Atlas, to be delivered to his customer in a mountain lodge (Chapter 1).

Bell Boeing Quad Tiltrotor. Proposed at the turn of the 21st century as a V-22 Osprey concept enlarged to the size of a C-130 Hercules. In 2038, eQuality CEO Jerold Cox uses a Bell Boeing Quad Tiltrotor as his personal transport in the Border States (Chapter 19).

AIRCRAFT—JETS

B-52 Stratofortress. An eight-engined strategic bomber flown by the US Air Force since 1955. The B-52 has seen combat over Vietnam, Yugoslavia, Iraq, and Afghanistan. As done with other US military assets, the new countries of Greater America divided the B-52 fleet during the early days of Civil War II. The Republic of Mojave had a unique opportunity to activate the big bomber as a dozen of them were in storage at the Davis-Monthan Air Force Base "boneyard" near Tucson.

B-52s drop paratroopers in wing suits (see above) to strike a base being used by America Blue to attack the Border States (Chapter 6).

Boom Overture. A civilian supersonic transport developed in the 2020s, the successor in spirit to the Concorde. With four engines slung under its delta wings, the Boom Overture resembles the American B-58 Hustler supersonic bomber developed in the 1950s. After driving to Canada on the eBahn, Gabriel Durand takes a Boom Overture from Winnipeg to Kyiv (Chapter 7).

C-17 Globemaster III. A four-engine military transport that entered service in 1995 with the US Air Force. Bren realizes military action is imminent when C-17s land at an eQuality logistics hub under the guise of civilian transports (Chapter 6).

CF-105B Arrow. In 2032, Canada deployed the CF-105B Arrow, an updating of its fabled Arrow interceptor jet that was cancelled in 1959 before coming into service. The new Arrow strongly resembles its delta-winged forbearer, with advanced engines powering the craft to Mach 3, a speed reached by few jets including America's SR-71. The interceptor features stealth coatings and a look-down/shoot-down radar system that can target ground-hugging hypersonic missiles. CF-105B squadrons patrol along the 49th parallel as part of NATO's defense against spillover from Civil War II (Chapter 6).

F-16 Fighting Falcon. In service since 1980, the American F-16 is the world's most widely used fighter jet, flown by the US Air Force and more than twenty allied nations. The plane's agility coupled with ongoing engine, avionics, and weapons upgrades ensure its viability through the middle of the 21st century. Bren and Mongo watch F-16s scramble (Chapter 12) after a false alarm triggered by the launch of a Sleigh cargo rocket (see following).

Textron AirLand Scorpion. In the 2010s, the Scorpion was proposed as a light attack jet. The plane found a market during Civil War II as the new nations of Greater America sought a low-cost alternative to legacy front-line fighters. Scorpions are part of the jet scramble Bren and Mongo witness (Chapter 12).

ROCKETS/MISSILES

Hydra 70. An unguided air-to-ground rocket introduced after the Vietnam War, based on the Mk4/Mk 40 rocket developed in the late 1940s, known as the Mighty Mouse. The Hydra 70 is typically fired from a pod mounted to a fighter jet or attack helicopter. Sparky and several Porch Pirates fire at Bren's Lightning with a Hydra 70 pod mounted on a flatbed truck (Chapter 18), a DIY approach seen in past conflicts like the Libyan civil war.

Romeo Hellfire. The Romeo variant of the Hellfire II laser-guided missile became operational in 2012. Hellfire is an air-to-ground missile that also can be fired from ships and ground vehicles. Drone-launched Hellfires became a symbol of the War on Terror during the first two decades of the 21st century. A Romeo Hellfire takes out a roadside mortar position as Bren drives to Fire Hub Sears (Chapter 9).

SPACECRAFT

Sleigh Cargo Rocket. eQuality's cargo rocket, part of a fleet that can transport VIPs and goods for customer delivery to any spot on Earth in less than an hour. The Sleigh is a two-stage vehicle—stage one is the booster with maximum thrust of five-million pounds, stage two is the orbital craft containing the cargo/passenger hold. The Sleigh's orbiter lands vertically and can launch without a booster for suborbital hops (e.g., Fire Hub Sears to eQuality central hub in Wichita). Jerold Cox, eQuality CEO, arrives at Fire Hub Sears aboard Sleigh 3 to commemorate the delivery drivers' first run from the facility (Chapter 9).

Icarus I. The first crewed spacecraft to Mars, which flew its inaugural mission in 2036. America Blue poured tremendous resources into the Icarus program to prove its technological dominance in Greater America, much as the Apollo program was meant to show the United States' superiority over the Soviet Union. Icarus I launched from the Kennedy/Johnson Space Center, a floating launch and control base built outside New York harbor to replace historic spaceflight facilities in Cape Canaveral and Houston lost to America Red.

Icarus 1 is a five hundred feet tall at launch, consisting of the first-stage booster with ten million pounds of thrust and the second-stage interplanetary command module. In cislunar space, the command module docks with pre-positioned service modules (contents: extra fuel, habitat components, surface rover, small nuclear reactor) to form the complete Mars vehicle. Bren brings Josh an Icarus I diecast model sent by Olivia in Gabriel's name (Chapter 13).

KEY TECHNOLOGIES

VIRTUAL REALITY—VR 2.0

In 2038, virtual reality has reached its second era, going mainstream with glasses that are nearly indistinguishable from ordinary eyewear. The frames deliver neural signals to users, imparting sensations of touch, smell, and taste to accompany the audio/visual displays. The United States of America may be shattered, but the metaverse is booming.

Main characters enter several virtual spaces using VR 2.0:

- **General meeting space**—a limbo for quick gatherings. Bren checks in with Madison using this space (Chapter 21).

- **Boardroom**—Jerold Cox uses this space to meet with officials from America Blue and the Border States after the former's military action to open the new enterprise zone. In this higher level of the metaverse, users can adjust their lifelike avatars for a more flattering appearance. The boardroom can convert into other virtual locations, allowing meeting attendees to experience different surroundings. During Cox's meeting, the boardroom changes to a war zone in the Border States and becomes Fire Hub Sears, depicting the site's origin as a shopping mall decades earlier (Chapter 7).

- **Project Archegos Sanctuary**—Bren and Madison attend Sunday service in the virtual sanctuary of Project Archegos, the Christian scientific enclave on Vancouver Island. Pastor Doug Wescott's message is interrupted by his brother Pastor Larry Wescott, who hacks the session to protest Project Archegos and the Deliverer (Chapter 7).

- **Excelsior Springs**—Pastor Larry invites Bren to a virtual version of his hometown, which was contaminated by a chemical plant, leading to his antagonism toward science (Chapter 15).

- **New Jerusalem**—Pastor Larry shows Bren the vision of a capital city, New Jerusalem, to be constructed upon America Red conquering the rest of Greater America and Canada. The city's grandiosity evokes the concept of Germania, a mega-capital planned in the 1930s by Albert Speer, Nazi architect and government minister, from which Hitler would have ruled the world (Chapter 15).

- *Gambrel*—The digital ballet Olivia creates and enters in the Prix de Gloire competition. She uses VR and motion capture technologies to choreograph the work and portray the avatar dance ensemble, all representing facets of her own personality.

TRANSPORTATION—TRANSIT PASS, eBAHN

Ground vehicles are preferred over airplanes for crossing Greater America due to air forces being on constant alert and independent militias possessing large stockpiles of anti-aircraft weapons. Two technologies ensure the safest ground transportation for those who can pay.

Transit Pass—a puck-shaped device that permits passage on protected roads. A transit pass costs more than a mansion or yacht and is much harder to acquire. Gabriel Durand controls his family's transit pass, making Olivia a prisoner in her home (Chapter 3, Chapter 5). Bren works as a delivery driver to save money for a transit pass, which will allow his family to travel legally and safely to Canada for relocation to Project Archegos (Chapter 7).

eBahn—the most secure road in Greater America. Built by treaty between the three Americas, the eBahn is a "smart highway." Electric vehicles recharge by induction when driving on its surface. The same charging system destroys any trespassing vehicles, with burned-out cars and electrocuted passengers left on the side of the road as a warning to others. Entry on the eBahn is only possible with a transit pass (Chapter 5).

3D Printing—Graphene, Home Printer Network

The 2030s have seen the commercialization of graphene, a "wonder substance" made of carbon structured at the nano-level to be stronger than steel, more conductive than copper, and more flexible than rubber. Several developments have enabled the graphene era:

Mass production of graphene. Graphene is derived from graphite, the crystalline form of the element carbon, used as an industrial substance since the Neolithic age. Prior to 2025, graphene, with its precise atomic structure, could only be produced in small quantities. Developed at Kansas State University in 2017, the "detonation technique" led to successful mass production of graphene by exploding graphite in a gas-filled chamber, producing graphene as the residue—a work process similar to an internal combustion engine.

In the 2030s, graphene refineries match the scale of petroleum refineries and are typically located alongside graphite mines to facilitate production (Chapter 10). Gigantic, automated excavators strip mine graphite seams, which are impregnated with carbon sequestered from the atmosphere to increase density. Ethylene gas is used for the explosion process, obtained organically from biomass waste. Heat from the controlled explosions drives onsite steam turbines to reduce plant demand from the grid.

Graphene as a 3D printing medium. To become a 3D printing medium, graphene coming from a refinery's production chambers is amassed in extremely porous layers, allowing the addition of a photo-reactive liquid to serve as the carrier. This graphene solution is pumped through pipelines, stored in tanks, and sent directly to home printers, much as water and natural gas are distributed to customers. During the printing process, a laser hits the graphene solution, burning away the fluid carrier and restoring the graphene to a solid that can be shaped into the desired item (Chapter 11).

Graphene's commercialization sustains consumerism during the deprivations of Civil War II. But people get bored with the goods they can conjure in the safety and convenience of their homes. The wealthy long for the old days of the brown box on the step, holding treasures that cannot be extruded from a printer. Delivery drivers, like Bren Van Allen, satisfy this need, often with their lives.

WARDER CHIP

The Warder Chip uses quantum entanglement to track a person without any observable transmission—no tracking devices on the person, no signal broadcast, no way to jam the tracking, no way to hide. The Warder Chip fulfills Einstein's theory of quantum entanglement, which he called "spooky action at a distance" in simplified terms. In this state, two objects share information and other properties instantaneously across any distance without being connected by conventional matter or energy.

The Warder Chip is a microprocessor, like conventional logic chips used in computers for decades. The chip matrix materials contain uptake receptors for DNA molecules. Introduction of the subject's live DNA—collected with a skin patch and then integrated with the device—activates the Warder Chip, the heart of a biomechanical quantum computer the size of a cell phone (Chapter 6). The chip and the subject are entangled. The subject is forever tracked across time and space.

By design, a standard 3D printer can produce the Warder Chip. Consumers will buy a kit containing the small biomechanical computer, printer operating software, a nozzle array, and a reservoir of chip matrix material. Once printed, the skin patch component has a shelf life of five days, during which the subject's DNA must be collected and integrated with the rest of the chip architecture (Chapter 5).

Gabriel Durand has created a device that realizes Einstein's theory of quantum entanglement, unlocking one of the greatest secrets of God's universe for dark purposes. His first test subject is his wife, Olivia.

BOOKS BY JASON WILLIAM KARPF

BRIMSTONE 1
STUDY GUIDE

JASON
WILLIAM
KARPF

WONDERS
of
the GALAXY

A COLLECTION
OF COSMIC
TALES

TE BRADFORD
MB DAHL
AARON GANSKY
BRETT HEASTON
ERICA MARIE HOGAN
TRAVIS W INMAN
JASON WILLIAM KARPF
STEVEN SOUTH
LG WESTLAKE